CHAPTER ONE

"FASTEN your safety belts, please," said the pretty air-hostess, walking alert as a fox terrier down the centre aisle. "We're coming in to land."

Inspector Cockrill looked out and down and saw nothing but a very small patch of grass which they were certainly going to miss and a very large building composed entirely of glass which they were quite certainly going to hit. The young woman on his right had immediately buried her face on his shoulder but this was no time for quixotic knight-errantry and he merely humped himself slightly away from her and gave himself over to prayer. The great rubber tyres bumped once upon the tarmac, bounced, bumped again, were still. Green to the gills, he shook off the clutching hands of the young woman, distastefully removed a long, curly red hair from the sleeve of his summer suiting and, as the aircraft began to taxi gently to its turning point, said with kindly pity: "There's nothing to worry about. We've landed."

"I don't mind when we're right at the top," said the young woman, raising her head and looking at him grate-fully out of large blue eyes in a face which, under a wealth of make-up, had gone exceedingly pale. "It's when you begin to see the land and the little houses and things and realize that you *are* up." She gave a sick shudder and half a dozen slick-looking feminine periodicals slid off her lap and down to the tilted floor of the aeroplane. She grabbed at

5

them with one scarlet-taloned hand while with the other she continued to pick automatically at the sleeve of his coat. "I'm so sorry. I seem to have moulted all over you, like a red setter." In the bright Italian sunshine he squinted at the mouse-coloured end of one of the hairs and she amended ruefully, "Well—like a setter."

"All right, all right," said Cockie crossly, aimlessly brushing at his sleeve. He left her and struggled out into the sloping aisle; and, stumping off across the landing strip to the little airport bus, he thought in despair: 'She's one of Them!' For Inspector Cockrill was setting out upon a Conducted Tour of Italy and ever since, his money being paid and withdrawal now impossible, he had received the assurance of the travel agency that he would find delightful friends among his fellow tourists, he had been contemplating their coming association with ever-increasing gloom. 'She and all the rest,' he thought. 'They're Them.'

'Goodness!' thought Louli. 'What a funny little man!' And fancy his having noticed so quickly about her hair. She thought it over rather wistfully, struggling down the aisle with her armload of slippery papers, trying to take her mind off the hideous feeling of sickness that heights always gave her. It was a brand-new rinse, and supposed to have been quite terrific. She had read about it in *Vogue* or somewhere: you applied it beaten up in yolk of egg and you could change your hair-colour half a dozen times a day if you wanted to, only the egg part was so revolting. She struggled into her place in the bus and all the magazines slid down to the floor once more. Scrabbling about under the seat for them, she noticed again that madly gay 'Billingsgate' stole. 'Beg a length of net from your fisherman friend down at Frinton,' commanded the caption, 'wash out excess tar, stitch gay white bobbles round the edge and wear thrown carelessly over your shoulder with an outsize straw hat.'

6

Tour de Force
by Christianna Brand

"You've probably never been presented with so many clues, all fair, all but a few deceiving. Try your wits."

—*San Francisco Chronicle*

"A larkish and quite diverting affair." —*The Spectator*

"Witty and wordy." —*Saturday Review*

Also available in Perennial Library

Christianna Brand's   GREEN FOR DANGER

CHRISTIANNA BRAND

*

Tour de Force

PERENNIAL LIBRARY
Harper & Row, Publishers
New York, Cambridge, Philadelphia, San Francisco
London, Mexico City, São Paulo, Sydney

To

PATIENCE ROSS

—dear Patience, who does
everything for my books except
take the credit

A hardcover edition of this book was originally published by Charles
Scribner's Sons. It is here reprinted by arrangement.

First PERENNIAL LIBRARY edition published 1982.

ISBN: 0-06-080572-2

82 83 84 85 10 9 8 7 6 5 4 3 2 1

"Brit-Slang" for "Capri"?

There was a picture of a young woman, taken in a London studio with a background of the Isle of Kerpree, wearing the net thrown carelessly over her shoulder. It was terribly dashing. She wished she had seen it sooner; before, in obedience to an earlier number of the same magazine, she had begged a red chenille tablecloth from her Edwardian aunt down at Bognor, washed out excess tea and ink stains, and stitched gay white bobbles round that. It was thrown carelessly over her shoulder at this minute and it really was dreadfully hot. She gave herself a shake to dislodge it and all the glossy magazines slid down to the floor again and shot under the seat in front as the bus started into action. Mr Cecil let go for a moment of his precious little red attaché case and stooped to pick them up.

Mr Cecil had noticed Louli already, at the airport in London. A wonderful figure for clothes; and she knew where to go for them, too—that vast circular skirt had not come off the peg and the white cambric off-the-shoulder blouse ('ransack the attics for Granny's old camisoles'), was the rage at the moment in all the Mayfair boutiques; he couldn't think where she could have found the stole but that deep red was an inspiration with her colour of hair. "My dear, do let me say that I think your stole's simply divine! Not Hartnell?"

"Oh, no," said Louli. "He did have some like it; but this one is real, it's my aunt's nursery tablecloth: I do think that's more fun." The only thing about it was that it was frightfully hot.

'Oh, but *worth* it!" said Mr Cecil. He himself had forced, but forced, ducky, all his clients into Toile de Vichy this year, that heaven-blue faded cotton that one saw on all those touching ouvriers and people in France; but one did get a teeny bit sick of it by the end of the season. His clients? "But I'm Cecil, dear, Mr Cecil, you know, of Christophe et Cie." He gave a modest wriggle and surreptitiously tucked his passport further out of sight. It really was too inconsiderate of one's passport to blazon one abroad—literally abroad, thought Mr Cecil, giggling privately at his own joke—as Cecil George Prout. "And you?"

"Well, I'm Louvaine Barker," said Louli, going a little pink as she always did.

Mr Cecil couldn't get over it. He had thought her—what had he thought her? One of the Bright Young Cookies from Mayfair, eking out Daddy's allowance with tentative dabblings in the deplorable new cult of do-it-yourself? But—Louvaine Barker! "My dear, I adore your books, I know them every one, positively bedside, I do assure you. Fancy—so distinguished! And you so young!"

"Twenty-nine," admitted Louli ruefully. When you had been in the public eye for—yes, it was ten years now—there was nothing to be done but admit. "Jolly nearly thirty: isn't it awful?"

"Wait till you're actually thirty-two, like poor me," said Mr Cecil. Mr Cecil had been in the public eye for twenty-five years, but he admitted nothing. He flung back a brassy forelock with a famous long white hand. "Too exciting for any *words*, my dear, meeting the fabulous Barker in the—in the flesh." He gave a tiny shudder; to Mr Cecil the flesh was something to be covered up as quickly as possible in Toile de Vichy. "Do tell all about it, ducky, every *single!*" It was his latest affectation to leave unsaid any obvious terminals; catching on like wildfire it was, among the Mayfair cookies and such good publicity for Christophe et Cie, at any rate as long as they still had the decency to add 'as Mr Cecil would say!' Louli, to his great delight, caught on immediately like the good little cookie she was, and unspoken last words littered or omitted to litter, her every sentence as, while the little bus bumped its way over the airport grass, she rapidly outlined the rise to fame—to distinguish fame as Mr Cecil had not untruly said—of Miss Louvaine Barker. "My first book was when I was nineteen; my dear, you can't imagine what a little drear I was! My publishers often laugh over it now, the first time I went to see them and sat there . . ."

Mr Cecil was beside himself with excitement. "But yes, I've heard Cannington tell about it, he dines out on it to this day! Mum as a mouse you sat and they couldn't get a word out of you, they were in despair, too Charlotte Brontë for *any!*"

"My dear, I was petrified. Mouse?—I was complete mouse, mouse hair, mouse voice, mouse mind and goodness knows, mouse courage . . ." But all that had changed, they had bought the first book and the reviews had been unbelievable; and then there had been a film and really and truly one did seem to have done a Byron and woken up one morning and found oneself famous. "So then the mouse courage perked up a bit and the mouse mind followed, not to mention the mouse hair; and as for the mouse voice, let them lead on the whole of Debrett, I just natter away and couldn't care less. I mean," corrected the neophyte, loyally, "I couldn't *care.*" She rattled on and on; she had told it so often that she knew it by heart, the words fell into place without conscious effort from her mind. Her mind . . .

Her mind could be given over to wondering, as she had wondered ever since they had left the London airport, about the man sitting three seats ahead of them.

The bus stopped at the great glass doors of the airport building and Leo Rodd was up and out before the rest of them and humping himself up the shallow steps with an exaggerated wrench of the right shoulder to propel him forward. He wished he had not come on this idiotic trip: thrusting himself into a whole new world which would gaggle at him and be sorry for him because he had only one arm—a whole new world to fall upon him and fawn upon him and wonder if he had 'lost' the other one in the war and refuse to believe him when he said, spitting it out at them with bitter venom, that no, indeed, dear lady, he had lost it falling off a bicycle one day in a country lane. Helen, his wife, walked beside him, tall, slender, elegant, wearing her air of quiet dignity like a queen; patient, considerate, silently sympathetic, relentlessly kind: carrying his brief-case as well as her own travelling bag, of course— because of his arm. 'Well, she will do it,' he thought. 'I can perfectly well carry the bloody thing myself but I just can't go through another scene about it.' There was nothing in the case but a score of the Scriabine Nocturne—Arranged for the Left Hand—and a bottle of Scotch in case there was none to be found in the wilds of Italia. Helen said, glancing back across her shoulder: "Here she comes: I don't think we're going to escape her."

"Here who comes?"

"The one you call The Bosoom."

"Well, why should we want to escape her?"

"I thought you disliked her, that's all," said Helen. Her arms ached with the weight of the two bags but she gave no sign of it.

"Of course I dislike her," he said irritably. "I dislike all women with dyed red hair and plastic nails and rubber brassieres. And what's more she's been fluttering her false eyelashes at me all the way over, longing to be womanly, no doubt, about my arm. But we can't run away from her all over Italy."

"Perhaps she's not coming with us."

"Don't kid yourself! She and the rest of them—every last one of them's on this blasted tour of yours."

"No tour of mine," she said laughing.

"You don't suggest that *I* wanted to come?"

"My father just thought . . ."

"I wish to God your father would leave me alone. *I* don't ask him to be for ever getting into a flap about my mental health."

Helen's father was in a flap about his daughter's mental health and nobody else's. "He only suggested that Italy would be a good place because we can fiddle some money here."

"Because *you* can fiddle some money. *I* haven't got any money—not any more."

"Oh, well," she said, "money doesn't matter. There's lots for two. And he just thought we might like a jaunt . . ."

"On a 'conducted tour'," said Leo. "Dear God. And look at them!"

They were very much like the members of any other conducted tour: thirty of them—gay ones, jolly ones, vulgar ones; refined ones looking down upon the jolly ones and hoping they wouldn't whip out funny hats and shame them at the advertised 'first-class hotels'; inexperienced ones who never could make out whether you called this place Mill-an or Mil-ann, experienced ones who phased them all by calling it Milarno and furthermore talking about Firenze and Venezia and pronouncing the island of San Juan el Pirata, San Hoowarne; robust ones who drank water out of taps and confounded the experienced ones by not going down with bouts of dysentery, anxious ones who refused all shell-fish, raw fruit and unbottled beverages and went down with dysentery before they had even started. . . . Pretty ones, plain ones, downright repellent ones . . .

Mr Fernando met them just inside the glass doors,

wearing an enormous label to show who he was. "Permit me, I introduce myself, Fernando Gomez, your courier, late undergrad St John's College, Cambridge University . . ." He was a Gibraltarian, five foot four inches high and very nearly as broad, tapering off, however, into narrow hips and infinitesimal feet which in turn tapered in ornamental brown and white shoes. "Permit me, I introduce myself . . ." He was radiant. His hair shone with brilliantine, his smile shone with gold fillings, his hands shone with polished nails and chippy little diamond and ruby rings; his eyes above all shone bright with enthusiasm and friendliness behind a pair of enormous yellow sun-glasses, keeping a sharp look-out for the one with the Park Lane address. "Happy to see you all, happy to welcome you, come all this way, please, we flash through the customs in a jiffy and the coach will be waiting outside. Then a jolly lunch in the town, a glance at the Duomo and off to the Riviera and stay there to-night. Miss Trapp, please, which is Miss Trapp? Miss Trapp, I introduce myself, Fernando Gomez, your guide . . ." Miss Trapp was the one with the Park Lane address. It was curious that she should wear a hat wreathed in withered brown brussels-sprouts and for a moment his confidence in her identity failed him; but he took off the sun-glasses and saw that the brussels-sprouts were red roses, really, and expensive red roses at that. "Come this way, please, Miss Trapp. I see you through the customs myself, we are through in a jiffy!" He picked up her suitcase himself, not waiting for a porter. It weighed half a ton but it was of solid crocodile leather and monogrammed in gold.

Mr Cecil was enraptured. He felt like a sheep, he cried to Louli in his gay, high voice as they lined up to go through the customs room: queueing up to be dipped. And his eye-lashes fluttered like butterflies in the wind, for this wonderful Fernando had shoulders like a boxer and did seem a perfect *pet!* But he had somehow got separated from what he called his attashy case and he was distressed about that, so afraid it might be feeling lonely and bewildered, poor thing, and feeling the heat. . . . With a thousand like fancies he beguiled the waiting flock while Fernando dashed up and down their ranks like a <u>sheepdog</u>,' sorting out baggage and owner, guiding both to a vacant spot at the customs counter, leaving them triumphantly there and dashing back for another pair. "At any moment," said Louli, "you expect him to lie down full-length with his nose on his paws."

"If only he'd put his silly paws on Little Red Attashy Case!"

"You seem in a flap about it," said Louli. "What's in it?"

There was nothing in it, Mr Cecil said, but drawing-paper and a few coloured pencils. This trip was not merely for pleasure, one was leaving the tour at Rome with a sheaf, but a *sheaf* one hoped, of scribbles inspired by the sunshine of Italy and San Hoowarne; and these would be finished off in the studio of one's Friend in Rome and shown at the exhibition of dress design there in the autumn; meanwhile, being executed in a thousand different exquisite materials for the coming London season. Mr Cecil was quite madly excited about it all and correspondingly worried about the attaché case; but when it turned up at last, he seemed oddly anxious that the customs officials should not see the paper and pencils. "You wouldn't get it through for me, ducky? Sangwidged in between all those *Vogues* and things, it wouldn't show at all."

"Oh, do you say sangwidged too?" said Louli, delighted. Mr Cecil, who knew no other way of saying it, was mystified but let it go.

The coach waited, true to Fernando's promise, outside the airport and there was a splendid confusion as they all found their seats, for the agency at home had blandly promised each of them a place in the front row, and Mr Fernando, moreover, was holding the seating plan upside down. "This single seat in front by the driver is kept free in case anyone may be sick on the journey . . ."

Everyone immediately assured him that in all likelihood they would be sick during the entire trip, a promise which with several of them was only too faithfully kept. "Now, in the front here, please—Miss Trapp; here, Mrs Jones . . ."

Louli Barker sat amidships, wrapt in gloom, penned against the window by an angular widow with a grievance at having been given a seat on the aisle. She looked round desperately for Mr Cecil or even her little friend of the aeroplane, and saw them sitting quietly in the back row. "Mr Cockrill, sir—here!" cried Fernando in a commanding voice. "And, Mr Cecil—you're here."

"Oh, but, my dear, no, I'm here," protested Mr Cecil. "And madly comfy, please don't make one move."

"This is a good seat I give you, Mr Cecil, in the back is not so good."

"Then nobody else will want to come here, so please be a kindy and let one stay!"

"Why can't they sit where they're told?" said the angular widow, who had fought and bled to avoid her place on the aisle. She handed a large straw hat to Louli and a folded coat. "I wonder if you'd mind having these on your lap? There's no room on the rack: someone's got a large red tablecloth up there and it's taking up all the space." The lady in front had brought her wardrobe on hangers, apparently, and now engaged herself in hooking them up along the window. A hand came over the back of her seat and tapped Louli on the shoulder. "Need we have these clothes hung in front of us? We shan't be able to see."

"We'll just have to sit and read the labels," said Louli. She rose abruptly to her feet. "Mr Fernando, could I sit at the back please?" She waited for no answer but hitched down the tablecloth from the rack, dumped hat and coat upon their owner and marched up the aisle where, in the privacy of the rear seats, she and Mr Cecil collapsed into a communion of effervescent giggling. The coach driver, suddenly getting fed up with the lot of them, started the engine, engaged his gears with a jerk that threw them all backwards, and, considering them now to be seated, triumphantly drove off. Fernando produced a hand microphone and, unconscious that his voice was being distorted to a meaningless bellow, described the passing scene. Inspector Cockrill stared glassily out at it, and longed for home.

One of the Simply Impossibles was Miss Trapp. She shared a luncheon-table in the restaurant in the broad arcades of Milan with a quiet young woman called Miss Lane. They were both on their own. "I prefer to travel by myself," said Miss Trapp, snapping her tight, prim mouth. She wore the expensive, if somewhat out-of-date, hat with the red brussels-sprouts and a depressing brown silk dress, and clutched tight up under her chin in one thin hand a large brown leather bag. She looked like somebody's housekeeper, spending the savings of five years of slavery on a so-far not very successful Holiday Abroad; but the bag was of real leather and bore a monogram which, if indecipherable, was at least of gold. Miss Lane looked round at the Jollies and the Vulgars, at the Experienced Travellers (loudly demanding Bitter Campari and Risotto Milanese) and the Inexperienced Travellers, nervously eyeing their plates and hoping there wouldn't be all that nasty garlic, and asked if one could really describe this as travelling alone . . .?

Miss Trapp folded her lips, hugging the big brown bag. She changed the subject abruptly. "Do you live in London?"

Something secret drew down over Vanda Lane's face.

She replied, however, that yes, she lived in London. She had a flat.

"Oh, a flat," said Miss Trapp.

"In St John's Wood."

Miss Trapp seemed not to have heard of St John's Wood. She herself lived in Park Lane—*quite* a small house. "I think the air is better there . . ."

Vanda Lane did not care two hoots about the air of Park Lane. She sat toying with her spaghetti and covertly watching the man with only one arm. She was in love. He was ugly and angry-looking and in a million years he would never so much as glance her way; but she was in love. 'I'm the slave type,' she thought, 'and he's the master type; and he's the only person in the world that I would want to be my master.' After all the years of existing upon vicarious romanticism, barren of personal relationship, suddenly, totally unexpectedly, out of the blue had come fulfilment —to worship like a dog at the feet of a man with a bitter face and sullen, contemptuous eyes. She dropped her own eyes before his casual glance: a secret creature with a closed secret face—with leaf-brown hair kept secret under a tight-fitting hat, with a good figure kept secret in a repression of corset and brassiere, with clothes whose excellence was so discreet that none but Mr Cecil would trouble to look at them twice: with far more good looks than ever the flamboyant Louli Barker could boast, kept secret beneath an apparently almost deliberate under-emphasis—devoid of make-up, tight lipped, unsmiling, chill. She lifted her eyes again and again dropped them before his glance; and Leo Rodd said to his wife that dear God, now there were two of them longing to sympathize with him over his arm; and added that there was one thing about all this pasta and stuff, he didn't have to have it cut up for him publicly.

Mr Fernando jollied them all out and into the bus again.

"Come along, come along, off now in a jiffy to lovely Rapallo on the glorious Mediterranean coast . . ." He knew that they would hate the glorious Mediterranean coast with its horrid dark grey sand carefully boarded off from its flashy little towns, and would compare it unfavourably with Tenby and Frinton and Southend-on-Sea, the cruder spirits even murmuring among themselves that they could have gone far more cheaply to any or all of those places—but to Mr Fernando nothing connected with Odyssey Tours could be less than perfect and he could not forbear from extolling the joys to come, while there was yet a chance of doing so uncontradicted. "Hurry up, hurry up, where now are all our ladies?" Their ladies were queueing up before the door of the single lavatory where indeed the gentlemen had recently been in a queue of their own, embarrassingly close. They arrived, breathless and blushing, in ones and twos, Miss Trapp last of all, hurriedly adjusting the khaki silk dress and the brussels-sprouts hat. The driver looked round impatiently, saw only one passenger still standing, and drove off with his customary jerk and she sat down with unexpected abruptness in her place; but not before Mr Cecil, rising from his seat in the rear had cried out, high and gay: "Why goodness, Miss Trapp—I do believe you're wearing a Christophe hat!"

Now whatever was there in that, thought Inspector Cockrill, to have made the poor lady turn so pale?

CHAPTER TWO

THAT very first night in their terraced hotel at Rapallo, already you could see the party sorting itself out, forming into groups: the Vulgars and the Jollies getting together over Americanos, the Timids being taken over by the Seasoned Travellers, the Neurotics turning pale together at the sight of heaped dishes of death-dealing green figs and peaches, the Hearties calling loudly for lo nachurelle and assuring each other that a smattering of French would take you all over the world. . . . There was a spinster aunt standing treat to a handsome niece who she was obscurely determined should remain as desolately maiden as herself— Grim and Gruff, Mr Cecil and Louli called them; and already a member of the party had been christened, for obvious reasons, Mrs Sick. . . .

Inspector Cockrill remained aloof from it all. He left the hotel and went inland in search of a pub; there were no pubs but he found a small square with chairs outside a café and sat down and asked for a bitter. The waiter brought him a Bitter Campari and, disillusioned, he stumped back angrily to the hotel. Louli Barker was sitting alone on the balcony. "Hallo, Mr Cockrill. Where are all the chaps?"

"I met Mr Cecil going along the front."

"He's in hot pursuit of Fernando; but I'm afraid it's no dice, poor pet, because Fernando is after La Trapp."

"Well, I'm going up to bed. If you can call it a bed," said Cockie, gloomily.

Their hotel was not only first, but luxury class. "What's wrong with your bed?" asked Louli, surprised.

"I don't know yet. I shall very soon find out." But he lingered a little. He could not help liking her: there was about her something as friendly and well disposed as about a nice child. Under all this silly, false exterior, he thought— she's real. Not like that other closed-in, secret creature with her unhappy mouth and hooded, downcast blue eyes. Louli's eyes were blue too, but by no means downcast, or if they were it was from the weight of her new eyelashes. You stuck them on with white of egg, she confided to him, and he could have no idea how hard it was to ask a chambermaid for white of egg in Italian! The trouble was that, what with the egg and all, they were as heavy as hell and she simply couldn't keep awake. From his balcony above, he later observed that she had, indeed, fallen into a little cat nap, sitting bolt upright on a white metal chair.

Most of the others had come in and gone up to bed by the time Louli awoke; nor had the cat nap been so profound that she had not been able now and again to open a wary eye and mark their departure. Only the man with the one arm remained, standing looking out across the dark bay. She got up and stretched and went over and stood beside him and said, "Hallo."

He started. He said, irritably, "I thought everyone had gone to bed?"

"Not me, yet. So I thought I'd come over and say hallo to you."

"Well, hallo," he said, getting it over, as to a tiresome small child.

"I thought we might as well meet one another, as I suppose we shall be travelling together . . ."

"Why should you suppose that?"

She ignored the obvious reply that they were in fact

travelling together. She said, refusing to be snubbed: "Well, let's say then that I *hope* we'll be travelling together."

"When you get to know me better," he said, "you will not regard that as a matter for optimism."

"As long as I do get to know you better," said Louli, "I'll take a chance."

She said it with the little friendly, half teasing, half indulgent air that had already conquered its corner in the arid old heart of Detective Inspector Cockrill. Leo Rodd accepted defeat. "We'd better have a drink on it." They were the only people left up and about, but the bar-tender remained with Italian enthusiasm, glued to his post. Leo signalled to him to come out and take an order. "Meanwhile my name is Rodd: Leo Rodd. And yours?"

"Well, I'm Louvaine Barker," said Louli, with the little blush.

"What an odd name," said Leo. "It sounds like a woman novelist. Here's the chap. What'll you drink?"

She said she was hungry and would have a Pimms No. 1. "It's divine here, masses of fruit and veg., a sort of a alcoholic minestrone." She glanced up at him from beneath the egg-white eyelashes, naïvely inviting admiration for her wit; but he had heard her swapping the same joke earlier in the evening with Mr Cecil and refused to be impressed. He took out his wallet and, laying it flat on the edge of the balcony before him, struggled to take out a note. She put out a casual finger and held down one side of it, but otherwise offered no assistance. He paid the waiter, picked up the wallet and, clumsily refolding it, replaced it in his pocket. "Thank you. You are the first woman I have encountered in the past sixteen months who would not have taken out the money, paid the waiter for me, folded the thing up and put it back in my pocket with a kind little pat."

"I know," said Louli. "I was watching you at dinner."
At dinner, Vanda Lane and one or two persons unknown
had shared a table with the Rodds. He gave a bitter smile
at the memory of it. "Miss Lane or whatever her name is
could hardly keep her hands off me; and as for my wife,
my wife is a dear, sweet thing, but my God!—if she could
predigest my food for me because I've only got one arm, I
do believe she would."

"It must be horrid," said Louli, "always having to
choose the things on the menu that don't have to be cut
up."

"Horrid," he agreed, sarcastically moderate. He added:
"I will forestall your next question by informing you that I
did *not* lose it in the war."

"No, I know," said Louli. "You fell off your bike and
got gas gangrene into it. I saw it in the paper and your
photograph, 'Concert Pianist Loses Arm' and things. It was
on a page where I had a review," she added candidly, "or
I don't suppose I'd have noticed it."

His eyes clouded over with the old, dark memories,
never far behind: the absurd, the ludicrous tumble off
the bicycle, the first stab of doubt, the uneasy fears, the
mounting terror, the ultimate long despair. Concert Pianist
Loses Right Arm. But she wouldn't have noticed except
that—something about a review. "You thought it was not
of any great importance?"

"Oh, yes," said Louli. "I cried." And she turned away
her head and bit her lip and mumbled that she was nearly
crying now, she had been nearly crying all the evening,
only she was certain that egg white would melt.

"*Egg* white?"

"My eyelashes," said Louli, turning her face into the
moonlight so that he could see.

They were terrible, they were like bent hairpins; but it

was true—the blue eyes were brimming with tears. Many women had wept for him, many had uttered words of tender pity; but here were words blessedly unspoken, here were tears that struggled *not* to be shed. Such as had been shed, had been shed in private, over a stranger, over a headline and a scowling photograph. "You cried? For me?"

"Well, not actually howled," she admitted, again with that odd little air of candour that, coming from so much determined sophistication was somehow so absurdly endearing. "Just sort of mizzled. But it seemed so awful for you— never being able to play the piano again. . . ."

"I see," he said. He turned away from her and stood again, staring out across the bay, black and silent now under the brilliant moon. "You looked at a photograph of my ugly mug and you cried—because a stranger couldn't play the piano any more." He thought about it. "Are you so fond of music?"

"Music?" said Louli. "Oh, no—it bores me stiff."

He burst out laughing. He stretched out his one arm and pulled her to him, suddenly, and kissed her lightly upon her painted mouth; and let her go. "Well, you're going to hear some now," he said. There was a piano in a sheltered corner of the balcony; two nights a week a stout Genoese lady played it for dancing there. He went over and sat down and twiddled on the stool a couple of times to adjust it to his height; and then, first with one finger, then with two, then with his whole, poor depleted complement of fingers, he began to play a little tune.

Standing in his striped pyjamas on his bedroom balcony above them, Inspector Cockrill looked down and listened and recognized the tune. Well, well, well, he thought; so this is a conducted tour! They don't waste much time.

He was by no means the only person in the hotel that night who heard and reflected upon that gay, that triumphant little tune.

And next morning there was a dip in the glorious, mud-coloured Mediterranean, sweetened by the sewers of Rapallo. Louli Barker bobbed and screamed, Mr Cecil bobbed and screamed, Miss Trapp in knee-length stockinette, dabbled her toes and squealed: Mr Fernando rolled like a porpoise, glistening with sun-tanned muscle, the Rodds swam out away from the rest of them side by side, she with the quiet elegance with which she did everything, he with a steady, overarm stroke which he had presumably evolved for himself since the loss of his arm. But Vanda Lane—Vanda Lane came suddenly into her own and, blue-black as a swallow in her tight black satiny bathing dress and cap, walked quietly out and executed three high dives as swift and graceful and exquisitely perfect as the swallow's own flight; and quietly retired again. They piled once more into the coach, en route for Siena. Miss Trapp, a little heady from the attentions last night of that rather *earthy* Mr Fernando, sat in her place of honour just behind him; further back, Leo Rodd and his wife dozed fitfully, he hot and cross, she elegant and cool, looking out indifferently upon the route through glasses as large and round and yellow as Mr Fernando's own. Behind them again, Vanda Lane sat in a dream of happiness to come, because Leo Rodd had congratulated her upon her performance and asked her to help him evolve some method of diving which might compensate for the loss of his arm. In the back row, Mr Cockrill irritably drowsed while Cecil and Louli Barker giggled over their collaboration in a travel book, to be entitled Incontinent

23

on the Continent, and dedicated to The Queues. In his seat beside the driver, Mr Fernando reached forth for his microphone. "Ladies and gentlemen, a brief stop now at Pisa, out for a jiffy to look at the Leaning Tower, and then to lovely Siena—three nights, ladies and gentlemen in Siena, expeditions through the country all about Siena; and after Siena, to the wonderful island of San Juan el Pirata which has been called The Cathedral in the Sea. En route, then, ladies and gentlemen, for Pisa. En route for Siena. En route for San Juan el Pirata . . ."

En route, ladies and gentlemen for—Murder.

CHAPTER THREE

MR FERNANDO's choice of 'first-class hotels' was by no means that laid down by the agency and appeared to vary startlingly between millionaire standard and a new low in third-rate pensions. The hotel at Rapallo had been in the very top grade, their three nights in Siena were to be spent in a dreary albergo that hit the very bottom. The angular widow felt it worst and became known to all members of Il Grouppa as Mrs Moan, a pair of timid schoolteachers travelling together and already regretting it, tried to pluck up courage to ask for their money back and abandon the tour, but without success, and Mrs Sick, gobbling her way through the curious evening meals, would then take possession of the one and only ritirata, to the discomfort of ladies and gentlemen alike, for the rest of the night. But Siena itself was breath-takingly lovely, seen for the first time in the light of an Italian summer evening and, as the dreamy days went by, even the handsome niece began to question her aunt's sagacity in matters of Romance; and Miss Trapp trembled on Mr Fernando's arm as he squired her on their conducted excursions or dawdled after the rest through the narrow streets of the town. They went on their last night for a farewell visit to the Duomo. "You do not come often abroad, Miss Trapp?"

No, indeed, said Miss Trapp, she had not been abroad for—for ages. Not since the war, really. The currency restrictions had made it hardly worth while. And then . . . "At my age, one does not care for travelling about on one's own."

"People may take advantage of your youth and inexperience," said Fernando gallantly; but she was no fool, he had found that out over the past few days and he said it with a smile, with a little teasing bow.

She longed to be easy and gracious, to accept the silly compliment at its face value, to handle the whole affair like a woman of the world. Instead, she felt a red stain spread over her pale face, and she said brusquely that she hadn't meant that at all: all she meant was that she didn't like going about alone.

"But you have many friends!"

"No, I haven't," said Miss Trapp gruffly.

"Ah—it is true. The rich cannot really have friends. I think, Miss Trapp, it is difficult for rich people to know who are their real friends?"

Miss Trapp's thin mouth took on a bitter line, a hurt and bitter line. "Yes, I think it is. Very difficult. There is always uncertainty; and then—suspicion, and once that's there, nothing can ever be the same again." He squinted at her uneasily but it was not meant for him, her mind was far away. "There's no happiness in having money, none. You can't be happy unless you have friends, unless you can trust people; but such a lot of them you can't trust, you get hurt and deceived so often that at last you come to believe that nobody cares about you at all, just for yourself alone."

"But you, Miss Trapp," said Fernando, gallantly, "so nice, so charming—*you* cannot doubt that your friends must care for you 'for yourself alone'?"

"I've just told you—I have no friends," said Miss Trapp.

He was nonplussed. It was difficult to progress in flattering attentions to a woman who refused to accept, who bleakly repudiated, the inevitable little implied untruths. He fell to boasting about himself instead. "No solitude, Miss Trapp, if one is a courier! One travels about—Spain, Italy, Austria, now for the moment my territory is Italy and San Juan el Pirata—and always with people, new people, people gay and on holiday; some dull, of course, some unattractive, some tiresome—between ourselves, Miss Trapp, always one or two Mrs Moans!—but so many, like Miss Trapp, very nice, very charming." He tripped them both up with another of his florid little bows as they walked along. "This way, come, I show you the Duomo in the moonlight. . . . Yes, Miss Trapp, they say to me in the office, 'Mr Gomez, you should not waste your powers going out with the parties.' But this is my pleasure, I don't want no stuffy office, I prefer to go as simple courier. You see—don't say it to the others, but I am not truly just a courier, I am partner in Odyssey Tours, I am the continental partner, based upon Tangiers. This, of course, you did not realize?"

"No, indeed," said Miss Trapp faintly. (Partner in a flourishing business—not just a courier!)

"You have not seen my dear Gibraltar, you do not know Spain? One day I take you there, I show you my villa, outside Gib. on the Spanish coast, a villa with white walls and terraces down to the sea, terraces of flowers, bougain-villea, jasmine, every colour of geranium. I shall show it to you one day, you shall come with me . . ."

Miss Trapp privately thought it in the last degree unlikely that Mr Fernando would ever have the opportunity to show her his villa by the sea. She replied politely, however, that it sounded most charming.

"Ah, charming yes; but for a poor bachelor like me, too large—and too lonely." Mr Fernando lifted up his face and appeared to be about to bay the moon. "You are not the only person who can be lonely, Miss Trapp."

Miss Trapp's forthright soul rebelled. "You've just said that *you* couldn't; because of being a courier."

Making hay with Miss Trapp was not a smooth-going affair. Mr Fernando, however, was glibly equal to all occasions. "Ah friends, acquaintances; but I speak now, to you of something else, Miss Trapp. I speak now of love."

Of love? And to her? Was Mr Fernando on this, the fifth day of their ever having met one another, speaking of love— and to her? Miss Trapp's good, common common-sense rebelled against so improbable, so ominous an idea. And yet . . . The black and white stripes of the cathedral swam and jiggled before her in the moonlight, her bowels turned to water in her thin, hungry frame. To be loved! For however base a reason—to be desired! He certainly was dreadfully shiny, dreadfully 'foreign,' quite, quite dreadfully earthy and masculine: and yet—to 'belong'! Not to be lonely any more, not to be solitary any more, to have this strong, this really almost repellently strong male arm to lean upon, to become Mrs Gomez and share the white-walled villa on the coast of Spain. . . . (To become Mrs Gomez and not to have to share the villa was no doubt more than any woman could ask of fate.) Her lips were trembling, she withdrew her hand from his arm abruptly and grasped at the handles of her big brown bag, hugging it tight up under her pointed chin. Mr Fernando looked, rather startled, into her face and saw that her eyes were brimming over with tears. "Miss Trapp —you are crying?" He stood before her, helplessly, his big arms hanging uselessly at his sides. "You are sad?"

"No, I'm not, I'm just stupid, that's all." She shook her head so that the tears were flicked out on to her cheeks. "Don't worry about me, I'm a fool."

"But I must worry." She lifted her head and looked back into his face and suddenly saw it no longer as the face of a bold, bad, braggadacio fellow: but the sagging face of a middle-aged man, anxious and kind—a face hag-ridden, moreover, by some secret anxiety of his own. It was only for a moment. He squared his big shoulders and gave her a flash of the old, effulgent, gold-studded smile: and yet a kind smile, almost a tender smile. "Come—I have made you sad with talk of loneliness: now we two will be lonely no more, we will be friends and I make you jolly again." He put out his hand to her. "Let us sit on the wall and look up at this funny old Duomo with its one foolish leg stuck up in the air, like the leg of an American convict in his striped suit; and I tell you all about San Juan el Pirata where we go to-morrow—I have mugged it up again in the guide book this morning." She did not take his hand, her own hands hugged the handles of the brown bag; and to cover the oddly lost feeling that it gave him to have his kindly meant gesture go unrewarded, he said, lightly, as they settled themselves on the wall: "What is in this old bag of yours that you will not let go of it for a moment, to take the hand of your friend?"

"What's in my bag?"

"You hold this silly bag so tight!"

"It's just a habit," she said. "There's nothing in the bag of any value." She sat for a moment staring at the pink and white, sugar-sweet façade of the cathedral with its slender, striped black and white tower. "At least—only one thing. And that wouldn't be of any value to anyone except me." She began to scrabble about with thin hands in the interior of the bag. "It's a letter; a sort of—farewell letter. I think, Mr Fernando—I think it would be a good thing if I were to show it to you."

He protested. "Miss Trapp, Miss Trapp, I was only teasing, for God's sake don't think I want to know what's in your bag. Come now, change the subject, I am your guide book, we sit here quietly and very soon you know all about San Juan . . ."

But she found what she wanted and put it into his hands

and he took the sheet of crested white writing-paper from the crested white envelope and read the few pitiful lines that were written there; and when they walked home that night down the narrow streets and across the incredible loveliness of the Campo and up more tiny streets to their albergo—Miss Trapp still knew very little about San Juan el Pirata but she knew all that she wished to know about Mr Fernando; and Mr Fernando knew all about Miss Trapp.

Mr Cecil meanwhile sought out Louli. She was sitting at a little table outside one of the innumerable cafés that edge the sloping scallop-shell of the campo. "Oh, there you are— I've been looking for you. Let me stand you a Grappa. We'll get on with The Book." Their fellow-tourists had seized with horrid avidity upon their project but had immediately split up into two equally undesirable parties, the Stuffies and the Downright Filthies and they had been obliged to give up discussion of their opus in public.

Louvaine seemed not over-anxious to pursue the matter, however. "Actually, I think I have an assignation of my own. It's tricky, because I don't really know where or when." She looked about her uneasily. "I thought the best thing to do was just go somewhere obvious and stay put."

Mr Cecil was all excitement. "An assignation? Who with?"

"With the lift of an eyebrow," said Louli, ruefully laughing. "I don't even know if it really meant anything."

"Oh, is that where you disappear to every evening? You don't waste much time," said Mr Cecil. He was aglow with interest and curiosity. But it was odd. "I thought it was usually the young woman who said where and when—not to mention whether. Not that I'd know," he added, hastily.

*Hindu ⟶ "memsahibs" = wives;
phonetically: "mem-sobs"

She shrugged, again ruefully. "I'm afraid this is rather a case of, 'Oh, whistle——' "

" '—and I'll come to you, my lad'?"

"That's about the size of it," said Louvaine.

Mr Cecil rapidly reviewed the various men in the party; there were two callow youths but they were after the handsome niece and surely too small fry for La Barker with all the worldly experience she must (at her age, let's face it!) have known; and for the rest, a couple of stuffy old colonels with their mems. and Mr Fernando, of course, and . . . "But *ducky*," said Mr Cecil, "*not* that ill-tempered devil with only one arm?"

"It's a pity about the one arm," acknowledged Louli. "But he does pretty well with it—don't you fret!" She said, a trifle anxiously: "You won't tell? I just have to talk about it to someone or I'll burst out at the seams."

"There's nobody to tell," said Mr Cecil. He said it a little reluctantly; to receive sacred confidences was, of course, delicious—but to be able to pass them on and so find oneself at the storm centre of a scandal was to Mr Cecil the breath of life. "Of course there's the wife," he added, "but she's one of these self-contained people, I don't suppose she'll care a fig . . ."

*HINDU ⟶ "sahib" = male leader;
phonetically ⟶ "sob"
⟶ more formally ⟶ "sah-heeb"

Leo Rodd stood at the entrance of the dreary little albergo. "Well—I think I'll—er—just go for a bit of a walk."

Helen was jaded and weary after two sleepless nights on the albergo beds. She missed her cue. "A walk?—we've just come back from one."

His hand dug into the pocket of his light jacket, the nails driven into the palm by the excess of his irritation, goaded on by the sense that he was deceiving and ill-using her. "Well—I'm just going off for another one. Any objection?"

No—she had no objection. She had pulled herself together by now and could smile and look into his face and say that the hotel beds certainly weren't very inviting; but that she thought that for her part she would go in: and to try not to wake her if he was—was late. And she *had* no objection: not really. These flirtations kept him happier, he pretended to be annoyed by outpourings of 'womanly sympathy' but he fell for them every time, there would be sentimental gaiety for a week or two, another week or two of increasing boredom and disillusion, a week or two of sulks and self-pity: and then he would come back to her. She smiled and lightly said good night and watched him walk away with his swinging, wrenching, exaggeratedly wrenching, shoulder-forward step, down the close little street, away into the lovely heart of Siena: and would not even let herself pray that this time it would be the same as all the other times—this time, despite the sudden sick stab of doubt in her own weary heart—he would still come back.

A figure detached itself from the shadows in the little square and dodged back into other shadows, lining the high street walls: creeping down, softly and swiftly, after him, an alley cat padding through city gutters to the mating call of the sleek, black tom, caterwauling on the tiles. . . . An alley cat! Her heart lifted within her, she could have laughed aloud at the folly of that stab of sudden dread. An alley cat —not the soft, shining marmalade creature with its proud head and the gleaming big blue eyes; but a secret cat, slinking along by its wild lone, avid and anxious, making for the rendezvous . . .

But men were curious creatures. Fancy, when that gay, that radiant creature, Louli Barker, was offering him her charming heart on a plate—fancy Leo going off to an assignation with a girl like Vanda Lane!

CHAPTER FOUR

THE island of San Juan el Pirata lies, as any regular traveller with Odyssey Tours must know, some twenty kilometres off the coast of Tuscany about level with the topmost tip of Corsica, in the Ligurian sea. It is perhaps seven or eight miles across and largely composed of volcanic upheavals of rock: a republic, self-contained, self-controlled, self-supporting, with a tiny parliament and a tiny police force and a quite remarkably tiny conscience in regard to its obligations to the rest of society; but with a traditionally enormous Hereditary Grand Duke. Juan the Pirate appropriated his foothold there two hundred years ago. Busily plying between Italy and his native Spain, he fell foul of both, established himself on the island, built his rock fortress there, defended it against all comers and, in 1762, retired there, gold-glutted, to die at last in the odour of sanctity, loudly declaring repentance for his abominable sins and in the same breath his right to hang on to the proceeds. Succeeding governments in both Italy and Spain have turned a blind eye, according to temperament or expedience, and to this day San Juan remains—on Italian territory in Italian seas—Spanish in thought and flavour; still using in highly bastardized form its founder's mother tongue and strictly upholding and maintaining his deplorable standards. The charming Peurto de Barrequitas, Port of the Little Boats, sends forth its fishing fleet night after moonless night and in the grey dawn welcomes it back with its contraband

33

cargo; all hands, including such members of the international anti-smuggling police as have not been out to sea with it, turning to, to help with the unloading. But even so it has proved, since the war, impossible to feed the insatiable maw of the contraband-hungry tourist trade, without recourse to the mainland; and San Juan reluctantly smuggles in, instead of through, the Swiss watches, American nylons, French liqueurs and Scotch whisky especially manufactured in Madrid, Naples and Cairo for this purpose. These are exhibited in the local shops with 'Smuggled' in large letters printed on cards in various languages; and such is their attraction that, in 1950, under the direct auspices of El Exaltida, the Hereditary Grand Duke himself, San Juan began work on the Bellomare Hotel.

The island, seen from the deck of the gay little vaporetto which plies between Barrequitas and Piombino on the mainland, looks like an outsize cathedral, rising abruptly up out of the sea. Perched fantastically at the tip of its spire is the fairy-tale palace of the Grand Duke. To the west, built up from the sheer rock face, is the prison—a dark, dank fortress where, in the splendid old piratical days, a countless toll of prisoners mouldered to merciful death; balancing it to the east is the Duomo which houses the illustrious bones of the founder, and to the north the cobbled streets thrust their way down to the quays of the fishing boats. But looking southward over the sunlit blue starred with a dozen tiny satellite islands, what would be the façade of the cathedral slopes down, crumbling and pine clad, to an indentation of little beaches: and here, above many-flowered terraces, stand the long lines of the Bellomare Hotel whose boast it is that every room faces into the sunshine and over the sea.

Despite this uniformity of excellence, there was the usual scrimmage for preference, round the reception desk when, late the next afternoon, the Odyssey party arrived. The rooms were strung out in three tiers, those on the first floor giving on to a balcony with steps leading down to the higher of two terraces. Vanda Lane, suddenly coming out of her shell, appeared ready to bleed and die rather than accept any but one of these rooms, number five; though nobody could see anything to distinguish it from any other, except perhaps that Mrs Sick was in the neighbouring number six; Louli Barker had studiously avoided it for this reason and bagged number four.

Mr Cecil was still inclined to be hurt at the spectacle of Fernando jockeying for position next door to Miss Trapp. "I've been put next to Cockrill," he said to Louvaine. "He's harmless enough. But Viceroy Sarah on the other side—I bet she snores. And you?"

"Other side of Viceroy Sal. Yes, I bet she does." Viceroy Sarah was a colonel's lady doing a recce, for her husband's coming leave. "Then La Lane in number five. My dear, I do think this place is *simply!*"

"Yes, *too!*" agreed Cecil. He repeated it. "Absolutely too!" It was a new high in brevity.

Inspector Cockrill, though still regarding the whole expedition with the darkest suspicion, could not but agree with them. He sat very pleasantly that evening on the lower of the two terraces under a swinging lantern, sipping a glass of the local Juanello, resolutely pronounced Hoowarnellyo by the erudite—deep in the latest adventure of his favourite Detective Inspector Carstairs, at present engaged upon The Case of the Leaping Blonde. All about him the members of Il Grouppa wandered, chattering. Lying on her bed in number six, no doubt, Mrs Sick was revelling in stomach trouble, in number three Viceroy Sarah would be writing home with powerful fluency to warn her husband that the people on these tours were definitely Not Pukka and the whole experiment an unsuccess and on the sand just below the terrace where he sat, Louvaine Barker strolled with Mr Cecil, 'just till he comes.' Inspector Cockrill cared nothing for any of it. Eyes narrowed to tiny slits, broad shoulders squared, Carstairs slipped through the murk of a London fog, brown fingers taut on the blue-black butt of an empty automatic—for to go armed when the enemy carries no weapon is to Carstairs, quixotic fool that he is, like shootin' at a sittin' bird . . . Inspector Cockrill flipped over a page and with a happy sigh, read on.

But Louvaine and Mr Cecil had come just beneath him, strolling towards a great rock jutting out across the sand to the sea, and even Carstairs was not proof at that short range against the two high voices clear in the whispering silence of the sand and the sea. "Louli, ducky, this is getting serious."

"Serious?" said Louli. "Well, what've I been telling you? Of course it is."

Goodness, thought Mr Cecil. What a fuss and scandal and him right here in the middle of it where he loved to be, such *fun!* "But what about him—him too?"

She was deaf to the tone of eager curiosity; wrapped in her own warm dream. She gave him a smile of purest radiance. "Oh, yes—him too."

"What, all in a couple of days?"

"In a couple of minutes. It's a madness," said Louli. "It just happens to you. You look at each other and—well, it's like Lem Putt says, in 'The Specialist': there you are—catched!"

"Lem Putt was talking about being in a lavatory, dear."

"But looking out through a little window, shaped like a star. That's me now—looking out on the whole of life through a window shaped like a star. . . ."

"And seeing nothing but this ugly, cross fellow, Leo Rodd?"

"Is he ugly?" she said. "To me he looks like the Angel of Light. And of course he isn't cross with *me*." The moonlight gleamed on the bright bent head, threw tiny shadows of curved false eyelashes across the high cheekbones; but it took the red dye from her lipstick and left her mouth dark and somehow rather sad. "Well, but, Louli—what happens now?"

"We get through the next two weeks as well as we can, and then when we're all home again, we sort it out: and then we'll get married or not get married, but anyway we'll be together."

"And his wife?" said Cecil.

She was silent. She said at last, "You see—the thing that happens is that you get this sort of—sort of a glory: and you can't see anything except yourself and the person you're in love with. You try to think about other people and mind about them, but it's like looking at them through the wrong end of a telescope, you see them as terribly tiny and terribly far away and you simply can't make yourself realize that their feelings aren't tiny and far away too . . ."

"But, ducky, surely it's just an infatuation?"

"If it is," said Louli, "it doesn't make any difference. It's real to us."

"Will she let him go?"

"You can't keep something that doesn't belong to you any more," said Louli. "One must just pray and pray and pray that she doesn't mind too much."

Cecil thought back to the recent defection of Francis—Francis who had been coming on this trip with him, who had suddenly up and rushed off to Majorca instead, with that horrid little ballet-beast Boris: to his own first meeting with Francis and the consequent quarrellings with Basil; to the first days with Basil and how ruthless Basil had been about Piers. . . . To all the scenes and the dramas, the

triumphs, the despairs, the pleasures, the pain. To all the
sordidness—for that was what it boiled down to in the end,
tricks and evasions and treacherous little lies. In the depths
of his heart he resented it because here was something that
lifted its head up out of the mire he knew; and he was
impelled to try to drag it down. "You and your Leo—don't
you feel just a bit—mean?"

"Oh, yes," said Louli. "About the little things. He feels
mean, sneaking off and meeting me in the evenings, I feel
mean being insincere to her. But not about the big things;
we can't help that."

They had come to the end of the beach, to where the
high rock cast its black shadow across the moonlit silver of
the sand. "And may one ask, dear, what you're thinking
of living on? I mean, the money is all hers, isn't it, they
make no secret of that?"

"*He* makes no secret of it. She never mentions it."

"Of course he used to make a lot, I suppose, but obviously
he'll never play the piano again, he'll never make a
farthing . . ."

"I'll make the farthings," said Louli. She smiled in the
shadowy darkness beneath the rock. "You don't think that
I can—but I will. You'll see!" And suddenly she started
forward. "Did you hear?—is that him coming now?"

But it was five minutes more before he came and found
her alone there in the shadow of the rock; and put his one
arm round her and held her as though he could never let
her go.

Away above the silver and black of the sea, the moon
hung like a silver lantern, tipping with silver the shining
edges of the oleander leaves, black shadowed by the night. At

the balcony rail outside the row of bedrooms, Mr Fernando leaned with Miss Trapp and like a troubled schoolboy explained, excused, promised reformation and at last with most unwonted diffidence, took her thin hand and held it in his own. In the pinewoods behind the hotel, Helen Rodd walked alone, anxious and sorrowful; through the scented gardens, Mr Cecil strolled and Vanda Lane hurried with pain and hatred in her bitter heart; in the shadow of the rock the lovers leaned in one another's arms and forgot the world and time. And on the terrace above them, Inspector Cockrill stirred restlessly in his deck-chair and tried to get back to Carstairs and could not concentrate. Carstairs never fell in love: perhaps because his eyes were so constantly narrowed that he was unable to recognize a pretty girl when he saw one. Inspector Cockrill, on the other hand, recognized a pretty girl only too easily and nowadays sometimes worried in case he should grow into a dirty old man; and he could not help being fond of this particular girl—and sorry to see her making such a mess of things. And yet . . . He looked out over the scented gardens, over a sea like wrinkled black treacle under the silver moon: and suddenly the magic and romance seemed all that was real, and England and his little world of crime and punishment, unimportant and far away. He could not know that he was looking at a stage set for murder; that the prologue had been spoken, that the cast was assembled, dressed and made up, in the wings: that to-morrow, when the curtain of darkness rolled back and the footlights flooded the stage in bright Mediterranean sunshine—the play would begin.

The pronunciation, in hybrid-Spanish-Italian, of the name of the hotel, phased even the Experienced Travellers who would have died rather than call the island anything but San Hoowarne. Mr Cecil and Louvaine called it frankly Bello-mare and had succeeded in convincing one or two of the more credulous that it referred to the lavish cuisine of the hotel and meant The Stomach of a Horse. Certainly the meals were gargantuan. Replete with tortilla and pizza, on the afternoon after their arrival, Cockie resisted all attempts to get him to join an expedition to see over the ducal palace on the hill and retired for the siesta. It had been amusing, he reflected as he stripped to his vest and underpants and lay down on the white-curtained four-poster bed in his close-shuttered room, to observe the skirmishings of those who, for less innocent reasons than an assignation with Carstairs, also wished to cry off. The outing had been arranged by the hotel and Fernando had been only too thankful to let his party go off without him for once, with the other guests. Miss Trapp, obviously prescient of this intention, started a positive epidemic of headaches. Helen Rodd, defensively clearing the way for her husband and his latest light of love, was the first to be infected; Leo and Louvaine, drifting in separately to announce the same affliction, discovered too late that she had been before them and that they were now all three condemned to spend the afternoon together after all. Vanda Lane, overhearing Leo's stumbling speech, succumbed immediately and only Mr Cecil, delighted at the possibility of mischief arising from this narrowing down of the party, struck out for himself and declared that ideas for Hoowarnese-inspired designs were simmering on the hob, duckies, and he must get out Little Red Attashy case and dash them down forthwith. They drifted to their rooms. Out in the blistering sunshine, the explorers moved off reluctantly upon their jaunt, the hotel staff retired to their remote and unbeautiful quarters to doze away the precious off-duty hours, and soon there was no sound or movement but the

hissing breath of the sea cooling the hot white sand. Inspector
Carstairs slid off the gentle protuberance of Cockie's full
tummy and lay with rumpled pages on the floor, and the
peace of the long Spanish afternoon siesta fell softly upon
the Bellomare Hotel.

It was an hour or more before Cockrill awoke. It was
pleasantly cool in the bare little cell-like room, but the
sunshine was streaming through the slats of the shutters
and he jumped up quite gaily and splashed about under
the shower in his tiny bathroom and put on a light jacket
and the hat which he had dashingly purchased in Rapallo
some days ago. Contrary to custom, he had bought it not
two sizes too large, but considerably too small and it sat
on his splendid head like a paper boat, breasting the fine
spray of his greying hair. He patted his pockets to be sure
of a stock of tobacco and paper for his cigarettes, tucked
Carstairs under his arms, and went out on to the balcony
whose rail was draped already with the bathing impedimenta of the hotel guests. Directly below were the main
reception rooms, their great doors standing ever open upon
the lovely terrace, roofed in with bougainvillea; two curving
flights of steps led down to the terrace from the balcony,
and from the terrace a central flight of shallow steps ran on
down and across a lower terrace, and so to the beach. To
his left as he looked seawards, a hump of rock jutted out
like a great nose at the level of the lower terrace, dividing
the beach from a little beach beyond; along its sharp ridge,
a narrow path had been worn by the bathers running out
to a diving-board which had been built into it, twenty feet
above sea level, at its tip. At the terrace end of the ridge, a
row of little bathing cabins had been erected; the upper
terrace ended in a short curve of steps leading through a
tunnel of flowering jasmine, down to the huts. In the angles
where the rock nose joined the face of the mainland, rough,

steep little paths had been worn, tippling down to the beaches below.

The beach was deserted but there were sounds of movement in the rooms strung out along the balcony and at the window of number four, Louli Barker stood with her bright head in a Tiggywinkle of curling-pins, drying her hair in the sun. She bobbed back when she saw him and simultaneously Leo Rodd and his wife appeared and, nodding to him, went off down the balcony steps to the terraces, turned to their left and disappeared beneath the bright flowers and twisted grey boughs of the bougainvillea that roofed it in. Deprived of her elegant clothes, she looked unattractively thin: her narrow shanks met the close-fitting legs of her bathing dress like the wooden limbs of an old-fashioned Dutch doll, joining its painted body. Leo Rodd carried a pair of rubber frog-feet and a mask with a small, bent, corked tube for underwater swimming; and over his shoulder was thrown, as though carelessly, a towel which covered the stump of his severed arm. Cockie had observed during their bathe that morning on the beach, the unobtrusive protectiveness with which his wife had gone to the water's edge with him and taken the towel at the moment that he plunged into the sea and let the blue waters close over his disfigurement—meeting him with it again, chucking it casually to him, just as he emerged. He wondered briefly if Leo's new love would be so constantly, so loyally, so ever delicately, at his irritable beck and call: and concluded, without much caring either way, that Louli would be more likely to bestow upon him one of her gay, sweet, careless smiles and say that honestly, ducky, nobody would care two hoots about his arm not being there, so not to fuss . . .

She emerged at this moment, red head gleaming, restored to its shoulder-length mass of curls, red poppies flaring on a diminutive white satin Bikini bathing suit. She looked at him, he thought, a trifle furtively, standing fiddling with the strap of her brassiere. "Hallo, Inspector. Have—have the chaps gone on?"

"Gone on?" said Cockie.

"To watch La Lane diving."

"Oh, I'd forgotten," said Cockie. At luncheon Vanda Lane, one eye on Leo Rodd, had promised to give an exhibition of her skill. Louli had turned pea green at the bare thought of anyone running out along the high razor-back of the rock and actually looking down—let alone leaping off into the sea; and he was a little surprised that she should contemplate watching the demonstration. He said however, that yes, Leo Rodd had just gone along, adding, somewhat to his dismay in a faintly warning tone: "*And* Mrs Rodd."

It checked her. She had started to move off without another word but now she stopped abruptly and her hand jerked on the narrow strap. "Oh, blast!—now I've split the thing." She stood looking down uncertainly, chin humped on breast, and finally moved on down the steps, one hand holding the split white satin together, the other swinging a gay red plastic beach bag. He saw the flicker of the red and white Bikini passing under the grey bougainvillea boughs. At the far end of the lower terrace, the Rodds emerged from the jasmine-tunnelled steps leading down to where the rock jutted out from the sea.

Miss Trapp and Mr Fernando appeared, popping out of their doors like a couple of cuckoos from synchronized cuckoo clocks. They presented a curious contrast, he stripped except for a pair of bright orange satin shorts on his narrow hips, enormously broad of shoulder, once-splendid muscle rippling under the sun-burned skin; she with a round rubber bath cap pulled down to her eyebrows, her stockinette bathing-dress almost down to her knees, tripping along, half dead with self-consciousness, at his side. Fernando was evidently concerned to excuse himself for his lack of diving prowess. "I am, however, great swimmer, Miss Trapp, Cambridge half-blue for swimming just missed: you see—fine muscles, big torso, very strong . . ." He hammered his magnificent chest with gorilla arms till his bosoms wobbled like the red-brown jelly from under beef dripping. Mr Cecil, appearing now at Cockie's side, leaned over the rail and watched them go, almost with tears in his eyes. "I do think he's rather gorgeous." In the afterglow of Fernando's sun-tanned splendour, his thin limbs looked like a tangle of over-cooked spaghetti. Under one pallid arm, he carried the precious red attaché case.

Vanda Lane came out of her room. It was extraordinary, thought Cockie, what it did for her to be, even temporarily, exalted over her fellows. In the sea and on the diving-board, she was frankly the admiration of all; she accepted it modestly but in this moment of trifling supremacy, she had lost her air of shrinking evasiveness, of resolute discontent: her face and figure were suddenly boldly handsome, out-lined in the close severity of tight black cap and tight, well-fitted black satiny bathing-dress. She wore black rubber shoes and carried a rolled-up wrap of white towelling, and the touch of white against the sheen of the blue-black gave her once again, as on the beach at Rapallo, the look of a swallow, exquisitely poised for flight.

Unwontedly friendly, she came over and stood beside them at the rail. "Have the others appeared yet?"

"Mr and Mrs Rodd have gone on," said Cockie. "Miss Barker went after them."

"No doubt," said Vanda Lane, dryly.

"Well, I mean . . ." But he would not make matters worse to make them better. "And Mr Fernando has just gone along with Miss Trapp."

"Still clutching the handbag!" said Cecil, gaily.

She leaned forward and looked at him across Inspector Cockrill. "I see you have yours too."

Just one's scribblings, said Mr Cecil. London was going all Hoowarnese next season or his name was not Cecil Pr.... Well, Cecil. Masses and masses of tiny frills from the knees down and terribly tight under the tail, they'd all have to walk about with their knees bent like Spanish dancers, it would be too new for any! The little red attaché case was crammed to the top, nothing elaborate, of course, nothing finished, just one's rough scribbles to take to Rome and complete in the studio but, and this was the vital thing, *ideas*. . . .

"Which you've gathered since you came to Italy?" said Vanda.

He went a shade white, gave a little startled yap like a small dog and like a small dog snapped round on her. "What do you mean by that?"

She put on an innocent face. "Does it suggest some special meaning?"

He tossed back the lock of gold hair but it was purely from habit, there was no room in him now for affectations. "I don't know. It seems . . ."

"Ah, seems," said Vanda. Her hands were fisted on the rail of the balcony, but loosely like the paws of a cat, and she kept up an air of easy bantering, only subtly touched with venom. "Ah—seems! But this is a holiday; and on holiday, nothing's quite what it seems. People aren't what they seem. Are they, Inspector? You're a policeman—you know that."

Above them the sun blazed down, below them the sea danced, sequined blue, the terraces were a massed glory of rose and oleander, of myrtle and orange blossom, of palm and pine; but suddenly there was a chill wind about them, ugly and chill. Cockie said flatly: "People are never exactly what they seem."

"But especially on holiday," she insisted. "Surrounded by people who don't know one. No give-away relatives, no childhood friends, no birth certificates, no diplomas, no marriage lines . . ."

"No police records," said Cockie.

"Exactly," she said. "Reborn. Reborn just for a couple of weeks, with a whole, new spick and span character to present to a whole new world. Starting with casual little showing-off lies to strangers—then the strangers become acquaintances, become friends, become patrons, perhaps, or even prospective employers, and it's too late to go back on the lies, they have to be strengthened, they have to be built up by other lies until at last there's a whole, great terrifying structure of lies to be lived up to for the whole, long holiday, perhaps even after the holiday, perhaps to the end of one's life . . ." She looked into their faces with cold, blue, disagreeably sneering eyes. "Don't you agree?"

"You're a student of human nature, Miss Lane," said Inspector Cockrill smoothly.

"I find it a profitable study."

"On holiday?" he suggested.

"And after. I keep up with my holiday acquaintances, Inspector."

"No doubt it pays to do so," said Cockie.

She gave him a brief, cold, secret smile as though at some private joke all of her own. "Perhaps!" She shrugged lightly; but he saw that her hands now were tightly clenched on the wooden rail.

Below them and to their left, they could see the little row of bathing huts and the base of the great rock nose where it jutted out from the forehead of the land. The Rodds were standing there chatting in their civil, impersonal way to Fernando and Miss Trapp. Cockie gestured towards them. "For example . . ."

46

"Oh, them!" She shrugged again, lightly. But suddenly the mask slipped, she said with a predatory gleam: "All of them with money, their own or somebody else's. All of them with secrets, all playing parts. Each one of those four people —hugging a despicable secret, deceiving the rest. That creature Fernando—if they did but know why we went to that albergo in Siena! And Miss Trapp—hoarding up her miserable fortune in a gold-monogrammed bag. And the other two—pretending; she looking into his eyes and pretending that she doesn't know what he's planning to do to her, he looking back, accepting her pretences, pretending there's nothing to know. All of them, all four of them, all the others on this tour, that Mrs Sick, pretending to be delicate and interesting when all the time at home she's as strong as a horse, that woman with the niece, Gruff and Grim as you call them, pretending to be generous and kind when all she wants is to get the girl under her jealous influence and force her life into a groove as solitary and sour as her own. . . . All of us, acting: all of us struggling to keep our mean little secrets, ready to die to protect them, ready to fight and cheat and lie . . ."

"And pay," suggested Inspector Cockrill pleasantly.

She whipped away from them, running off abruptly down the wooden steps on soundless, rubber-soled feet, and away under the bougainvillea boughs. They saw her emerge from the tunnel of jasmine that covered the steps from the upper terrace to the lower, pause for a moment to fling her white towel into one of the bathing huts, and run out along the ridge of the diving rock, bounce once on the springy board and soar out—out and down to the blue water, twenty feet below.

The sea sent up a feather of triumphant spray: and closed in over her.

*   *   *

Sharply, as a razor blade slitting through stretched blue satin, her white hands cut their way up through the surface of the water. She swam back to the shore immediately, shaking the drops from her shining black costume. "I hope she feels—cleaner," said Mr Cecil, still standing at the balcony rail, staring down at her.

"Yes," said Cockie. He thought it over. "What a very curious conversation!"

"Very revealing, don't you mean?" said Cecil.

"Yes, that's just what I do mean." She had climbed up the path in the angle of the land and the rock and now appeared on the terrace, they saw her go up and speak to the group standing watching her there. She pointed down to the beach and they began to move off, down the steep path up which she had come. "They're going to watch from there," said Cecil. "She's going to show Mr Rodd a dive that he could do. Let's go and watch too." His face had lost something of the pasty look that terror had brought to it, he was returning to a nervous desire for action, he was longing to talk, to confide, to protest, to exclaim. "Where's Louli? We'll go and find *her*." They went down the central steps together and joined Helen Rodd and Leo, now standing on the sand looking upwards at the diving board. Vanda Lane had gone out there again and was standing, gently springing, deep in thought. As they watched, she turned sideways to the board's end, her right arm stiff to her thigh, the left curved upwards over her head: and so sprang high into the air and forced herself up and out and down. But she hit the water rather flatly, surfaced almost at once and, as she scrambled ashore, stood for a moment and gave her head a little, uncertain shake. Leo Rodd ran forward to meet her. "You didn't hurt yourself?"

"No, but . . ." She blew out her breath and patted her diaphragm. "I'm winded, that's all. I came down a bit flat." A faint stain of pink was slowly creeping up over her shoulder and arm where she had hit the water, and she raised her knee and hugged it, blowing out her breath again. "I say, I do feel bad about this," said Leo. "You were trying it for me."

She protested. 'No, no, I'm perfectly all right; but the truth is, the board's too high for experimenting. It was stupid of me."

"Yes, well don't try any more. I'm sorry," he said again. "I do feel guilty."

Miss Trapp and Fernando arrived at this moment and Miss Trapp was suddenly galvanized into womanly concern. She thought Miss Lane looked not at all well, she thought Miss Lane should lie down for an hour or two, she thought Miss Lane should take a drop of brandy or some aspirin at least. . . .

A civil wrangle followed between two schools of thought those who considered that Miss Lane should certainly take brandy and lie down, and those who could clearly see that she had had the wind knocked out of her for a moment but was already practically restored to normal health. Miss Trapp, however, was adamant, threatening to march Miss Lane back to the hotel herself, tuck her up with a couple of aspirin and mount guard over her to see that she didn't get up. Vanda, quite obviously horrified by this well-meant offer, finally consented to change out of her wet things and perhaps have a rest on her bed. Cockie, looking on with a lack-lustre eye, suspected that she was not entirely sorry to be forced to give in. She toiled back up the little path to the top of the rock and paused there for a moment, apparently to speak to Louli Barker; for Louli, a couple of minutes later, came flying down the path, looking rather white, but loud with exaggerated accounts of the hideous time she had had cowering in one of the huts while they all nattered outside, holding together the split in her already not very adequate bathing suit. However, she said, in a rather forced, high voice, fortunately that clever Miss Lane had had the brilliant suggestion of tying it up with a handkerchief, which was not frightfully safe but on the whole doing quite well . . .

"In one of the bathing huts?" faltered Miss Trapp.

Louli gave her a wink which considerably imperilled the safety of one set of the preposterous eyelashes; but Cockie could not rid himself of an impression that she looked rather white and strained and, as Cecil rushed up and poured out his confidences into her ear, he saw her jaw drop, her eyes grew wide and startled, she began to gabble in reply, returning confidence for confidence, looking back over her shoulder to the top of the rock; looking at the rest of the party, now swimming or floundering in the sea as their custom was—at Helen and Leo (she shook her head vigorously)—at Fernando, at Miss Trapp. . . . At Cockie himself. After a moment they came to some agreement about Cockie; and so parted and fell to an exhibition of bobbing and screaming whose forced gaiety quite outdid the bobbing and screaming of the earlier bathe at Rapallo. So, thought Cockie, they're going to confide in me that Miss Lane is trying to blackmail them; and I shall reply that she is merely taking a malicious pleasure in frightening them and that they are silly to go and give away, by their very response, that they each have something to be blackmailed about. And then they will decide that I am only a stupid old codger, and leave me to read in peace.

And sure enough, as soon as the bathe was over, Louvaine appeared, sauntering up the shallow steps to the lower terrace where he had established himself in his deck-chair. "Oh, hallo, Inspector. I didn't know you were here."

"Didn't you?" said Cockrill, sardonically.

"Goodness, you are cosy! I shall come and join you."

She sat down on the pebble-patterned terrace at his feet, shaking out her mop of red hair. He observed with amusement that with all the bobbing, not one drop of water had been permitted to endanger the wisdom of a dozen magazine articles on How to Keep Lovely in the Summer, accumulated on her charming face. To make quite sure, she dived into the recesses of the scarlet beach bag and, producing an outsize flapjack, peered intently into the looking-glass, added yet another layer of sun-tan powder, attended to the left set of eyelashes which had become seriously unsettled by her earlier wink at Miss Trapp, and removed excess grains of powder from both with a licked fourth finger. "That is a disgusting habit," said Inspector Cockrill severely.

"Well, some people actually put them *on* with spit. I do use my white of egg." She added some quite unnecessary lipstick and fished in the bag again. "Do you mind if I do my nails?"

"If it involves the smell of pear drops, I mind very much," said Cockie.

"No, that's taking off. I'm putting on." Unvarnished, the inch-long nails looked like an extension of her fingers, they made the whole hand seem very narrow and inordinately long. "Repellent, aren't they? Like poor, dead hens' hands, I always think, hanging up in poulterers' shops." She produced a bottle of violently bright varnish and a little brush. "I say, Inspector—do *you* think Miss Lane's a blackmailer?"

"Is that what you came up here to ask me?" said Cockie.

"Yes," she said frankly. "Cecil and I agreed . . ."

"I know you did. Well, the answer is—no. Not for money."

She looked up at him sharply, one hand half-painted, held with fingers apart to keep from smudging contacts. "Goodness, Inspector—what a clever person you are!"

"I think what she does, she does for the kick she gets

out of it. It gives her a sense of power. Herself, she's unsocial and ungregarious, she's an introvert: she doesn't like to see other people free and easy and happy, and so she tries to spoil things for them, that's all. She's clever at putting two and two together, she finds out things or she just guesses and if the guess doesn't come off, there's no harm done. But it often does: most of us have a bone or two at least, in the skeleton-cupboard."

"You think she just likes to see us wriggling on the hook?"

"Us?" said Cockie. "You too?"

She bent her head over her hand again. "Well, you see— I don't know if you know that Leo Rodd and I . . ."

"Yes, what about it?" said Cockie.

She seemed surprised by his level tone but after a moment's hesitation she went on. "Well she—she sort of referred to it. Look—I'll tell you what happened. You know when you talked to me on the balcony up there?—well, you didn't know it but you said something and it made me give a sort of jump and I was fiddling with my bra at the time which was a tiny bit torn at the top and I must have given it a jerk because the damn thing started to split right down. Well, my dear, there isn't much of it at the best of times and by the time I'd got down to the diving rock it had gone a bit more and it really was *not* quite the thing! So I dove into one of the huts because it was a trifle embarrassing, Leo being there with Mrs Rodd and all, so I sort of skipped round the back and dove in and thought I would try and fix it; but I had nothing to fix it with and it wasn't all so easy, and by that time Fernando and La Trapp had arrived so I couldn't go out and there I was . . ."

"And there you were, as Lem Putt would say—catched."

She looked at him in innocent astonishment. "Good lord —how extraordinary that you should say that."

"Is it?" he said, a little guiltily.

"Well, yes, because I . . . Well, I'll go on telling it straight through. There I was, as you say, catched. Well then by the sound of it The Lane appeared and she must have put something into the cabin next to me because I called out to her, hey, you haven't got a pin of sorts, have you? but she evidently didn't hear because she just went on. So I peeked out, holding the bra together with one hand, but by that time it really was most unsafe; and I saw them all watching her going out along the diving rock and she dived off and disappeared. Then she came back and she told them she'd try and do one that Leo could manage, and to go down and watch it from the beach. So I thought good, then I can hop out and run back to my room and sew the thing up. But just as they were going—Miss Trapp, the last, being most gallantly handed down by dear Fernando—she must have said something very quietly to Miss Trapp, because Miss Trapp went most terribly white, at least she went mud grey actually, and let out a sort of squawk and just stood there. Miss Lane didn't say anything more, she walked out along the rock and did her dive and I wish she'd come a bit flatter, that's all. But anyway, meanwhile Fernando had come back up the path to see what was happening to his lady love, I suppose; and there followed the most shy-making conversation which I really cannot bring myself to repeat; and I realized that they didn't know I was there. But not one word from the Trapp about La Lane. That was peculiar, wasn't it?"

"Under the circumstances," said Cockie, "perhaps not."

"Well, perhaps. Anyway you can see that I was more catched than ever and by this time I was doing a St Lawrence in my little hut, just now and again turning a flank to get the roasting even." She wriggled her shoulders under their protecting stole of hotel towel. "I sunburn terribly easily and the roofs of those things are only sort of slats: I shall be striped like a zebra-crossing to-morrow."

"Oh, yes?" said Cockie, vaguely. It was certainly odd that three minutes after Miss Trapp had been reduced to mud-grey by a word from Miss Lane, she should have been so extravagantly solicitous for the lady's well-being. "And then?"

"And then?" She screwed into an ungraceful huddle, squinting ruefully over a reddened shoulder to try to esti-mate the extent of the sunburned strips. "Oh, yes. Well then, as Miss Trapp seemed slightly distrait and not madly responsive to Fernando's declarations, he gave up for the time being and said they had better go on down to the beach, to which proposition, I can assure you, St Lawrence responded with one tiny half-baked cheer. My dear, I look like something off one of those silver grills in the posher restaurants."

"Never mind your back," said Cockie. "What happened then?"

"Then I went out and practised breathing, which I had practically forgotten how to do, and hung back a bit so that they shouldn't know I'd been there and feel embarrassed at my having overheard their conversation, which I can assure you they had every cause to do; and then I was just going to bolt up to my room when the Lane came up the path to the top of the rock and I tottered forward on my poor charred stumps of legs and said had she got a pin or anything? She said rather unfriendlily that she didn't carry a housewife when she went bathing and hadn't I got a scarf I could use? So I groped about in the old red plastic and dug out a handkie and here, as you see, it is; but while I was fixing it, I was drooling on with what I thought was a gay account of my sufferings in the hut and she suddenly interrupted me and said—well, Inspector, what do you think she said?"

"I should think she said, 'And there you were—catched'," said Cockie. "Like I did." He added, equably: "Everyone quotes 'The Specialist.' "

She considered that. She gave a little shrug. "Well— could be. But then she said something more and she said it very significantly, sort of looking straight at me but *not* quite straight at me. And then she walked past me and up the steps to the top terrace and never even glanced back." She gave a little shudder. "It was the way she looked at me!"

"But what was it she said?" said Cockie.

"It was something out of 'The Specialist' too. Come on— as you're so clever, you guess again. What do you think she said?"

"I think she said that there wasn't even a window to look out of this time," said Cockie. "A little window, shaped like a star."

No rabbit pulled out of any hat had ever enjoyed a more gratifying reception.

The long, hot afternoon wore on. Flat on the terrace beside him, Louvaine slept, her curly red head on her arm. Down on the beach, Miss Trapp had shaken off the attentions of Fernando and with the aid of a bathing towel and a large beach umbrella, established a sort of private nudist camp at the foot of the diving rock, and there genteelly sunned herself. Fernando in a series of porpoise wallowings by no means fulfilling his boast of a missed half-blue for swimming, had managed to reach the big wooden raft which was anchored five or six yards from the shore and lay spreadeagled upon it, unafraid of the sun: as the raft dipped and swayed with the ripples of the incoming waves, Cockie caught glimpses of the great, red-brown torso, glistening like satin with its only too natural oils. In a rubber boat, shaped like a duck, Mr Cecil drifted lazily up and down, paddling himself with languid white hands at the ends of slowly reddening thin white arms. The Rodds had thrown themselves down under the sun-shed—a long, narrow roof of dried palm leaves, supported on four-foot poles,

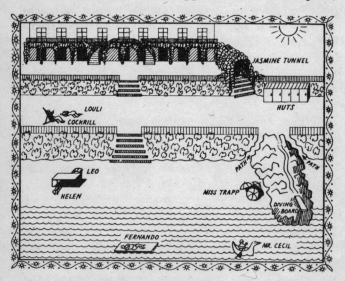

open-sided except at the short ends, where one could lie half in, half out of the shade. From where he sat, Cockie could see the backs of Helen's Dutch doll legs sticking out straight and shapeless towards the sea, and the rope soles of her bright yellow canvas espadrilles; at the opposite side, away from the sea and nearer to him, Leo's head and shoulders appeared. He had brought down some manuscript music with him and, his wife's yellow sun-glasses perched on his nose, was holding it against the sky, lying flat on his back, reading upwards; but after a bit, evidently tiring, he

56

relaxed his arm, propped the manuscript over his face like a sort of tent and presumably went to sleep beneath the lot. Miss Lane had evidently taken Miss Trapp's advice to have a nice lie down, for she did not appear. Inspector Cockrill applied himself joyously to the adventure of Carstairs and the leaping lady.

At seven o'clock they began to drift up from the beach. The sun was still high but they could not accustom themselves to the idea that dinner would not be served one minute before nine. Louli, wakened by people stepping over her legs, put out a lazy hand and caught at a passing ankle. "Who's this? Oh, you, Cecil! My dear, what on earth have you been doing? You look as though you'd been boiled in cochineal."

Mr Cecil was in a terrible taking. "I went to sleep in my duck, my dear, *silly* me!—and I must have been drifting and drifting about getting redder and redder every minute. . . ."

"Most peculiar, ducky, because the back half of you's quite white; you can almost see a seam where the red and white join. . . ."

Fernando arrived, springing up the steps after his inamorata, glittering with health and vitality. "Ah, ha, Miss Barker, Inspector, this is where you hide yourselves, is it?—sleeping together all afternoon on the terrace." He nudged the Inspector in the ribs with an elbow like a well-cooked pork chop. "I have been wide awake all the time," said Cockie austerely.

Leo Rodd bowed to Louvaine. "Under the circumstances, that was only gallant." His glance met hers and shifted away at once. He added rather hurriedly: "Has anyone seen Miss Lane?"

Nobody had. "I hope she's all right; I feel a bit guilty, she was trying the dive for me."

In view of his conversation with Louli, it was quite

fascinating, thought Cockie, to watch Miss Trapp go into her routine as the solicitous, the know-all nurse; apparently sincere, apparently truly concerned, and yet with the oddest underlying air of absolute insincerity, of not caring a damn whether the patient lived or died. But that in itself was queer; for if it were true that Miss Lane had uttered to her one of those oddly baleful half-threats of hers, would Miss Trapp be really so detached about her health, would she not rather wish her ill than well? As it was, she led the way up the long, shallow steps to the upper terrace, up the curved wooden steps to the balcony, in a ceaseless twitter of brandy and aspirins, cups of tea, eau de cologne and nice lie downs. At the door of Miss Lane's room, she paused and listened and, as though caught by some imperceptibly rising tide of hysteria, they all paused and listened too. "Not a sound. I wonder if . . . Should I just give a teeny knock?"

The teeny knock was not answered, nor were teeny cries of enquiry and concern and gradually heightening alarm. Fernando shrugged his broad shoulders. "She is in her bathroom or she has gone out."

"I hope she's all right," said Leo Rodd again.

Louli Barker leaned back on her elbows against the rail of the verandah. "Why don't you just look in and see?"

"Well, but, ducky, would she *like* that . . .?"

"I don't see why not," said Louli. "Either she's there or she isn't. If she's there, why doesn't she answer? If she isn't, she won't know that we looked." The sun gleamed through the tangle of the curly red hair tossing about her shoulders; against the white satin of the Bikini, her skin was almost as smoothly white. She twirled the gay red plastic bag by its gay red strings. "Go on, Miss Trapp, I dare you—have a bash!"

A crimson shawl had been thrown across the bed so that, with her dark hair, still wet from the bathe, spread all about her head, she looked like some modern Ophelia afloat on a lake of blood. But the four tall posts, the looped back white curtains, made of the bed a catafalque; and upon the catafalque, she had been ceremonially laid out, pale face composed, pale feet placed neatly together, pale hands loosely clasped upon her heart: wrapped in a long white garment like a shroud, laid out ceremonially upon a crimson shawl, with something that looked like crimson rose petals scattered upon her breast. For a moment you might think it some monstrous joke, might suppose it simply a girl asleep on a curtained, four-poster bed: until you caught sight of the dagger handle between the lax fingers—and saw that the crimson rose petals, were not rose petals at all.

CHAPTER FIVE

COMMUNICATIONS on the island of San Juan el Pirata are inclined to be slow; but there is as a last resort the telefono and by this extravagant means a message was finally conveyed to El Gerente de Politio just as he was about to board his ship with the rest of the smuggling fleet. The Gerente, torn between regret and excitement, collected his men from their various vessels and despatched them off home to change back into uniform. All except Jose: Jose had better stay behind and prepare Number 1 cell for reception of an inmate—the bales of illicit tobacco could go into the corridor, the hashish had better be put in the safe if it could be crammed in and the coffee must stay where it was—it wouldn't leave much room but criminals couldn't be choosers. The goats must certainly be accommodated elsewhere. If the she-goat had kidded, Jose must use his discretion as to what had best be done with mother and child, but they couldn't go into the office, it didn't look well. . . . Puffed up with these triumphs of organization, he hurried off home to change too.

Meanwhile, at the hotel, aghast and bewildered, the handful of tourists who—however slight the acquaintance —had best known the dead girl, huddled together in the chill shade of her murder. Horrible, terrifying, shocking, incredible—but true! At half-past four on that sun-baked afternoon, she had left them, walking off, splendid and vital in her blue-black bathing suit, up the narrow path to her hotel room. Less than three hours later, they had found her there—dead. "And it was I who made her go," sobbed Miss Trapp, sick with the shock and distress of it. "If I hadn't made her go . . ."

"Don't upset yourself, Miss Trapp, think rather of me who must arrange all these matters. The Company—the Company will want investigations," stammered Mr Fernando, grey to the gills.

"So incongruous," said Mr Cecil, wretchedly. "Lying there dead, with all that sunshine outside!"

"And the dagger still—still . . ."

"A dagger like the ones we bought in the town."

Louvaine sat white and silent in her wooden armchair, out on the flower-gay terrace, not a stone's throw from where the girl lay dead—dead and murdered, laid out ceremonially on a four-poster bed. "I suppose I was the last person who ever spoke to her."

"Except for the murderer," said Leo quickly.

"Except for the murderer. But otherwise—I was the last."

"I don't know that I'd insist upon it, ducky; considering the nature of the conversation. I mean," said Mr Cecil, looking round with rising excitement, "I suppose we're all suspects now, my dears, *aren't* we?"

"Together with some fifty other souls," said Leo Rodd. He looked for confirmation to Inspector Cockrill. "I should think the local talent will find itself a trifle daunted when it does arrive."

The Gerente, marching in some time later at the head of a straggle of men, was inclined to agree with him. The choice of possible culprits amounted to sixty—a depressed and anxious bunch of British tourists, assorted guests of various nationalities and fifteen members of the hotel staff. These last, however, he speedily dismissed with not a stain on their characters: they were natives of San Juan, the men, out of the tourist season, valued members of the smuggling fleet, and men and women alike very properly provided with two hundred pelire apiece, done up unobtrusively in little paper packages; and loud with promises of more to come if that were not enough. He sent them all off rejoicing. So! Ten minutes work and already the list was reduced to forty-five. It only showed what a man could achieve, who understood his job. He eyed the rest of them speculatively.

A senor stepped forward, very splendid, with teeth of solid gold, weaving his way with rigidly outstretched arm, dividing up the company into two uneven clumps like a host about to institute some intricate drawing-room game for the reluctant amusement of his guests, and broke into eloquent Spanish. The Gerente, who spoke only the Spanish-Italian argot of the island, understood about half of what he said; but it did seem that the larger group had been, without possibility of doubt, far away from the premises at the relevant times, on a jaunt to the palatio, safe from suspicion beneath the very wing of El Exaltida himself. They would have to be released. He made a tiny but unmistakable sign to the beautiful senor with the golden teeth and the senor sighed and regretfully shook his head. It was bad, but it only confirmed his doubts: he must positively let forty rich suspects go and not a pelire the richer himself.

And now they were seven. In the centre of the great, cool, white-washed room with its shining wood floor and elephantine Iberian-Abbotsford furniture, Fernando argued, his arms nearly wrenched out of their sockets by the eloquence of his gesture. The rest drew together in a sort of protective huddle, Cockie resentful and cross, the Rodds and Miss Trapp very grave, Mr Cecil and Louli gone suddenly madly gay. "I feel," said Leo Rodd to Cockie, struggling with his one hand to light a cigarette, "that all this is coming unpleasantly near."

Cockie produced tobacco and paper and rolled a cigarette for himself. "It's as well to get rid of the lot that were up at the palace. They're obviously out of it."

"Still, while they were in it, they did serve to complicate the issue."

Cockie looked up, bright eyed, over the first puff of his cigarette. "Do you want the issue complicated?"

"I only think," said Leo, "that all this may be very comic-opera and engaging, but it's too terrifying for words."

Mr Cecil and Louli burst into their patter. But their hats! Their cloaks! Those guns, my dear! That dog!

Their hats were apparently made of black patent leather, with circular crowns and circular brims, and the circular brims were broken sharply across the back and turned up flat against the circular crowns. The cloaks were of midnight blue, too utterly dramatic, said Mr Cecil, only just the wrong length to be really smart. They were worn over dirty white trousers with cylindrical legs; and even dirtier bare feet, except in the case of the Gerente whose dignity was served by the addition of a pair of filthy white tennis shoes. They carried what appeared to be flintlocks, splendidly chased in silver and black. The dog was a fearsome Alsatian bitch with an angry eye, obviously bred on a diet of human flesh. "My dears, up to one's room for one's sketching books this *min*ute, if only one dared!"

"Well, I agree with Leo," said Helen Rodd. "I think it's not funny at all, but most terribly sinister."

"You surely don't imagine . . .?" said Miss Trapp, mud-grey once more.

"I just didn't care for the look of El Exaltida's prison."

"What would our position be?" said Leo Rodd to Cockrill. "Are we subject to Spanish law or Italian or what?"

"You're subject to the law of San Juan el Pirata," said Cockie. "If a crime is committed here, it's their affair."

"But surely international law . . . I mean, our Government . . ."

"That *is* international law," said Cockie. "It's on their soil and it's their affair. The British Government will no doubt represent and request and all the rest of it, but the Exalteeder or whatever he calls himself, doesn't give a tuppenny damn about the British Government, I don't suppose, or any other government: so I quite agree with you, it's not funny at all." He added with some relish that the penalty for murder here, was hanging, same as at home; and that after the intervening weeks of Juanese justice, it was understood to come under the general heading of a Merciful Release.

In the centre of the room, Fernando continued to argue, flinging expostulative arms. Now and again he pointed to one or other of them, identifying, explaining, defending—promising? "Really," said Louli, "did you ever feel more like slightly unsaleable fatstock at a market fair? 'What—twenty pelire for that poor spavined old scrag . . .?' Oh!—sorry, Miss Trapp, I didn't mean you."

"I hope not, Miss Barker," said Miss Trapp icily. Inspector Cockrill hoped so too. It was not like Louli to be unkind; not that kind of unkind.

"The Gerente is looking at *me* rather doubtfully," said Cecil. "What can Fernando be saying?"

"Oh, yes, and Inspector, now it's you. He's looking at you most oddly!"

Inspector Cockrill was not used to being looked at oddly. He arose, stubbed out his cigarette and marched across to Fernando. Behind his back, Cecil and Louvaine went into a comedy act, thumbs into armholes, knees bend, shoot out one leg, 'ere, 'ere, 'ere, wot's all this going on? It appeared to afford them a good deal of entertainment; the rest of the party contained their mirth without any visible effort.

Mr Fernando was exhausted. He wiped the sweat from his glistening brow with the sleeve of his summer suit. "Inspector—I fight. I fight for my party, I fight for my helpless ones." He made an encircling gesture with his arm, though he had hardly strength left to lift it. "All my tourists, they are my people, they are in my care."

"Never mind the others," said Cockie crossly. "You fight for the ones that were not at the Palacio. That's us."

Fernando lifted his arms and flopped them down again immediately, though whether from sheer despair or because he could no longer hold them up, Mr Cockrill could not discern. "Inspector—I tell you: I fight. I fight for Mr and Mrs Rodd: the senor has but one arm, poor man, the senora is beautiful—be merciful, Gerente, I say, and let them go. Besides, they are rich, and shall they not be grateful? And the young senorita, a great book writer, Gerente, and she also is beautiful and also rich. And the pale senor, like a lady, he has many shops in London, shall he not send you dresses, Gerente, when he gets safely home, beautiful dresses for your Inez, your Isabellita, your Carmen, your Pepita . . . I searched for the name of his wife, Inspector, you understand, but his Spanish is not good, he thought that I told him the poor Mr Cecil is the father of many daughters." He lifted his weary shoulders only half-way to his ears. "However, it was the same in the end. The Gerente too has many daughters. Also I told him that Mr Cecil is rich."

"And Miss Trapp is rich?" said Inspector Cockrill.

Fernando looked slightly uncomfortable. "Ah—Miss Trapp. You understand, senor, that with Miss Trapp it is a matter of delicacy. The Gerente is sympathetic towards Miss Trapp."

"Well, I trust the Gerente is sympathetic towards me," said Cockie. "Nobody need think *I'm* rich."

"No, no, Inspector, but you are agente de politio, to him you are a brother."

"Thank you," said Cockie. He looked about him and finally enquired, delicately: "Then who . . .?"

Fernando looked about him too, cheerfully smiling. "There are still . . ." But there was no one. His smile grew less, he began to tick them off rather feverishly on his fingers. "Mr and Mrs Rodd; yourself, Inspector, Miss Trapp, Mr Cecil, Miss Barker . . ." There was nobody left. Fernando had fought for his helpless ones, not wisely but too well, and now was a helpless one himself; and what friend would fight for *him?* The Gerente made a sign to his men and two of them stepped forward purposefully. Fernando said in a voice that was suddenly sharp with fear: "Inspector—he says that I shall go with them."

"Go with them? But why you?"

"After all," said Fernando, reasonably, "there is no one else."

"Then he must begin again."

"Why should he?" said Fernando, quite seeing the Gerente's point, "when he has *me?*"

Inspector Cockrill thought swiftly. "Tell him—point out to him that if you aren't here, there'll be no one to interpret for him."

Fernando translated. "He says that the Hotel Manager, El Diretore—he knows some English."

"Tell him I don't understand the Dirrytory's English. If I can't have you to interpret, I shan't be able to assist him with his investigations."

Fernando looked unhappy. "Inspector, he replies that he does not need you to assist him with his investigations."

"Have you explained to him who I am? Tell him I'm a

police inspector, tell him that's a very high and important position, higher than his own . . ."

But Fernando was already telling him. He looked more unhappy than ever. "Inspector, he says—he says that you are too old."

"*Too old*," said Cockie, in a voice of doom.

"In San Juan, a policeman of such rank would have retired long ago, Inspector, very rich. All policemen of any rank are rich—the smugglers must pay them bribes and with the bribes they may buy more boats and need not themselves pay bribes. It is only because of so many daughters that El Gerente himself has not retired; and," said Fernando, frankly, "it can be seen that he is much, much younger than yourself, Inspector."

"You mean that he does not believe that I am a policeman?"

"A policeman, yes; but—what is a policeman? That you are a Gerente, higher than El Gerente himself—well," said Fernando, regretfully, "no."

Inspector Cockrill decided that the time had come when he must speak—and speak in Spanish. He stepped forward, looked into the Gerente's beaming face and, banging himself smartly on the chest, said very loudly: "Me—Scotalanda Yard!"

The Gerente's face lost it's complacency. "Scotalanda Yarrrrrrda?"

"Very big," said Cockie, spreading his arms like some euphoric angler looking forward to the day's catch, "very important. Importanta!" He had been to Scotland Yard perhaps half a dozen times in his life, on visits to other people.

The Gerente gave Fernando an enquiring glance. "Si, si, si," said Fernando, eagerly. "Scotalanda Yarda!"

It was electrifying. The Gerente fell upon Cockie's neck

and embraced a blood brother, bussing him upon his withered cheeks till, in their seats in the stalls, Mr Cecil and Louli had to stuff their handkerchiefs into their mouths, to stifle the hysteria of their laughter. But Inspector Cockrill, extricating himself from the enveloping folds of the Gerente's cloak, agreed with Leo Rodd: it might be all very comic-opera and amusing, but in its very absence of all sense, all reason, all responsibility, it was so utterly sinister as to turn him cold with fear; murder and the suspicion of murdering, were not, after all, very funny.

Mr Fernando did not think so either. He stood there between his squat guards, not smiling; and suddenly even the giggles in the background ceased. Brown faces, black-whiskered as brigands, shadowed beneath shiny black-mackintoshy hats; blue cloaks, mysteriously folded, glint of gold ear-rings against swarthy cheeks, glint of silver chasing upon evil glint of steel: bare brown feet shuffling beneath grimy stove-pipe trousers—shuffling in eagerness to be off and away, off and away with the prisoner, any prisoner, the innocent, the guilty, anyone who would serve to string up, some convenient day, upon the old gallows in the market-place; or moulder away, forgotten, in the dank, bottomless grave of the black old fortress on its rocky cliff. For questioning? There would be no questions, or none that the Gerente, in his need for a victim, would not ask and answer to his own satisfaction; no evidence taken, or none recorded; no public trial, unless, possibly, the Gerente should think it politic to get hold of his friend the Magistrato and agree to squeeze one in, some time before Easter—there is always a little spare time about then for, though it would be too much to ask the Juanese to give up smuggling for Lent, it is a fact that, profoundly pious, they do almost universally refrain on all the special days of fasting and abstinence and right through Holy Week . . .

"Tell him," said Inspector Cockrill firmly, "that we will go up to the girl's room now, and I will assist him in his investigations. Tell him that you will come with me as interpreter."

It was half-past nine. Outside on the terrace, the Stainless Ones were at the trough, heads down, eyes bright with divided excitement and simple greed. Leo Rodd summoned El Diretore who arrived pale and breathless, in evident expectation of being murdered on the spot if he failed in giving immediate attention to these foreign savages. "We can't eat out there," said Leo Rodd to him, gesturing towards the diners on the terrace. "Put a table on the balcony above and send something up to us there. And send up some wine, molto vino or whatever you call it, and a round of double Juanellos, or whatever anyone fancies." He led the way through into the central hall and up the stairs, through his and Helen's room and so out on to the balcony. "We'll make them fix us up in this corner here, and then we can be out of the way of those goopers, and at the same time keep an eye on the Inspector and his boy friend and their goings-on." To Miss Trapp's anxious quackings he replied briefly that *they* were not yet murdered and while they yet lived, they must eat. "My dear, I do think your boy friend is so masterful," said Cecil to Louvaine. "*Some*one has to act," said Louli shortly.

"One must be forgiven for being just the least mite jittery; you may not know it, but one has been here before!"

"What do you mean, here before?"

"Oh, but a murder, ducky. Years ago, in Christophe's, one of the girls, you can't think how horrid. Police investigations and all sorts. I mean, what is Inspector Cockrill going to *think?*"

"He'll think that your many daughters will soon be orphans," said Louvaine, cheering up.

Out of the chaos of the hotel staff, El Diretore organized a sufficient service to the improvised dining-room on the corner of the balcony. "Under the circumstances," said Leo Rodd as they settled themselves unhappily round it, "I suppose 'Here's to crime' would not be a suitable toast."

"I don't know about anyone else," said Cecil, "but I for one am frankly a frightened boy."

"I think we should be five frightened people," said Leo. "But Mr Rodd . . ."

Leo put out a hand for the cigarette his wife had lighted for him. "Look here, Miss Trapp—we simply must face the situation and it isn't a comfortable one. Everyone else on the tour is definitely out, and so are the rest of the people staying in the hotel. Anyway—we were the only people who knew her at all: as it happened, our little group did seem to see a bit more of her than the rest, and of course we were the ones concerned—however remotely—with her last hours. She was bathing with us at half-past four, at seven o'clock she was dead."

"Yes, but just because we casually spoke to her, on a conducted tour—I mean, how can any of us be connected with her in any way?"

"I simply say that people are going to ask questions and we'd better team up and think what we're going to answer."

Further along the balcony, Inspector Cockrill leaned against the rail looking on with exquisite disapproval as the politio of San Juan went about its task. Miss Trapp unhappily sipped at her Juanello. "The servants . . ."

"He's sent the servants away."

"Of course," suggested Cecil hopefully, "he may have sent them away to dungeons or somewhere."

"Nonsense, ducky, they're roaring round with osso buco and ratatouille down on the terrace before your very eyes. And anyway," said Louvaine, "why should any of the servants have wanted to kill La Lane?"

Miss Trapp thought there might be a dozen reasons. Everyone knew that foreigners were dishonest. "They might think she'd be down on the beach with the rest of us and go into her room . . ."

"But why kill her?" said Leo.

"If she caught them pilfering . . ."

"They wouldn't kill her, surely?" agreed Helen Rodd. "They'd only have to slip half the proceeds to the Gerente, to get away scot free, and I dare say all tourists are pretty fair game. And anyway, why her room rather than any of the others? None of the others seem to have been touched: and it wasn't as if hers was the first or the last or anything: why begin there?—I mean, if they had been on a thieving expedition. And it isn't as if she wore a lot of jewellery or had anything ostentatiously valuable."

"Mind you, that coat of hers is Victor Stiebel," said Cecil; it had always been a sore point.

"Do you think the criminal community of Barrequitas would be likely to recognize that?"

Mr Cecil cheered up at the thought that a Stiebel model might pass unnoticed. Louvaine said: "What you mean is that her things were expensive?"

"You don't wear a coat like that and have other things cheap. Fifty or sixty, Mr Cecil, would you say?"

Miss Trapp thought it would be nearer sixty. "That's a real Chinese silk tussore, Mrs Rodd. Christophe's, I know, would charge sixty, if not more." She suddenly blushed scarlet. "Oh, but Mr Cecil could better speak of that."

Leo Rodd drew irritably on his cigarette. "Aren't we getting away from the matter at issue?" But in the gathering darkness, further along the verandah, Inspector Cockrill, all ears, thought to himself that maybe they were not so very far off, after all; and longed to know, as a matter of private interest, whether they were talking in shillings or pounds.

"So, if not a pilfering servant, Miss Trapp—what then?"

Miss Trapp looked down her long nose. There were—other things. A young woman, defenceless, alone . . .

"But why kill her," insisted Leo. "Why kill her?"

"If she put up a struggle?"

"I don't think she did," said Helen Rodd. She gave a little shuddering shake to her head, but she controlled herself at once, sitting upright on the wooden balcony chair, very cool and composed, a charming grey moth in her soft grey dress. "I—when we went in and looked at her, I looked at her hands. I always do seem to notice people's hands. Her hands were—clasped round the hilt of the knife, you remember? They were very clean, like a little girl's hands that have just been washed to go to a party: she kept her nails rather short, cut square, no nail varnish or anything. Well, they were perfectly clean too, not torn or broken or anything, and you could see her arms up to the elbows and they weren't marked in any way. I'm sure she hadn't—fought with anyone."

"And anyway," said her husband impatiently, "if just servants—why the ceremonial?"

"The ceremonial?" said Louvaine, blankly.

"For Pete's sake! The girl was laid out on that horrible bed, her hands folded, her feet together; her hair was spread out all round her head in a sort of fan—and underneath her had been spread a great red shawl. I say again—why the ceremonial?"

"Well, but, ducky," said Louvaine, "the Spanish are a madly ceremonious nation."

He made a swift impatient movement. In the shadowed lamplight, his face took on the old angry, intolerant frown, he pushed away the plate of hors d'œuvres before him with a movement of irritable revulsion. "This is so terribly serious —couldn't we just for a moment be spared the double-talk?" She flung up her head and met the hostility of his bright, dark eyes; and Cockie, watching them from his place along the balcony, thought that she looked back at him with something like terror. Helen said smoothly into the shattering silence: "But do you think it really *was* 'ceremonial'?"

He switched round upon her, obviously grateful for a less immediately—or less obviously—vulnerable object for his uncontrollable irritability. "Of course it was 'ceremonial.' Laid out on that ghastly bed, wrapped in a thing like a— like a shroud."

"Yes, but was she in fact 'laid out'? Don't you think we may all have imagined it? After all, she was only lying on a bed. It happened to be a four-poster bed, that's all."

"Why put her there at all?"

"She may have fallen there when she was killed," said Cecil, going over to Helen's side.

"Of course she didn't," said Leo. The waiter swooped, uncomprehending about them, gathering up the almost untouched plates of black olives and smoked ham. "She fell by the little table, right across from the bed in the corner under the window. The chair was pushed back, there was blood on it . . ."

*   *   *

It was a small, square, wooden table, a plain wooden chair. In the room along the verandah, the Gerente was even now examining them, with a splendid disregard for spattered blood and possible fingerprints: he had in fact been astonished to find that Scotalanda Yarrda seemed to set store by these extravagances. After all, blood was blood, a young woman had been killed in this room, they all knew that: and here was blood—but naturally, señor! As to prints, there had at one time been some powder and an insufflator down at the prison, but goodness knew where they were now. For after all, when you had gone to all that trouble, what then? He knew everyone in San Juan el Pirata without having to look at the tips of their fingers! The Gerente Inglese must not take him for a fool, said the Gerente de Politio, laughing heartily at the bare idea. Inspector Cockrill had scarcely time to note the shape of the splashes on the table, before a uniformed arm, sweeping casually across them, smeared them half out of existence . . .

". . . you mean you think she was lifted on to the bed?"

"Even if she was," said Helen, "that might not mean anything much. It seems to be a sort of instinct to lay dead people out flat—or injured people, for that matter, although it does the dead people no good and often makes the injured people worse."

"Yes," said Miss Trapp. "That's true."

"But that white shroud . . ."

"It was only her kimono, Leo. She'd probably put it on when she changed out of her wet bathing things. I know, *I* lay down for the siesta just in a thin dressing-gown."

"I see, yes," said Leo, slowly. "They just heaved her on to the bed, pushed her feet together, which would be the normal instinct, I suppose; and her hands—well, her hands were on the hilt of the knife."

"She may have been trying to pull it out," said Helen, shuddering again.

Inspector Cockrill looked and listened, grimly smiling. Very comforting, he thought: no shroud, no catafalque, no carefully laid-out body, nothing ugly, nothing inexplicable, nothing bizarre. He kept one wary eye upon the room where El Gerente went his slapdash way, but across the intervening space he tossed, with almost malicious pleasure, a pebble of discord into the still pond of their returning confidence. "Aren't you forgetting about the shawl?" he said.

It was true. They had forgotten all about the shawl. Helen said quickly: "You don't think that was—just an accident too? Like the bed being a four-poster." But she suddenly went very tense; she said sharply: "Only it wasn't *her* shawl. It was . . ."

Leo Rodd said something to her, savagely, out of the corner of his mouth. "It was my shawl," said Louli.

Louli's shawl. The chenille tablecloth that a few brief weeks before she had wheedled out of the Bognor aunt; the red chenille tablecloth with the gay white bobbles—laid out, smoothed out beneath the murdered body, a lake of blood for a floating corpse with outspread, dank dark hair. "It was my shawl. I thought you all realized." She moved a little closer to Cecil in a rather pathetic gesture of reliance upon that acidulate, bloodless comradeship that was all he had to offer her. "I must say, it makes me feel quite sick."

"I'm sorry," said Helen, distressed. "I didn't think what I was saying."

But Louvaine was not one to bear a grudge. "I know, ducky, don't worry." She repeated, "I thought you'd all have recognized it."

"What was it doing in her room?"

"It wasn't in her room," said Louli. "It was in my room. They—the murderer, must have got it. It was folded over the back of the chair." She added that her room was next to Miss Lane's, number four. "I bagged it so as not to be next to Mrs Sick."

Mr Cecil did so understand that. "But how could they have *got* into your room?"

"Well, just through the door," said Louvaine. "The door into the corridor wasn't locked, I never lock doors; and the one on to the balcony was wide open."

"Nothing else was touched?"

"No, I changed afterwards, out of my bathing dress. Nothing else was touched at all."

They were all silent, miserably considering it. Miss Trapp said at last: "Miss Lane had a shawl of her own, if they wanted a shawl. At least a stole—a blue and white one."

"Would it be the same size as Miss Barker's?"

"I think it was more a proper stole," said Louli. "I had to fold mine, actually, it's square." And *act*ually, she added, a tablecloth and not a stole at all.

Presumably a murderer who felt compelled to lay out the victim according to some ritual of his own, might equally be obliged to choose a shawl of a certain shape and colour, might even find some horrid significance in preferring a tablecloth. But that presupposed some knowledge of where such a thing was to be found. "We've all seen the shawl, Louli," said Leo Rodd, forgetting in his concentration all about 'Miss Barker.' "We saw it at Milan and you wore it the other evening in Siena. But here?"

Louvaine considered. "No, I haven't worn it here. It's a stupid thing, actually, idiotically hot."

"So that the hotel staff wouldn't know it? Or any of the

hotel guests? They wouldn't realize that you'd got such a thing in your room?"

"The girl who does the rooms would," said Miss Trapp, clinging desperately to her own theory of a sort of inverted noblesse oblige.

"Still and all," said Leo, "it does seem to narrow things down."

At ten o'clock, the murdered body of Vanda Lane was wrapped in a piece of black bunting, by no means thus employed for the first time, and carried off without undue ceremony to the prison, which apparently combined the functions of morgue and police station, as well as those of civil and criminal courts and dungeon gaol, the customary end of appearing there at all. Cockrill joined them at the table with a subdued Fernando who remained, faute de choix, suspect No. 1, but was permitted a restricted freedom on a sort of ticket-of-leave arrangement, Inspector Cockrill standing Prisoner's Friend. "Have you all eaten yet?"

"We've toyed with hors d'œuvres. The Diretore's whipping up a paella or something for us."

Appetites might be impaired but the paella when it came was hot and steamy, rich with pimento and tomato, with onion and garlic, with fish and chicken and dear little chopped up squids. "Eye of newt," said Louli, fishing out a rubbery tentacle tip, "is one thing, but toe of frog I simply will *not!* Have you heard, Inspector, that mass escapes have been taking place right, left and centre?"

Inspector Cockrill had been in the dead girl's room during the commotion on the terrace, vainly trying to convince the Gerente that, before the body was removed, it might be handy to call in someone who could even roughly guess an estimate of the time of death. "The entire staff, Inspector, left in a body, and were all marched back again, positively clanking with hotel spoons and forks, and nobody seemed to mind a bit." But when the thus belated paella had been cleared away and the waiters, who certainly seemed not a whit the worse for their foiled excursion, had brought the little cups of thick bitter chocolate and bowls of thin sweet cream, and left them to themselves, all their forced hilarity ebbed away. "Now do tell us, Inspector, what on earth's going on?"

Above them the sky was dark with a clear, star-studded darkness like a spangled veil, below them the sea was a-glitter with the firefly lights of the fishing fleet, pair by pair; all about them the air was balmy, sweet with the scent of jasmine, mimosa and rose. But Inspector Cockrill, heaving himself sideways to dive into his pocket for papers and tobacco, wished himself fervently back in England again, on a nice chilly, damp July evening, holidaying decently in a Herne Bay boarding house. "Well, I'll tell you what I can. It isn't what I'm used to," said Cockie, resentfully, "but it seems to me that you'd better all know what there is to face." He completed the cigarette and lighted a small bonfire at its wispy end. "Very well. I will describe what I've seen; you can draw your own conclusions. First: the room."

"Just like all our rooms?"

"Just like the rest of them. There are ten in a row, in this angle of the hotel building, and this was number five; that you know. A small, square room with nothing in it but a bed, standing out from the centre of one side wall, and along the other wall a built-in wardrobe. The balcony wall, as it were, has a central door and a small window on either side, rather high up. Under the window on the bed side, there's a small dressing-table, under the other window there's the small square table and a plain wooden chair. The floor's uncarpeted, bleached white wood: and all the furniture's in plain bleached wood. The curtains, the bed curtains, the counterpane, are all just white cotton stuff—the whole thing has a sort of monastic effect, presumably to be cool and clean. The back of the room is divided off to make a tiny bathroom, leaving a narrow passage to the corridor door. I take it your rooms are all much the same?—mine is."

Double or single, the rooms were all the same: into some a 'matrimona' had been squeezed instead of a single bed, but that was all the difference. "Very well. In the bathroom there's only a wash-basin and a shower: the shower is just an overhead sprinkler surrounded by a curtain, with a rim round the drain underneath."

"Whoever peddled those shower things through Italy," said Louvaine chattily, "did a wonderful job. They're simply everywhere." The only thing was, last night she had forgotten her bath-cap and hair-dye had simply spouted all over her, positively rivers of blood . . .

"At any rate they sold one to the Bellomare Hotel for Miss Lane's bathroom," said Helen, pleasantly smiling, pleasantly leading back to the subject on hand. Her husband sketched her a tiny mock bow. "Thank you, my dear; your heart is in the right place—whatever they may say." But Inspector Cockrill thought that underlying the mockery was a gleam of purest gratitude: of rather astonished gratitude that for his sake, she should protect his love from so signally making a fool of herself at a moment when light-hearted folly was very much out of place: should protect himself from that first sick stab of disillusion and doubt. "You were saying, Inspector . . .?"

Inspector Cockrill had, as it happened, finished with what he had been saying. "We come now to her possessions.

They're as I think you'd expect—very neat, nothing out of place: everything of excellent quality, no discrepancies in that respect. I was only able to have a very cursory glance round; but I could see that the dress she wore this morning was hung up in a wardrobe, there were some underclothes in a corner of the bathroom, presumably for washing. Her bathing dress and the rubber cap and shoes were rolled up in the white towel—a hotel towel—and hung over the edge of the balcony rail outside her door. There were two novels, closed, on a corner of her dressing-table, no sign anywhere of sewing things, manicure things, pens, pencils, paper and so forth—they were probably in the dressing-table drawers." He eyed them with a glint of teasing. "You will make what you like of all this as I go along.

"Now, the body. The body was lying as you saw it. There seem to be no marks of any kind, no scratches or bruises, nothing—except the one stab wound. This was made by the paper knife, as you saw. Several of the tourists bought these knives this morning in the town . . ."

Mr Cecil had bought one himself, too divine for one's desk at Christophe's with that wrought black and gold handle, so decorative; and Louvaine had bought one, because Leo had admired it; and thought that one day she would give it to him and say, 'Little did they realize when I bought it flat out in front of them all, that I was buying it for you . . .' for on such foolish secrets her secret love of necessity for the time being fed; and Miss Lane had bought one. They were labelled exuberantly, 'Butifull Toledo steel works, mad only in San Juan,' and it was not for tourists to enquire how Toledo steel came to be made only in San Juan, or where were the foundries and workshops necessarily implied.

"The blade is five inches long," said Cockie, "and thin

and sharp. It could penetrate the breast without undue force being used."

"You mean that a man *or* a woman . . .?"

"Certainly," said Cockie. "Now, the point of penetration is fairly low on the left breast, over the heart, but not more than an inch from the central line of the breast bone. The kimono thing she was wearing has straight edges; it would be tied round her waist by the sash and form a sort of deep V. The knife hasn't penetrated the stuff, it has gone between the two edges of the V." He added that they could make what they liked of that: and furthermore that she had nothing on under the gown.

"The coverlet under her is rumpled a bit, of course, and there are a few smears of blood on it. The disarrangement suggests that she was lifted on to the bed from the side away from the windows, which is a little odd because the shortest way from the spot where she was killed, in the table corner, would be to the other side of the bed. The front of the kimono is spotted and smeared with blood, but not as much as you'd expect; and the blood seems rather pale and watery there, as if it were diluted." He held up a hand to ward off premature interruptions. "The wound would probably have spurted blood. If she'd put up her hands to defend herself, her hands and arms would have had a good deal of blood on them; but in fact they seem quite clean except for a few small smears. The shawl underneath her is quite clean, except for a damp patch where her head lay; and as we know, her hair was still quite wet.

"That's the bed. Now, the table and chair. The table has been pulled out into the room a bit, and the chair is behind it: as you go in through the balcony door, they're in the right-hand corner, but the table had been moved so that anybody sitting at it would be looking, as it were, slantwise, towards the balcony door; and anybody standing half turned in the doorway would be talking to the person across the little table. The chair is pushed back as though someone rose quickly from it: I only say 'as though' but I think Miss Lane was a very tidy person and in the ordinary way, she would probably have replaced the chair. The chair has a few smears of blood; but the table is spattered all over with blood—except for an oblong patch, roughly in the centre which is free of any blood marks at all. The spots of blood, as I stood in the doorway, were tapered in my direction, if you see what I mean." No one appearing to see what he meant at all, he amended crossly that they were shaped like tadpoles with their tails pointing towards him.

"Couldn't be clearer," said Cecil, sotto voce to Louli; but Louli had learned her lesson by now, and looking nervously at Leo, she mumbled to shut up and listen.

"Turning to the bathroom," said Cockie, not deigning to throw them a glance, "I found blood smears almost everywhere. The shower had been used since the maid did the bathroom, the hand towels were damp and blood-stained, just dropped about anyhow. One of the bath-towels, we know, was outside on the rail with her damp bathing things: the other was rather interesting—it was very damp and it was stained with blood all along one edge. There were smears on the wooden floor between the bathroom and the bed, where blood had been washed off or water mopped up; and the same between the table and the foot of the bed." He stopped abruptly and tilted back his chair, his toes just touching the ground. A glass of Grappa was standing full before him and he emptied it, coughing, at one gulp.

Mr Cecil thought that it was all madly interesting, but didn't tell them much.

"It tells us a very great deal," said Cockie severely.

Leo Rodd had a bash. "It tells us that—let's see. She

came up from her bathe—no, go back earlier than that. She came in from lunch, she changed into her kimono, possibly with her undies still on, and presumably lay down like the rest of us. Then she put on her bathers, tossing her underclothes, then or before that, into the bathroom to be washed. When she came back from the bathe, she put her wet things on the rail and slipped on her kimono with nothing underneath it. She pulled out the little table from the window a bit and was sitting there when . . ."

"What for?" said Cockie.

"What for?"

"Why did she sit down at the little table?"

"Well, *I* don't know—to write some letters or something."

"But there were no writing things on the table," said Helen. "Or sewing things. Or manicure things."

"M'm. I see," said Leo.

"Perhaps she was reading," suggested Louvaine, reasonably.

"One doesn't sit at a table to read," said Miss Trapp, "and her books were on the dressing-table. And anyway, she'd come in to lie down." Miss Trapp herself had sent her in to lie down.

"Perhaps she *had* lain down. After all, she was in her room for two and a half hours before we found her. Then she got up and sat down at the table."

"I say again—what for?" said Cockie.

"Perhaps she sat down to talk to the murderer?"

"Leaving him standing up? There wasn't anything else in the room to sit on."

"That would suggest a servant," said Miss Trapp, eagerly; but nobody bothered about Miss Trapp and her servant problem any more.

"Then what was on the table?" said Cockie.

"You've told us yourself that there was nothing on it,"

said Leo. But he remembered. "Ah!—but you said there was a patch that wasn't spattered with blood—an oblong patch."

"Like ferns in a book," said Louvaine. She shied away from that dawning, irritable frown. "No, no, I'm not talking nonsense: don't you remember when one was a child, one used to put leaves and things down on a clean page and spatter ink with a comb? It was heavenly. And then you lifted up the leaf and all the rest of the page was speckled."

A slight altercation followed between those who had never heard of it in their lives, and those whose childhood rainy days had been made exquisite with ink and comb. Mr Cockrill continued to draw on his wispy cigarette. He considered it his duty, in the very curious, not to say dangerous, circumstances in which they found themselves, to tell them the facts. If they could not trouble to use the information, that was no affair of his.

Miss Barker, however, was getting quite well trained. She nervously brought the subject back from the realms to which her simile had consigned it. "I only meant that the square patch was like the leaf. In other words, Inspector, there was something on the table when the table was spattered with blood; and it's been taken away."

"Yes," said Cockrill.

"Something square: a book or a box."

"Something oblong, actually; if a book, possibly an open book."

"There were two books in the room?"

"Neither of them is bloodstained."

"Now that I do call exciting," said Cecil. "A book or a box—and the murderer's taken it away. Whatever can have been in it?"

Inspector Cockrill had a very shrewd idea of what might have been in the book or the box and thought Mr Cecil too might be less than sincere in his wide-eyed wonder. But they moved on, away from that particular problem. "Well, anyway, Inspector, she was sitting there in her white kimono and the murderer came in through the balcony door . . ."

"Why the balcony door, Leo?"

"Because of the way the chair was facing, the way the table was turned. Aren't I right, Inspector?"

"You'd make a good detective," said Cockie; higher praise no man could bestow.

"They faced each other across the table. The murderer was—was either a man *or* a woman," said Leo, slowing down. And he added, tentatively, but encouraged by Cockrill's recent praise, "But probably a woman—or a man whom Miss Lane knew pretty well."

"Very good indeed," said Cockrill, surprised.

"And about her own height or a little taller; and right-handed."

"Now you're simply showing off," said Mr Cecil.

"He's doing very nicely," said Cockie. "But you'd better explain your deductions, Mr Rodd, to these simple minds."

Leo deprecatingly obliged. "As for the height and the right-handedness, you could see from the hilt of the knife, when she was lying there, that the thrust went from right to left and slightly downwards and any detective story tells you what that shows. As to the murderer being a woman or a man—well, it's true that a man would be the likeliest to be taller; Miss Lane wasn't short by any means." He gave them his bitter smile and added that he trusted they would balance the fact that he was the only man present of the requisite height, against the fact that he could hardly be called right-handed. "But I still think it may have been a woman, and that's because of the kimono. If the knife didn't go through the kimono, if it went between the two edges, then the kimono must have been fairly wide open, or anyway, open a long way down; and I should think Miss

Lane was the sort of girl who would automatically pull it together if she was in the presence of a man—unless she knew him extremely well, and even then I think she'd probably just hitch herself tidy and comme il faut."

There was a loud chorus of admiration. "Elementary, elementary," said Leo. "Come on, Mr Cecil—you have a go now."

"There's nothing left to have a go at," said Cecil, a little bit put about by all this fuss and adulation over somebody else. "They talked across the table—not for very long, because the other person didn't sit down . . ."

"There was nothing for them to sit on; they just had to stand up."

"They could have gone and sat on the bed," said Cecil, crossly. "I mean, if it had been a real discussion, a real heart-to-hearter. Anyway, I say it was a short discussion, they quarrelled, the paper knife was on the table, because after all it was a paper knife and anyway it was new, she probably just put it down there to look at and gloat over a bit like one does with anything new: and the murderer picked it up and lunged at her, hence the tadpoles, and . . ."

"Here, hoy, why 'hence'? Explain your deductions, as the Inspector would say."

"Oh, but anybody knows," said Cecil, his good humour returning, "that if you flick a paint-brush or a pen, the drops fall into a little round dobble that tails off *away* from the thing that's flicked. She was standing behind the table and the blood sort of—well, squirted out and the drops on the table do taper away from her, as it were. But it only confirms that she was standing behind the little table, facing towards the balcony door, and that we know."

"That we deduce," said Cockie.

Cecil thought it was all too horrid, anyway, quite sickening, and that they should *hurry* on to the bathroom. "You won't find the bathroom any more attractive," said Inspector Cockrill.

"Well, as it happens the only interesting thing there is the bath-towel," said Cecil. "I mean, obviously the murderer went in there and cleaned up; he may even have had a shower, he may even have washed his clothes, though how he could walk about afterwards all damp one doesn't quite see . . ."

"Unless, of course," said Cockie, sweetly, "he happened to be in a bathing dress."

"A bathing dress?"

"My dear Mr Cecil—the six suspects chosen by the police of San Juan are sitting round this table at this moment; and at the time that the crime was committed—isn't it a fact that all of you were wearing bathing dresses."

"The six . . .? But, Inspector . . . I mean, you don't really think . . .?"

"I don't think anything," said Cockie. "I'm talking about what the people here think, and unfortunately it's what they think that matters. And I simply say that it is perhaps a slight—confirmation—that the murderer was able to wash himself clean of bloodstains and then walk about with damp clothes without attracting notice. It does suggest a bathing dress."

"Of course if it was one of the other hotel people, Inspector, they could have gone to their own room and changed."

"Yes, but Leo," said Helen, "then surely they'd have gone and washed in their own room as well? Why stay on the scene of the crime?"

"Because the scene of the crime was the one place where it was safe enough to leave traces of blood. Isn't that true,

Inspector? If the murderer had gone to his own bathroom, there would probably have been some traces, however faint, and the police would have discovered them."

Inspector Cockrill privately thought that the Hotel Bellomare could have been transformed to a blood bath before the police of San Juan would have taken the slightest notice. He agreed, however, that the murderer, as long as he was fairly safe from interruption, was wise to remove all traces of the crime on the spot. "Now, Mr Cecil—you were commenting on the bath-towel, and you're quite right to do so. Very damp; and with bloodstains all down one of the long edges, lengthways, that is."

"M'm," said Mr Cecil. "Very damp. Well, bath-towels often are very damp; and we don't know that it wasn't Miss Lane herself who used the shower, before ever the murderer came near the room. But the thing is—the blood." He gave a distasteful shudder at the ugly word, but was really too much concentrated upon the subject before him to do more than token service to his delicate susceptibilities. "There was blood on it—but only down one edge. And the other thing, that sort of goes with it, is that there wasn't much blood round the knife and the edges of the kimono and it seemed to be a bit diluted. So, Inspector, I should say that—yes, that the towel was sort of folded, or rolled if you like and, as it were, ringed round the hilt of the knife; so that there wouldn't be too much blood spilled about when she was moved on to the bed. When she was on the bed, the towel was removed, her hands were put back round the knife—they were only quite laxly curled round it, they weren't gripping it—and the towel was chucked out into the bathroom." He eyed Cockie like an alert sparrow; and Cockie reflected, as he had earlier reflected about the Gerente, that it never did to underrate people. He said graciously that that was very good indeed. Mr Cecil went quite pink with gratification, thought over the problem and said that that was all.

Cockie switched off his graciousness like a lamp. "All?"

"I can't think of anything else of interest."

Nobody else could either. "Good heavens!" said Cockie. "You amaze me." You told them everything, you put the facts before them fair and square: they discussed them all intelligently, made some superficial but quite well-reasoned deductions—and then totally ignored the most interesting; possibly the most important, certainly the most unaccountable—of the lot. He was disgusted with them. He got up abruptly from the table. "Well, I shall go to bed now and get some rest. I advise you all to do the same. You're going to need it." They understand nothing, he thought, marching away from them impatiently: they don't even understand the danger they're in. Well, I'm supposed to be on holiday —let them get on with it! He stood on one leg at his bedroom door, to crush out the stump of his cigarette on the sole of blue canvas, Juanese espadrille. There arose a repellent stench of burning rope.

CHAPTER SIX

L EO RODD sat on the edge of the four-poster bed, tugging
     with his one hand at the lace of his shoe and waiting,
     nerves scraped raw, for his wife to offer to do it for him.
'In one minute—in one minute now, she'll stop fiddling
with her hair and turn round and pretend to notice for the
first time and say, "Shall *I* have a go?" as though it were
some sort of competition, something that we could do about
equally well, a sort of jolly puzzle . . .' He wondered whether
a day might ever come when Louvaine would get on his
nerves like this: sweet, feckless, gay Louvaine, with her
casual hand put out now and again to his assistance, without concealment, without apology; would she too one day
have evolved this grating formula of delicate tact, shall-
I-have-a-go, let-*me*-try-darling, can-you-manage-all-right-
my-pet . . .? 'At any rate,' he thought, 'she'd have done
something by now, not stood there fiddling with her hair
for the past half hour.'

Helen glanced at his reflection in the looking-glass, standing there combing and recombing her perfectly set brown
hair. 'Whatever I say will be wrong. If I offer to do it, he'll
say that for God's sake, he isn't an infant in arms. If I wait
any longer he'll ask if I happen to have noticed that he's
recently lost one of his hands.' But one could not stand there
all the morning. She put down the comb and turned away
from the table, pretending to see for the first time that he
was in difficulties. "Shall I do it, darling?" She knelt down

and steadied his foot on her knee like a girl in a shoe-shop. "There you are. Give me the other one." She stood up again and covertly looked him over to see that there was nothing more he needed. "Well, I'll go on down now, and wait for you on the terrace . . ." ('And then you can meet your girl on the balcony, quite by chance,' she thought, 'and start your day with a word of love—as you're longing to do.') She went out on the balcony and down the wooden steps to where the tables were laid for breakfast out on the terrace. Nobody was there yet but Mr Cecil, exquisite in white linen trousers and a peach coloured shirt. "My dear, did you hear the departures? They've all rushed off, quacking with excitement, down to the quay. Fernando has arranged for some of the smugglers' boats to take them out for joy rides and all I can say is, I hope they're sick, unfeeling beasts."

"One of them will be at any rate," said Helen, smiling.

"Poor Grim's had a terrible night, dear, positively haggard. Do you want me to order some of this repulsive bread and jam for you?—it's all there is." He fished out a book of Useful Phrases in Italian, Spanish and Juanese. "This language! Wouldn't you think 'despacio' meant 'be quick'? But no, no, on the contrary it means slow, and heaven knows, there's no need to tell them that." He contented himself with some signs which the waiter apparently understood for he departed with the customary despacio. "He'll be hours; but anyway, it'll be horrid when it does come, so why fret?"

"You seem rather jaundiced this morning, Mr Cecil," said Helen. It was a relief to have someone so easy to talk to.

"I didn't have a very good night. Mrs Rodd," said Cecil, suddenly, "was Miss Lane blackmailing you too?"

She went very white, putting her hand up to her long throat, holding it there very still, staring at him.

"Blackmail?" It was as though the idea had never dawned upon her; but, dawning, did so with a vivid and terrifying significance. "Well, no, Mr Cecil. What do you mean?"

"Didn't Louvaine tell you?"

"No," she said. "She didn't tell us."

'She may not have told you,' thought Mr Cecil. He suggested, casually: "She may have mentioned it to your husband."

"Oh, no," said Helen, quickly. "He'd have told me."

'I wonder,' thought Mr Cecil again. But Miss Trapp had come up, clutching her bag, and sought permission to join them. "Oh, yes, do, Miss Trapp—all poor criminals together, and all the rest have rushed off down to the sea in ships, mean things, revelling in their freedom. Do you want me to order you bread and jam? Mrs Rodd and I have been looking it up in the little book but we can't find anything except 'I would like to be shown the toilet,' a horrible suggestion so early in the morning." He repeated his pantomime for the benefit of the waiters. "Except that it's called the excusado, which I do think is rather charming. I was asking Mrs Rodd," he went on, prattling gaily away without a pause, "whether Miss Lane had been blackmailing her too?"

"Blackmailing?" said Miss Trapp, also apparently astonished.

"Well, she was trying it on Louli Barker and me and you, so I thought . . ."

"On me?" said Miss Trapp, her fist tight up under her chin clinging to the handles of the brown bag.

"Well, wasn't she?"

"Certainly not," said Miss Trapp sharply. "What could she have to blackmail me about?"

"I wouldn't know," said Cecil. He thought back to that strange conversation up on the balcony when she had looked down at the four of them, standing talking on the terrace by the rock. 'All of them with money—their own or somebody else's . . .' She had added that she knew what 'miserable fortune' Miss Trapp hoarded up 'in a gold-monogrammed bag.' 'Louli's right,' he thought, 'she doesn't go pale, she goes quite grey.'

Up in his room, Leo Rodd, listening, heard the quick, light step and the little cough and came out on to the balcony. "Louvaine!"

"Oh, Leo—my love!"

"We must talk quickly, darling. You realized that I couldn't come to the beach last night? You didn't go?"

"I strolled about for a bit, just in the hope—but I knew it was quite insane. Can we to-night?"

"God knows that if it's possible, I will. But the whole place is humming with spying and questioning, we'll have to be careful. If the worst comes to the worst, we'll just have to wait till all this is over and we get away from here."

"After all, there's no hurry—we have all our lives," she said.

He stood by the door of his room, his hand on her wrist, looking down at her. "Oh, Louli—I wonder if really this is right?"

She was terrified. "You haven't changed your mind?"

"No, no, my heart, of course, of course I haven't changed my mind. I only wonder. . . . There's a devil in me, Louli, ever since this—this business of mine. It's not really me, I used not to be like this, I was on the whole quite a decent-tempered chap. But now—I'm so afraid that one day I'll be unkind to you, too, like I am to poor Helen: drive you into a shell, make you afraid of me and then be angry with you for being afraid of me."

"I'm never afraid of things," said Louvaine.

"That's what I thought. You were always so—so particularly unafraid, Louli. But you see, already it's beginning.

Last night at dinner, I was annoyed because you and Cecil fooled about . . ."

"Yes, darling," she said, "you *were* rather cross."

"And you were afraid, Louli. You looked frightened. It's simply haunted me."

"I'm afraid of not having you," she said. "Not of anything else in the world. But I'm afraid of that."

He raised her hand and kissed her clutching fingers; and felt, with a little pang of fear and presentiment of fear, how they shook within his grasp. But Mr Fernando came out of his room and their hands dropped guiltily, they started into motion, strolling with great unconcern towards the wooden steps. Fernando looked as though he too had slept badly, but he switched on The Smile and together they all went down to the breakfast table. Mr Cecil was sitting there gaily dispensing rolls and apricot jam and the frankly rather horrid coffee which everyone would recall as so infinitely superior to anything one got in England; but his companions seemed not enormously interested in his bright chatter. Helen Rodd looked up anxiously at her husband, not sparing any glance for his lady love, Miss Trapp raised lack-lustre eyes in response to a flash of ivory and gold. "Goodness," said Louvaine, pulling out a square wooden chair and hitching it close to the table with herself caged inside it, "you do all look glum!"

"Yes, we are glum; and if you want bread and jam, Louli, you can order it yourself, I'm worn out with Dumb Crambo. But imagine, ducky," said Mr Cecil, pushing back his brassy hair, "we've been talking about blackmail and neither Mrs Rodd nor Miss Trapp had any *idea!*"

Louvaine opened her blue eyes very wide and gave Miss Trapp a startled glance, as though over the tops of a pair of spectacles. Leo Rodd said sharply, "Blackmail?"

"Hadn't you told Mr Rodd, dear?"

"No," said Louli, "there hasn't been a chance."

"Blackmail?" said Fernando. "Miss Lane?"

Cecil pushed back his hair again with a comb of white fingers. "I thought you were telling people, Louvaine?"

"I was going to, but how could I? The murder happened and there's been nothing but ta-ta-ta about that, ever since."

Leo Rodd had no truck with Dumb Crambo. He called over a waiter, pointed to Fernando, Miss Barker and himself and said loudly, "El café, el pan and el jam if you haven't got anything else and despacio, no I mean the other thing, de prisa! Oh, sorry, Fernando, I'd forgotten you could do it but never mind, he's gone now." To Louvaine he said: "You didn't think that all this—about blackmail—might have fitted in with the ta-ta-ta about murder?"

"I thought it might fit in most uncomfortably," said Louvaine. She added that anyway, she *had* told Inspector Cockrill before the murder. "He said she probably wasn't a blackmailer, really; she probably only enjoyed seeing people wriggling on the hook."

"Oh, well," said Leo. You could see the care falling away from his shoulders.

"Some people are like that," said Helen Rodd. No doubt Miss Lane had thrown out little hints about Miss Barker's goings-on, had thrown out little threats of what she could tell the injured wife. It was extraordinary, she thought drearily to herself, how people always assumed that the wife went through it all blinkered by blindness and stupidity —as though one wasn't always the very first person to know, sometimes before even the guilty parties themselves! "It gives them a kick," she said, "to think they have the power of making other people unhappy." Did they suppose, she wondered, that they had the monopoly in that?

Inspector Cockrill came down the verandah steps, a trifle self-conscious in the panama hat and a suit of crumpled alpaca. He looked with repulsion upon the remains of the rolls and jam, and the cups of thick coffee. He was sick of Abroad. "You go to your Dirrytory," he said to the waiter, loudly and clearly, "and tell him to arrange a pot of tea for me and some bacon and eggs, bacon and eggs, understand?—bacona and eggsa." He sat down heavily in one of the square wooden chairs. "Well?"

Mr Fernando had spent a busy night getting things worked out and he now had a plan to put before Inspector Cockrill. All the Gerente wanted, he said was—a culprit. But supposing it could be proved to the Gerente that not even a culprit was needed. He heard, Fernando heard, for the first time this morning, that yesterday Miss Lane had given herself away—had allowed two people, and one a policeman, to learn that she was a blackmailer. She had run off and had her bathe; but later, in the quiet of her room, thinking it all over—must she not have been overwhelmed at the realization of what she had done? The moment they returned to England, the Inspector would warn the authorities; investigation would be made—not only was her future means of livelihood reft from her, but her past would come surging up, and what would be left to her but prison and disgrace? What horror, what despair, cried Fernando, all teeth and eyelashes. She sits there at her little table, her head in her hands. Her eye falls upon the knife. She lies down upon her bed and composes herself for death: one sharp thrust—and all is over.

"Does she then get up and fetch the red shawl?" asked Cockie, fascinated by this résumé, "or did she get it first? And why the sacrificial sprinkling of the table? And what has happened to the oblong object that was on the table? And why did she mop up the floor and why did she do all that washing in the bathroom, and how did she manage it after the stab wound—which has every appearance of having caused almost instant death—had been made?" He added, agreeably, that he only wanted to know.

"Ah, *you* want to know, Inspector," said Fernando. "But the Gerente wants to go out in his boat with the fleet. These inconvenient questions will not trouble him." He looked at his friends, his Helpless Ones. "You are all on a jolly holiday: would it not be best if the Gerente were to accept this solution? After all—she was a blackmailer: do you care so much who killed her? Do you really wish that for this, someone should rot away in the San Juan gaol? Say nothing to the Gerente of this blackmail: I will tell him we all believe she committed suicide. Inspector—you agree? What Scotland Yard says will be of importance."

"If you don't mention the blackmail," said Cockrill, "what motive will you suggest for the suicide? Or won't the Gerente care about that either?"

Fernando thought that the Gerente would care about nothing but getting on with his smuggling. He shrugged and smiled. "Young ladies fall in love. A hopeless affair . . .?" He put his head on one side. "Mr Rodd—was not the lady just a little devoted to yourself?"

"She may well have been," said Leo. "Most ladies with nothing else to do at the moment, fall in love with my missing arm. But I've never had a suicide on my hands yet —or shall we say my hand?—and I'm not going to begin now. You can look elsewhere for your motive. However, I'm all for saying nothing about blackmail and lots about suicide, and getting out of San Juan as quick as we can go. Upon which proposition, I suggest a show of hands."

Through a forest of hands, Inspector Cockrill watched the approach of the Gerente, down the verandah steps. He looked very splendid, the sun glinting on the black patent leather hat and the silver chasing of his ancient gun, the blue cloak flowing about rumpled trouser legs, innocent of any creases save those of much wear. He was followed by the hotel manager, carrying a small brown book.

Five feet from the breakfast table, he stopped. He motioned to the Diretore. The Diretore stepped up to his side and opened the little book. He held it out in front of him like a choir boy with his musical score, and began to read. "Meesa Trappa," read the hotel manager, unhappily contorting his face over the difficult, clipped English syllables. "Ochenta Parka Lana, speenister . . ." He broke down, he read out several lines in a rapid gabble in his own tongue. "She writes that Miss Trapp appears rich," translated Fernando, muttering anxiously to his friends, "she says that she carries her—her treasure—in a brown bag, she says—she says that the monogram on the bag is not—is not . . ." He broke off, wretchedly faltering. He said to Miss Trapp: "She writes that the initials on the bag are not yours."

The Gerente stopped the flow. He stubbed a dirty finger towards the bottom of the page. El Diretore looked at it, hesitated over it, finally announced: "Poundsa cincuenta." But something more puzzled him. He turned the book round and showed it to Mr Fernando, pointing with his finger to a large figure circled in ink, at the bottom of the page. "Fifty pounds," read out Fernando in a sick voice. "With a question mark."

"With a question mark? What on earth can it all mean?"

"It can only mean one thing: is Miss Trapp's secret good for fifty pounds?"

The Gerente silenced them with a commanding hand. El Diretore turned over a page. "Meester Thetheelah. Ch-rees-topy . . ." But he could not. "No importa," said the Gerente. He stubbed with his finger again. The Diretore, one eye on Fernando for guidance, read out: "Poundsa ciente?"

"A hundred pounds," said Fernando.

"A hundred pounds—*me?*" said Cecil. His pale face was dreadfully white, his hair was the brassy gold of ormolu against the colour of old ivory. "Ask him—don't ask him what it is, just ask if—if she—thinks she knows anything against me?"

The manager translated the English slowly to himself, repeated it in his bastard Spanish. "He says, yes," said Fernando, retranslating. "He says it is about—your shop. He says . . ."

Louvaine came loyally to the aid of a friend in trouble, perhaps about to be shamefully (though they could not all help rather longing to know!), exposed. "Don't let him read it out. It's no business of ours."

El Diretore had settled for the easy way out. He turned over the pages and translated to himself and so to Fernando. "This one is about you, Miss Barker," said Fernando. "You come on the last page. Your name, your address." He listened attentively. "Then much about . . ." His eyes slid round to Leo Rodd.

"Don't tell me, let me guess," said Louli. "But—how much?"

"Feefty pounds," said the Diretore. He turned a page. "Meesees Roddha."

"No," said Helen quickly.

Fernando listened again. "He says nothing against you, Mrs Rodd. Much about—Mr Rodd. She asks . . ."

"Never mind what she asks," said Helen.

"She asks only if you love your husband, Mrs Rodd. She asks what would be your attitude if you knew . . ."

"That's enough," said Helen, sharply.

"At the bottom of the page is written five hundred pounds." The Diretore tipped the book so that they could see it written there; but this time there were no question marks. "It might seem," suggested Fernando, "that this was not to be so much a price for silence as a price for speaking." He turned another page. He said quietly: "And here is Fernando. There is something against me too. And the figure fifty pounds."

"And me?" said Leo.

The Gerente took the book. He flicked the pages and showed them the heading 'Leo Rodd.' There was very little more, and there was no figure at the bottom of the page. He turned another page and put the book into Inspector Cockrill's hands.

His thumb stuck in the open place, Cockie turned the book over. It was a morocco bound notebook, more or less square: he observed that, lying open, it might well have covered the oblong space on the table that had been protected from blood splashes. It was written throughout in the elegant, upright, Italianate script which it had recently become fashionable to adopt, especially among those with uninteresting or illegible hands of their own: easy to learn and, with practice, fluent and quick. It was exceedingly neatly set out, the headings underlined, the margin regular —and theirs were by no means the only names in it. He turned back to the open page, headed with his own.

Miss Lane had a pretty turn of phrase. For a moment the Terror of Kent had a glimpse of himself as others saw him— a dusty brown sparrow that had somehow got mixed up with migratory birds and was ill at ease and unhappy in the raw, red, sun-drenched countryside, far from his English lanes. He was a Detective Inspector (a Det. Inspec., she wrote it), he was small and stooping, and his hair was grey: and after this was a query and an exclamation mark. There were little digs at the ever-present mackintosh, the detective stories, his dentures which he had hitherto held to be quite secret, the purchase of the too small panama hat. Beyond this, however, there was nothing: no hint of illicit passions, of false pretences of wealth or position, no reference—he breathed a sigh of relief—to certain small adventures in pelire in the tobacconists' shops of Barrequitas which did business, open and unashamed, trafficking in currency there. But at the bottom of the page was a figure, ringed in an ink circle: fifty pounds. And the white paper was flecked with brown marks, a school of little brown tadpoles, disturbed and wriggling away from him, across the open page. He had seen dried blood too often before this, not to know what the brown marks were.

They went for a bathe that morning. It was terribly hot and anyway there was nothing else they could do. Leo Rodd and Helen swam, Mr Cecil and Louvaine Barker and Miss Trapp went through their routine bobbing and screaming, Fernando gambolled in his porpoise fashion from the shore to the raft and back. Inspector Cockrill hitched up the stovepipe trousers of his alpaca suit and went for a long, long paddle all by himself, the straw hat perched on the top of his noble head.

And afterwards, they lay in a long line under the sunshed, drawn together by their common situation, and talked and talked and talked. Cockie, coming back from his paddle with ankles pink and puckered from their long immersion, stopped and looked down at them. Miss Trapp and Mr Fernando lay side by side, muttering together, he a vast, quaking, reddy-brown sea anemone, naked and anything but ashamed, she wrapped in striped towelling like an angel on horseback, a very thin prune in a very large rasher of streaky bacon. Mr Cecil lay on his back, his front still sore from yesterday's sunbathing: as Louli had said, you could see, literally, a line of demarkation where the pink ended and the white began—could see too the little daubs of sun-tan make-up in the wrinkles round his eyes, and the false tint of the yellow hair that flopped away from his head on to shoulders as white as a girl's—as white as Louvaine's own white shoulders, lying next to him with her red head on her forearm, scratching 'I love you' in the sand for Leo Rodd to see and, seeing, smooth over with a warning frown. Helen Rodd was at the end of the row, lying with eyes closed behind round yellow sun-glasses, Dutch doll legs and arms spread-eagled, half in, half out, of the sun. And one of them thought Inspector Cockrill—a murderer. For there was no escape now—no easy talk of servants, of intruders bent upon plunder or rape, no nonsense about suicide. The book had been on the table, the book that had held their names and against their names, some of their names at least, details of secrets known to the murdered woman. No Spaniard, no Italian, no San Juanese could have known what the book contained, or, knowing, need have troubled to hide it away. The Gerente had found it, tucked under the lining of a drawer of the wardrobe; he had told his blood brother so much, but refused any glimpse of the contents, marching off proudly with his booty back to his gaol. "He says he will come again," Fernando had translated; and doubtless he would. Doubtless he would come again. And meanwhile one of them—one of these six people lying chitter-chattering like a row of starlings, under the sun-shed—arguing, guessing, confiding, playing half-seriously at being anxious and terrified but not nearly as anxious and terrified as they had every right to be—one of them was, in fact, a murderer. But he did not know which; and since it did not then occur to him that by just glancing once more at them, with a little more attention, he should have been able to tell, he left them to it and went back up to the hotel.

CHAPTER SEVEN

IT WAS midday. The voices of returning tourists roused
Cockie from his deck-chair, loud with their triumphs in
the smugglers' boats whence they had returned laden
with spoils stealthily slipped into their hands by the sailors
(by order of their captains, who took forty per cent) and
which they could have bought for half the price in the
Barrequitas shops and half that again anywhere outside
San Juan el Pirata. Grim was still being grim, Gruff was
torn between loyalty and love, Mrs Sick had been sick and
so, though they made less parade of it, had nearly everyone
else; one of the more obscure Jollies had been assaulted by
one of the sailors in a Nasty Way and the rest of the women
were treating her as Untouchable and wishing like anything
that it had happened to themselves. Inspector Cockrill
decided to go for a walk.

He had forgotten about the guards at the hotel gate but
the word had gone round and they fell back with respectful
cries of Scotalanda Yarrrda and seemed not even to expect
a bribe. He strolled down to the quay and watched while
the last bales of illicit tobacco, the last sacks of illicit coffee
were hauled ashore under the supervision of the Gerente,
who had absented himself from his labours on the murder
case, until this imperative duty should be completed. The
Gerente was delighted to see him. He took a couple of
watches out of his pocket and offered him either at a very
low figure, finally pressing both upon him for the price of

one. Scotalanda Yarda proving adamant, he flung his arm about the shoulders of his brother and with a windmill of gesture begged him to come back for a glass of arguardiente. Cockie, who had pictured Carmen or Isabelita dispensing little glasses among the geraniums in a white-walled patio at El Gerente's home, discovered himself, too late, at the prison gates.

The prison had been built by San Juan himself in his less regenerate days and had undergone little improvement since. El Gerente's apartments, however, in contrast with the rest, were tremendously cosy, with ingenious gutters of cockled-up tin to catch the moisture which dripped down the six-foot walls, and a window in each room which would positively have let in light and air, had not storks for some generations built their nests, undisturbed, just inside. There was a splendid smell of illicit coffee and a jug of it was brewing on an open fire—the smoke escaped through a hole in the ceiling or at any rate enough of it to have produced a chronic and unattractive cough in the inhabitant of the room above; and Jose had disobeyed orders, for a prematurely born baby goat was curled up on a bundle of rags in a corner. The Gerente lifted a ponderous key from a nail in the wall and, after great exertions, succeeded in opening the safe. From it, pushing aside sundry packages of noxious drugs, he produced a bottle of arguardiente and, pouring out liberal glassfuls, proceeded to toast his guest with such warmth that Cockie expected at any moment to have his veins opened for a ceremonial mingling of blood.

Intelligent conversation, however, was difficult. The Gerente gave it up at last and sent for an interpreter. The interpreter proved to be a light-hearted brunette who leaned against the Gerente's knee and tickled his ears in the intervals of her work. Her first duty was to warn the blood brother that now he and El Gerente were friends and he must not tell El Gerente's Pepita what an attractive interpreter he was obliged to employ. Inspector Cockrill felt fairly safe in undertaking silence upon this point. Since they were so chummy together, however, he felt that the moment was ripe to put in a word for the Helpless Ones.

The Gerente was delighted with the theory of suicide, translated—amid gales of inexplicable laughter—by Lollita. But it would not do. He produced the morocco-covered book. Nor was Cockie the only person who had appreciated that point about the non-English-speaking. It was very clear, translated Lollita in transports of merriment, that the senorita had had some hold over one or other of the present short-list of suspects, and that that person had, naturally enough, seized the opportunity to make away with her. She added without prompting that there were many killings in San Juan and the Gerente always caught someone in the end. It obviously did not very much matter whom.

Cockie had thought it all out carefully during his paddling hours that morning and—allowing for the increasing effects of the raw eau de vie—he had it off pat. He got to work with paper and pencil. The senorita had last been seen at four-thirty, going up this little path here (he stubbed with a nicotined forefinger at a rough plan of the hotel and gardens whose perspective grew progressively wilder as its details and the glasses of arguardiente multiplied). At that time all the—very well, suspects—were gathered or were gathering together on the beach. And *from* that time to the time when, two and a half hours later, the body was discovered, they had all remained together on the beach: first bathing in the sea, then sunbathing on the sand. He, Inspector Cockrill, had sat during the entire two and a half hours, on the lower terrace—here—and, after thinking it very carefully over, he was prepared to say that not for one single moment had any of them been out of his sight.

Mr and Mrs Rodd had lain under the sun-shed, Miss Trapp over here at the foot of the diving rock, Mr Fernando on the raft several yards out to sea, Mr Cecil in a rubber boat further inshore, and Miss Barker on the terrace by the side of his own deck-chair. No, he had not slept—not a wink. Others had slept, perhaps. Miss Barker had slept. Mr Cecil said *he* had slept: Mr Fernando too, spreadeagled on the raft. But Inspector Cockrill had not slept, insisted Cockie with a vague, arguardiente-hazy idea that to have done so would in some way have let down the honour of Scotalanda Yarda. And he could assure the Gerente that all the six people concerned had been, throughout the entire afternoon, on the beach. "I saw them," said Cockie simply, "I know."

The Gerente looked somewhat put about by this reverse. He humped the brunette off his knee and told her crossly to get a chair for herself. She returned with something apparently left over from the Middle Ages and sat down meekly at a corner of the desk. The Gerente spoke sharply, all trace of gaiety suddenly gone and she sharply interpreted. "Gerente says—you see *all?*"

"All," said Cockie firmly.

"All time?"

"All time. I mean, yes, the whole time."

"You no sleep?"

"No sleep. I was reading a book."

"Ah, ha!" said the Gerente.

"Gerente says, Ah ha!"

"What does he mean, Ah ha?"

"Then your eyes were on the book!"

"I do not read a book for two and a half hours without lifting my eyes. The murderer would have had to leave the beach, pass up the central steps quite close to me, or cross the beach to the little path up the corner of the rock; he would have been gone at least—at the very least, three-quarters of an hour. I could not possibly have failed to miss him—even if I did not see him go or return."

The Gerente was silent. Deep in thought, he sat staring at the desk before him, putting out an automatic hand to refill the arguardiente glasses and pass them round, dirty fingers bunched over the tiny rims. He downed his own at one gulp and leaned back in his wooden chair, holding the morocco-covered book open, before his face. He put the book down, still open, on the desk and spoke to the girl. She translated: "Gerente say—they could not then have killed?"

"No," said Cockie.

"Gerente say—because you could see them all?"

"Yes," said Cockie.

"Gerente say," said the girl, and now there were no giggles, no more meaningless laughter, "Gerente say, very well then—but who could see *you?*"

Inspector Cockrill sat stock-still. The fumes of the brandy, heavy and hot, clung about his brain, he was like a man treading in treacle who cannot shake himself free; but he forced himself violently back, at last, to cold sanity: and discovered sanity to be cold indeed. Once again, through the farcical trappings, the ugly truth stood bare and his very bowels felt sick and chill within him. He said, sharply: "I could see *them:* they could see *me.*"

"Gerente say no: you were above, you could see down. They were below. They might not see you."

"Miss Barker was lying there close beside me."

"He say, yes—asleep."

"As soon as I stood up, anyone from the beach must have seen me. I would have had to walk to the higher terrace, up these central steps, here."

"He say you can move along terrace to the jasmine tunnel here, and go within the tunnel to the upper terrace."

"What was I supposed to do if Miss Barker woke up?"

The Gerente shrugged, Lollita interpreted the shrug. "There is no reason why a gentleman should not get up and go."

"On all fours along the terrace? Well, never mind, let that pass," said Cockie. "Suppose she had woken while I was away or while I was coming back: after the thing was done?"

"Gerente say—dead senorita knew bad secrets about Senorita Barrker. Senorita Barrrker would be content to— have slept."

It never did, it never did, to underrate people. "Tell the Gerente—tell him that *I* had nothing against this senorita. There is nothing against me in the book. Why should I kill her? Why should he think I might have?"

The Gerente kept his eyes on Cockrill's face. He stood up, reached for a piece of writing paper, placed it in the centre of the desk; lifted his glass of arguardiente and with a swift movement shot out the dregs across the paper. The drops fell in longish splashes, tapering away from their source. He glanced down at them with satisfaction, his eyes returned to Cockrill's face, he pushed aside the paper and slowly replaced it with the morocco bound book. It was open at the page headed with Cockrill's own name. Not thinking what he did, Cockie also rose and stood looking down at the book.

The bloodstains, spattered across the written page, were like a little school of tadpoles: scuttling . . .

With a second swift movement, El Gerente turned the book. Cockie could read his own name now, Vanda Lane's comments about him, the figure she had ringed at the bottom of the page. And the tadpoles were scuttling—away from him.

Away from him.

But on the small wooden table, the stains had run the other way. The book had been turned on the table.

She sits at the table. The blackmail book is lying there before her and the Toledo steel knife. The knife is there by chance; not so the book.

Somebody comes in and stands facing her across the table. She opens the book—she or the intruder; the book is turned on the table so that the intruder can read. The intruder reads—and snatches up the knife.

Whoever had lunged across that little table and thrust the knife into Vanda Lane's heart—had stood looking down at the blackmail book opened at the page which bore Inspector Cockrill's name.

He stood there, staring down at the blood-spattered page and, for the first time for many, many years, knew what it was to be afraid: uncertain and afraid. He opened his mouth to speak: and shut it again. One wrong word, one false move. . . . And yet one could not stand, speechless and motionless, and let the trap close. For, once this trap closed, he knew that the helpless victim might struggle till death: unheard, unseen, only too soon unremembered. England no doubt would clamour for her own; but who in San Juan el Pirata cared about England? They were within their rights. A murder had been committed, a culprit had been—selected; the requirements of justice had been satisfied; and El Exaltida and El Magistrato and El Gerente de Politio must ask to be excused now, for the smuggling fleet would soon be going out or soon be coming in and there was important work for them to do. Indeed, if all this agitation was going to continue, it might be expedient, come Holy

Week, to string the prisoner up with as little fuss as possible and so put a final end to the argument.

He looked up and into the Gerente's eyes. The Gerente smiled uncertainly and lifted winged arms in a tremendous shrug; really, it was the blood brother's own silly fault, said the shrug. He glanced at the clock; the clock said, probably untruthfully, that it was after two o'clock and he made a wry face—evidently two was his dinner hour and Pepita was going to be cross. Two guards came into the room in response to a fist banged on the table. Cockie said, panic-stricken: "What does this mean?"

Lollita asked the Gerente and the Gerente openly meditated what answer would soonest placate the prisoner and finally replied that the politio wished to offer the Gerente Inglese some lunch. It was a pressing invitation; for they were one each side of him, gripping him tightly by the upper arms. The Gerente gave him an apologetic smile and went off to face Pepita. Detective Inspector Cockrill of Scotlanda Yarda went down to a cell in the bowels of the Barrequitas gaol.

In contrast with the blazing sun outside, it was very dark down there; dark and dank and very chill. There were no cockled tin gutters here to catch the moisture trickling down the walls, the floor was green and slimy with two hundred years of it. There was a rotting wooden bench along one wall, what little space was left was taken up by great sacks of what appeared to be coffee beans: there was a strong smell, and several other signs, of goat. The guards went away with a tremendous banging of door and turning of key: ten minutes later one of them returned with a bowl of savoury rice and a two-horned glass drinking bottle of raw red vino corriente, from the few poor straggling grapes on the further side of the island; and went away again, yawning and with rather less noise. Inspector Cockrill ignored the rice but he drank half a carafe of the wine. The sacks of beans were drier than the bench and he sat down on one of them, to think.

An hour later he was still sitting there. His mind was frozen, he could not think at all, could not plan, could not decide, could not look forward, could not look back. El Gerente would not appear again at the hotel. By the next morning, perhaps, Fernando would institute some enquiry. The Politio would reply that all was now settled, Odyssey Tours was free to proceed upon its way. Fernando would argue a bit, no doubt, would ask for explanations, would protest; but his own troubles were not so far behind him that he would be likely to dare a great deal, and he would eventually shrug his broad shoulders, report back to his company in England, and proceed as his duty was, with his party, all only too thankful to scuttle away leaving behind a hostage, they would argue comfortingly among themselves, well placed and well able, to look after himself. Meanwhile. . . . Meanwhile, numbed with despair and dread, one simply sat; as one had sat inept and stupid, since last the door had slammed and the key had turned . . .

The key had turned . . .?

So very much noise, the first time. So very much less, the second time. He got up quietly and went across to the great, wooden, iron-hinged door.

San Juan el Pirata was running true to form. The guard had gone off, late for his afternoon siesta, and forgotten to lock the door.

He went out quietly into the shivery corridor, up the dank, twisting, slimy shallow stone steps, through the cool, dim hall where the politio peacefully slept, their heads pillowed on their folded arms; out into the clean, bright, glorious light of the day; and walked through the little town as though all the hounds of hell had been after him; and so to the Bellomare Hotel.

The Gerente got there at five o'clock. The Inspector was sitting with Fernando on the terrace, and leapt to his feet, all hypocritical smiles. Through Fernando he thanked the Gerente unreservedly for the charming hospitality of the politio; he had enjoyed his luncheon immensely—but then, feeling drowsy, had strolled back to the hotel for his siesta without waiting for his friend—the Inspector felt sure El Gerente would understand? El Gerente understood perfectly; but it was he himself who had instituted the idea that it was all a jolly luncheon party; and nothing had been said about the Inspector remaining under guard. He really must have a word with Pedro about leaving that door open: Pedro was a good man, one of his best men—in a rough sea, under dangerous conditions, perhaps the best; but really, a fellow must keep his mind on his jobs. Meanwhile . . .

Meanwhile, reunited, the Helpless Ones drew together as never before. Il Grouppa took possession of the beach and made all hideous with British bathing cries; the seven poor suspects conducted an emergency meeting among the pines.

Detective Inspector Cockrill made a short speech. He said that from this moment on, it was every man for himself and what the French called sorve qui pert. One of six persons —seven if they liked to count him in, and they were welcome to—was a murderer. He, Cockie, was not going back to that dungeon to save the neck of any murderer; and he was not going to let anyone else go. No innocent person should end up in the Barrequitas gaol if he could help it; if he could help it, the guilty should not end their either, but come back to England and there stand a fair trial and have a fair chance. "But that's all the mercy he'll get from me," said Cockie. "From this moment I'm against him: whichever of you six people it is. And if you've got any sense, you'll be against him too. Whatever you may think of the rights and wrongs of murdering a blackmailer—if she was a blackmailer—the fact remains that by letting the blame fall on the innocent, the killer is a danger to us all. I'll help you all I can; but you'll have to help *me*. And I give you fair warning, that my neck isn't out of the noose yet, not by a long chalk; and I'm going to do everything I possibly can to find out the true murderer, and protect myself." He sat down abruptly on the intricately pebble-patterned seat in a little clearing in the pine trees, and took out his tobacco. They were silent, sitting on the pine-needled ground in a ring round his feet like children listening to a bedtime story; but the story was too grim for children at bedtime and they were startled and shocked at the cold vehemence in his voice. Into the anxious silence, he repeated it. "This isn't funny, not a bit; and man, woman or child, I'll get whichever of you six people is the murderer. I'll go back to that place for no one. I warn you now."

"Yes. But Inspector Cockrill," said Leo Rodd, "taking as read that we don't for one moment suppose that you are the murderer—you did, yourself, give the Gerente an alibi for all the rest of us. And it was true. We *were* there, you *could* see us all. You said you had thought it over carefully . . ."

"I have thought it all over a great deal more carefully since," said Cockie, "and it only goes to show that one should not work to preconceived notions of things. When I wanted none of you to be guilty, I soon convinced myself, quite sincerely, that none of you could be guilty, that I could give you an alibi. Now I want one of you to be guilty, and I can clearly see that none of you had an alibi after all."

Except one. One of them had an alibi; and at the bottom of his arid old heart, he knew that he was glad of it. For there was, in Louli Barker, that quality which in these young creatures always had power to move him—that quality of gaiety and courage, hiding under however garish an exterior, a humble and deeply vulnerable heart. He was glad that she had an alibi; had slept through the long, sun-drenched afternoon, lying at his feet with her red head pillowed on her arms. Louli Barker was Out. For the rest of them, it was definitely sorve qui pert.

CHAPTER EIGHT

THERE is no room on the island of San Juan el Pirata for a burial-ground. For some decades, this constituted a drawback in its amenities, but at last the inhabitants were made happy by the discovery of a current which could be relied upon to deposit a corpse—in not less than five days from its launching—upon the Ligurian shore; and, thus delicately blackmailed, Italy agreed to cede a plot of ground just north of Piombino, complete with landing-stage. Here the Juanese built a high wall in the Moorish fashion still prevalent in Spain, pitted with narrow recesses like overlong bread ovens, where the dead might be popped, head first, to bake slowly away into nothingness, decently sealed in with the paraphernalia of Christian piety. The little Vaporetto del Muerte plies between Barrequitas and the landing-stage, exquisitely gloomy in dingy black and silver and all a-flutter with purple drapery and ostrich feather plumes. By this means, on the second day after her doing to death, Vanda Lane of St John's Wood, London, was taken—weather not only permitting but insisting—to her last resting-place.

Telegrams had been exchanged between Inspector Cockrill and Scotalanda Yarda, to the infinite astonishment of the Gerente who appeared to regard the whole thing as a species of witchcraft; but so far nothing was known of close friends or relatives of the dead girl. A considerable company, however, followed her coffin, inappropriately gay in their summer

115

holiday clothes; and stood with muffled curiosity among the sentinel cypresses while Mother Church, on the off-chance that this might be one of her children, conditionally performed the last rites. Mr Cecil, half hidden behind a cypress and hardly less sorrowfully dark in trappings of full Juanese mourning bought for the occasion and really too amusingly chic for words, scribbled away in his sketch book with ostentatious surreptitiousness and confided to Louvaine that probably this was the best turn La Lane had ever done to anyone in her *life*. . . .

"Only it's in her death," said Louli.

Louvaine, also, was tremendously decorative that day, in a skirt of bold patchwork lined with scarlet and a scarlet blouse to match, that nobody else in the world would have dared to wear with that hair. "I think one should go a bit gay at funerals," she confided to Miss Trapp, who caught up with her as they trailed along the dusty white road back to the landing-stage. "I know *I* shan't want people going around in black when I die, folding their hands and looking piously down their noses . . ."

Miss Trapp stifled any inclination to say that she thought the chances of Louli's friends observing the proprieties at her obsequies, were remote. She said instead that, as she found Miss Barker alone—so difficult usually, she was always so surrounded by—er—friends—she would be glad of a word with her. "Miss Barker, I wish to ask you a question, straight out."

"A question?" said Louvaine, looking round rather desperately for one or any of the doubtful friends.

"Yes, a question. Miss Barker—that day, while we were watching Miss Lane diving (poor creature, this is all so dreadful, one can hardly believe it, even yet!)—you—you mentioned that you had been in one of those bathing cabins some of the time . . ."

The road was long and straight, bordered with depressed villas in hideous shades of burnt siena and arsenic green and a crude rose-pink. The heads of the straggling procession were dappled with the flickering shade from the laced branches of the bordering trees. "I was in one of the cabins, yes, fixing my bathing dress."

"That would be while—while Mr Fernando and I were talking? The others had gone on down to the beach by then."

"I didn't hear what you were saying, if that's what you mean."

"But, Miss Barker——"

"You were standing quite a little way from me, Miss Trapp, the other side of the steps from the top terrace. I wasn't eavesdropping, I do assure you; I heard nothing."

Miss Trapp's nervous hand fidgeted on the handle of the brown bag. She wore yet another of her expensive silk dresses, which surely had never been designed to have a V neck. "Yet you told the Inspector that Miss Lane was blackmailing me."

"I told him she spoke to you when she came back up to the top of the rock, after her first dive."

"You could hear that too?" said Miss Trapp with an edge to her voice.

"I couldn't hear any of it. Mr Fernando had started off down the path and she said something to you as she passed you; but I didn't hear what it was and so I told the Inspector."

"Well, all she said to me was, 'The tide's on the turn.' "

"That doesn't sound very blackmailing," agreed Louli.

"That is what she said," declared Miss Trapp firmly.

"O.K., well, that's splendid. Just tell the Inspector that that's what she said, and then don't fuss any more."

"I have told the Inspector," said Miss Trapp. "He

replies that you told him I went white and gave a startled exclamation."

Louvaine had actually reported that La Trapp had gone mud-grey and let out a great squawk. She did not labour this distinction, however. "I had only just opened a crack of the door, Miss Trapp, and peeked through, and I saw Miss Lane say something to you. I do hope you realize," said Louvaine a little anxiously, "*why* I told Inspector Cockrill all this? It was only to protect you: it was before the murder happened that I told him, you know. She tried the same thing on me a moment later. I told the Inspector about me and about you at the same time."

"But there was nothing to tell."

"All right, then there wasn't," said Louli. "In view of the fact that she started in on me one minute later, perhaps I was only being wise after the event and imagining that you sort of cried out. Mr Fernando came back up the path and asked you what was the matter . . ."

"He did not ask me what was the matter. He merely turned back to see if I was coming; Mr Fernando has good manners," said Miss Trapp, tossing her head in its depressing brown straw.

"Well, all right, he didn't ask you what was the matter," said Louli, getting cross. "I don't see why you should be in a state about it, anyway. Anyone would think I'd accused you of murdering the woman."

Miss Trapp went mud-grey once more. "I was on the beach while she was being murdered. I could not have been anywhere near her."

Louvaine was hot and weary, the white dust kicked up through the open straps of her sandals, unpleasantly dry and scrunchy beneath her toes, the red hair hung hot and heavy about her white neck. She said irritably that that was not what Inspector Cockrill believed: he had said that, after all, any of them had had opportunity to kill. "You could have gone up the path by the rock . . ."

"I was on the beach during the entire afternoon. Inspector Cockrill could see me there."

"He could see an enclosure of towels and beach umbrellas," said Louli. "You needn't have been inside it, after all! You'd built it right up against the diving rock, you could have chosen that place on purpose, you know; you were better placed than anyone for going up to her room, you only had to skip along the bottom of the rock, up the steep little path in the corner where it joins the terrace, and so on up through the jasmine terrace and all the rest of it; and scuttle down again." Mr Cecil overtook them, exquisite in his tapering black satin trousers and billowing black cotton blouse, tucking away the sketches in his red attaché case as he walked. "Oh, Cecil, do come here and rescue me! Miss Trapp's being so cross because I'm supposed to have told Cockrill that La Lane was blackmailing her, when all the time it turns out she was only remarking chattily that the tide was on the turn."

"Hardly an observation to have made me turn pale," suggested Miss Trapp with heavy irony.

"Oh, but, my dear, I couldn't agree less," said Mr Cecil, promptly. "Too pale making for words! I mean, whatever can she have meant?"

"Have meant?" said Miss Trapp, beginning to falter.

"But the Mediterranean, dear: no tides," said Mr Cecil.

well!! I learn something every day!!!

Drinks, of course, were available on the Vaporetto del Meurte and might be taken with great wedges of pizza, rich with garlic and onion and tomato and waxy, melted cheese, to the accompaniment of mournful music played by an ordinarily cheerful small brass band. Helen Rodd, who seemed to find some ease of spirit in the cool, impersonal, heartless friendliness of Mr Cecil, joined him at one of the little tables and accepted an Americano. Leo Rodd left them and went and leaned over the rail at the stern of the boat, looking out over the scummy white wash slashing the shining blue silk of the still sea. Louvaine, joining him there, repeated her remark about going gay to funerals, leaning on the rail beside him trying surreptitiously to touch his hand. "I mean, I think one should wear something not too depressing."

"So I see," he said rather coldly, and he moved his hand away from hers. "Damn it, darling—not now!"

She whipped away her own hand as though it had been stung and once again there came to her face that look of sorrowful foreboding that had come to it when he had snubbed her on the evening of Vanda Lane's death. "Oh, Leo . . ."

"I'm sorry," he said. "But the woman's dead. We've just left her, lying there all alone, and I do think we might have some thought for her, just a little pity. Nobody with her but a pack of strangers, poor wretched woman, not a soul who loved her."

She gave a little shrug. "Oh, well—as to that, I don't think you need really worry."

"Not worry?" he said, roughly. "What do you mean?"

She was frightened again. "I only mean—well, you go on and on about nobody loving her: what does it matter, she's dead now, why should you care?"

He thumped with his one hand on the painted black wooden rail. "My God, Louvaine—not you too! Not you too—jealous and possessive, fighting off even a kind word for another woman: and a dead woman at that! For God's sake, I didn't care two hoots for the girl, I don't care whether anyone loved her or not, I dare say no one did, she was an unlovable creature at the best of times. I only say that she lies there now, alone in a grave in an alien land—don't you think she's just to be pitied a little for that?"

The wind lifted the heavily-curling mass of red hair, swept it back from the face that was suddenly no longer the face of his gay and lovely love but the face of a stranger, only dimly to be recognized. Once again, as on the first evening that he had known her, the great blue eyes were abrim with unshed tears. "Pitied?" she said. "No, I don't think she's very much to be pitied. She's dead, and I'm alive—but sometimes I think I envy her, with all my soul." She waited: but he was not looking at her, he was examining the palm of his hand where he had whacked it down on the wooden rail. He said, absently: "I'm sorry . . . I seem to have picked up a splinter. Just a second . . ." He went over to the café bar, and she saw him hold out his upturned hand, like a child, to his wife.

She turned and walked away, along the dirty decks, among the plumes and the beaded wreaths, the tarnished silver and the mourning draperies, past the garish uniforms of the funeral band; and stumbled as she went.

CHAPTER NINE

LUNCH on the terrace that afternoon was not a very festive affair. The exculpated tourists were to continue their itinerary next morning, in the care of a new guide who had been deflected from another tour after much to and fro cabling between Gibraltar and England; and already their minds were filled with apprehension as to whether the canals of Venice would smell and what would happen if they failed to have their baggage outside their doors the next morning at seven-thirty, as required. Several of the guests who were to have filled their vacated rooms had heard of events in San Juan and, apparently assuming murder a natural hazard of holidaying there, had cancelled their bookings; and the hotel management, though they had easily filled the rooms up with 'chance trade,' were not pleased with Odyssey Tours. Mr Fernando, of course, remained behind with his helpless ones, and appeared by no means elated at the prospect; his eye was shifty and he wore a hangdog air. Louli Barker was white and silent, Leo Rodd ominously black-browed and his wife alert and anxious; Miss Trapp was altogether absent, having declared her intention of going to lie down, not obviously comforted by Mr Cecil's reminder that this had proved in the past to be not necessarily the safest thing to do. Only Cecil himself was up to scratch socially, twittering away to Inspector Cockrill over espressos on the terrace, ticking off on tapering white fingers intriguing points against Miss Trapp. "A

Christophe client, Inspector, but *I* don't recognize her, never seen her in one's life, I do assure you. Shopped by proxy, perhaps, but then why? If one's not coming in one-self for fittings, why come to a couturier?" Under such circumstances, said Mr Cecil, blenching at the bare thought of it, one might as well simply get things off the peg. "And then why go all funny when I recognized her hat?" He considered it. "Mind you, it's a very old hat."

Cockie sat perched on the wide balustrade of the terrace, with his coffee cup beside him, swinging his short legs, his back to the sea. "Is it? How old?"

"Well, but I mean, my dear—roses: three seasons ago, it gives one the actual *date*. And come to think," said Cecil, "everything she's got is at least three years out of fashion. It's odd. She goes to the big houses, she spends a lot; but she gets nothing new for at least three years. Now, why?"

"Perhaps she can no longer afford to," suggested Cockie.

Mr Cecil cradled the shallow coffee cup in his long white hands. "It might be. Everything she has is madly expensive —but old. Of course some people like things like that, we have lots of old drears who think it's not chic to be smart." He went off into a whinney of high-pitched laughter. "Oh, dear—not chic to be smart!—I do think that's rather good!"

"Miss Trapp still lives in Park Lane."

"Can't get rid of the lease, dear. Or wants to keep up appearances till the last ditch. Hoping and hoping that something may turn up."

"Such as a husband?" suggested Inspector Cockrill.

"A husband!" He put down the cup with a rattle in its saucer. "A rich woman, Inspector, rich and lonely but not minding being lonely because of being rich. But something goes wrong, she begins to take fright about her money; and while it still lasts, she decides to go forth and use what's left to get herself a husband." But, to be honest, it did not sound like Miss Trapp. "Or a husband just comes along . . ."

"Who wouldn't be a husband if he knew . . ."

"That the tide of fortune was about to turn," said Cecil, triumphantly.

And it had been Miss Trapp who had insisted so importunately that Vanda Lane should retire to her room that day. Of course, reflected Cockie, himself retiring to his room and throwing himself on the four-poster bed for the siesta, there would be no intention to murder—not then. Get the girl out of the way for the moment, would be her impulse, till one had time to think things out; and very neatly she had gone about it, with every sign of concern—and it was true, as he recollected it, that the concern had sounded oddly impersonal, oddly insincere. Then, safe for the moment, the bathe. And after that . . . He could picture the poor thing, crouching in an agony in her nudist camp for one, deciding at last to creep up and see the girl, to discover for herself the real extent of the danger: to plead, to promise, to threaten; at last—to kill? The book turned on the table perhaps by the blackmailer at the first threat: beware what you do, there's a policeman among us. . . . But, blind with rage at the blighting of hopes so lately grown infinitely dear, she would lunge forward with the suddenly snatched up knife. He thought of the improvised catafalque of the bed, the outstretched figure, the hands composed, the outspread hair. The work of a woman, her mind deranged by horror of what she had done? But there had been little sign of derangement in the methodical removal, in the bathroom, of stains of blood. He reflected again that it had been convenient for a murderer that they had all been wearing bathing dresses which could be washed with impunity and would cause no comment if they appeared still damp; and thought wistfully of Scotalanda Yarda, of post-mortems and fingerprints and analysis of garments for traces of blood.

Mr Cecil was not one to keep his mouth shut when he was excited about anything. Mr Cockrill, having ventured out as far as the raft, was sitting sunning himself there after the siesta that afternoon, when he was approached by Fernando, rolling out from the beach like a well-baked golden porpoise, hoisting himself up beside him and turning upon him an agitated, round brown face. "Inspector, forgive me, I trouble you, but I am in a great worry, I have heard bad news. Inspector, I ask you now as man with man—is this true?"

"Is what true?" said Cockie.

"This which I have heard: to me it seems impossible that anyone can think of such a thing."

"I don't know what you're talking about," said Cockie.

"Ah, ha, Inspector, you refuse then to answer me, you avoid my question?"

"I don't avoid your question at all—I simply don't know what your question is."

"Then I must ask it again," said Fernando, heavy with irony. "And here it is, I ask it, please this time to listen, Inspector; do you believe that Miss Lane was killed by— Miss Trapp?"

"By Miss Trapp?" said Inspector Cockrill. "No, I don't."

Mr Fernando was absolutely flabbergasted. "You don't believe this?"

"No, certainly not. I'm quite sure she wasn't killed by Miss Trapp."

"But I thought—I heard—I understood that you had built up a whole case against her?"

There was something black and wet and shiny on the raft near Inspector Cockrill's hand. He picked it up idly and looked at it as he talked, turning it over and over, not thinking about it. "There's a big difference, Mr Fernando, between building up a case and building up anything else. When you build—for example, a house—you start with a certain number of bricks and if you need more you get more; and if there are any over, well, you put them aside, you use them up some other time. But in building up a case, you must work only with the bricks that you find on the scene of the crime—and if there are not enough, then your case falls down; and if there are any over then, once again, your case falls down. There are two bricks left over in the case against Miss Trapp, two bricks that try as I may, won't fit in any-where: and so the case against Miss Trapp falls down."

It was almost pathetic to see the relief, the incredulous joy and relief on that bland, round face: the dawn of doubt, the dawn of conviction, the sunshine of gold teeth flashing in a smile as broad as the break of day. To Inspector Cockrill's horror, two huge tears gathered in the soft, brown eyes and rolled, unimpeded and unashamed, down the sunburned face. "Two bricks?" said Fernando, foolishly babbling. "Two bricks?"

"One brick is the red shawl. Why should Miss Trapp have laid out the dead body on the red shawl? How would she have got the shawl anyway, why should she have gone into Miss Barker's room?" The other brick, the real brick, the gold brick as one might say, was the brick that he had placed under all their noses, when he described the scene of the murder to them: the brick they had failed to recognize as relevant at all.

But Fernando did not really care two hoots about the bricks. "I am so thankful, Inspector, for this poor Miss Trapp. One word from you about this, and . . . you understand, Inspector, El Gerente grows impatient, already there is trouble about the murder, the hotel is complaining, bookings are cancelled and this island lives largely upon the tourist trade. There has been an order from—from higher up," said Fernando, glancing back nervously to where, literally higher up, the palace of the Grand Duke sat on its pinnacle of rock. "The matter is to be cleared up without more delay, the murderer is to be found and the rest of the suspects must be sent home at once and the whole thing wiped over and forgotten. I tell you, Inspector, the Gerente is very anxious—very anxious indeed." The complaint was evidently catching for he added in a voice of positive awe: "El Exaltida has decreed."

"Oh, *has* he?" said Cockie, deeply interested.

"So the Gerente must strike soon; and, Inspector, the choice is not very great. You are out, for El Exaltida has said that he does not wish for trouble with the British police who might put the island out of bounds for tourists. Miss Barker is out, because we know that she was with you. This left Miss Trapp, Mr Cecil, Mr and Mrs Rodd and me. Now you most happily say that Miss Trapp is out. I also am out, so that leaves only those three." He looked not unduly downcast at the thought of their plight.

"Why are you out?" said Inspector Cockrill bleakly.

"*I?*" said Fernando, incredulous.

"Was not Miss Lane trying to blackmail you too? There was a figure against your name in the book."

Mr Fernando shrugged deprecatingly. "No use, Inspector, to blackmail a man with no money."

"Unless he has—rich prospects," suggested Cockie.

He shrugged off that one too with an odd little smile. "In any event, Inspector, I could not have done it. I lay all the afternoon here on this very raft, you say it yourself."

It was a large raft, built at two levels with a sort of wide step on two sides of it. Now in the light breeze blowing up over the glinting blue sea, it rolled a little, breasting the gentle waves. "I saw you sunbathing on the raft. I didn't see you leave the raft and I didn't see you swim back to it, it's true. For this reason, I assumed at one time that you'd been here all the time; in my anxiety to look after everyone's interests, I assumed a good many things, too readily. But if you watch this raft carefully from the terrace for an hour, as I've since been careful to do, you'll realize that most of the time—especially in a breeze like this—you need not actually see the whole surface of the raft at all."

Mr Fernando's smile faded, he sat deflated, his hands on his knees. "But, Inspector . . ."

"I don't say you did leave the raft. I just say that you can't so definitely count yourself out. You *could* have left. You could have swum to the shore, to the little beach on the further side of the rock, you could have gone up to the bathing cabins from there and so on up the steps to the top terrace and to her room. I don't say you did," repeated Inspector Cockrill, "but I do say that you could."

From far out to sea, Leo Rodd drifted lazily back from a solitary swim, his head dark against the breeze blown blue. "Inspector—just glance over there, just lift your head for one moment and then down again. Can you miss him? Can you miss a swimmer, can you not see the dark head bobbing, a blot where all is so blue? You did not sleep that day; how was I to have known that *any*one would sleep, was I not to suppose that all might be alert, looking out idly over the nice blue sea? How could I have dared to swim half across the width of the bay to the rock, knowing that, by any or all of half a dozen people, I would almost certainly be seen?"

"There is such a thing as underwater swimming," said Cockie.

Fernando made a rude noise. "Who, Inspector—me? From here to that rock?" He leapt to his feet, dangerously tilting the raft. "Come with me, Inspector, we go into the hotel, we ring up Gibraltar, you speak there with my friends. Ask them, here is a thing that a man's friends can say in a jiffy, here is no pretence: ask only, 'Can Fernando Gomez swim under water a distance of even five yards?' Ask at my swimming club—in Gib. we all go, all my office, all my friends, to the swimming club. Here is a thing they must know."

"All right, all right," said Cockie. It was true that here was a thing that members of a swimming club could say about another member, one way or another. A man can swim under water or he cannot; and Mr Fernando, failed half-blue for swimming at his university, was not one to have kept this talent dark from his admirers.

Inspector Cockrill swam by no means under water himself, but with a style retained from his boyhood gambollings along the coast of Kent—reared up half out of the sea, practically horizontal, and hitting out wildly with his hands at the surface of the water, like a dog. By this means, leaving Fernando to dash off, reassured himself, to reassure his lady-love, he propelled himself shorewards and, as though casually, intercepted Leo Rodd as he swam in. "Here you are, Mr Rodd—I believe this belongs to you."

It was the black rubber mask with its corked breathing tube from Leo Rodd's frogman's suit. "Good lord, thank you," said Leo. "I'll lose the thing one of these days, I'm always leaving it washing about on that raft." He still had the black rubber fins on and, like a seal, flopped along in them across the hot sand. "Come and lie in the sun and dry, Inspector, and tell me what's all this nonsense about poor Miss Trapp."

Inspector Cockrill, unwontedly communicative, outlined

the cases—now largely exploded—against both Fernando and Miss Trapp. "Fernando couldn't have swum from the raft right across to the rock without my noticing him," he ended. "He kicks up a spray like a fountain every time he moves in the water and I remember it was like that, way back in Rapallo, it isn't an act that he's put on since all this blew up. So he'd have had to swim under water. Well, either he can swim under water or he can't: he says he can't, and offers to confirm it, and I believe it's true. So Miss Trapp is out; and Fernando is out . . ."

"And then there were three," said Leo, narrowing down the list of suspects as Fernando had done, but with considerably less complacency. "Mr Cecil, my wife, and me." He sat with a towel hung across his maimed shoulder and stared out to sea. "Well, I never was awfully fond of that Cecil," he said.

"Mr Cecil was floating up and down in a rubber duck," said Mr Cockrill. "In the sight of all."

"You wouldn't say that the rubber duck popped round to the far side of the rock for a short time?"

"I wouldn't say it didn't," agreed Cockie, readily. "But not for a long time. Not for half an hour."

"It certainly would have taken half an hour to—to stage that thing up in that room?"

"Yes," said Cockie. "And to get up there and down again. Probably longer, far longer; but at the very least and narrowest calculation half an hour."

"Which would narrow things down even more?"

"It would appear to," said Cockie. He asked, offhandedly: "Where is Mrs Rodd this afternoon?"

"She didn't come down to swim. She was still asleep when I left so I didn't disturb her." He did not add that Louli Barker had besought him to meet her during the siesta hour, that he had taken advantage of his wife's being asleep to slip off quietly to the pinewoods and there go painfully through a reconciliation scene that had been truly happy and satisfactory to neither of them. He leaned on his one arm, lying twisted sideways on the hot yellow sand. "Inspector: let me get this straight? By no silly chance are you suggesting that my wife . . .?"

"Then there were two," said Cockie. "You calculated it yourself."

"And *I*'ve got no right arm." He gave a sort of snorting half laugh, unconvincingly unconcerned. "Of course you don't really believe she had anything to do with it?"

Inspector Cockrill sat up on his narrow hams, feet flat on the sand, knees raised, hands dangling between them holding the inevitable untidily smoking cigarette. "I have to be impersonal. I simply consider facts."

"Well, the facts are that my wife was under the sun-shed with me the whole blessed afternoon. She never moved."

"You can't be sure of that. You admit you were sound asleep."

"And *you* admit that you could see her there."

"I assumed," said Cockie wearily, "that I saw her there. What I actually saw, was the rope soles of a pair of yellow espadrilles. I could see the roof of the sun-shed and the shoes sticking out at the far side, towards the sea."

Leo Rodd made an impatient gesture. "She could have got up while everyone on the beach was asleep," insisted Cockrill, steadily, "and moved along under the wall—I wouldn't have seen her there—and up the corner path to the cabins. The only time I need have seen her—if I'd been looking, only I was not for that moment—would have been while she crossed to the wall: just a few feet. Everyone else was asleep."

"How could she possibly have counted on that?"

"I don't suggest for a moment that she did, Mr Rodd.

The same thing applies to everyone: it isn't suggested that the murderer went to Miss Lane's room with any preconceived intention of killing her. He may have left the beach, originally, with no intention of seeing her at all; wanted to go to what Mr Cecil calls the huh-ha, or something. He probably left the beach quite openly, it was probably the merest chance that I didn't see him go, and that everyone else was asleep. But he will have noticed on his way, that they were asleep—and he couldn't see me, from below, sitting reading on the terrace; so—having, on an impulse killed the girl—he would take advantage of their being asleep, to creep back to his place."

"Why come back at all?"

"It was a risk," agreed Cockie. "But the murderer might think the risk worth taking—and so it's proved. The alternative would be disastrous: to be without an alibi when everyone else was known to be on the beach." He added that in Mrs Rodd's case, she would probably have taken particular care even when she was—quite openly, as far as her intention went—leaving the beach: so as not to waken her husband.

Leo Rodd's fist was clenched on a handful of warm sand: that broad and beautiful musician's hand that would never again find its full satisfaction in creating music. He said stonily, "And then?"

"The supposition would be that then Mrs Rodd, having gone up to the balcony, either on a private errand or intending to see Miss Lane, did in fact see her and—again, I emphasize on an impulse—killed her."

"You suggested the same fable about Miss Trapp but Miss Trapp's out because she wouldn't have gone to Louvaine Barker's room and got the shawl. Well—that applies to my wife as well as to Miss Trapp."

"Except," said Inspector Cockrill, with some temerity,

"that Miss Trapp could have no—no grudge against Miss Barker."

"You mean . . .?" His hand tightened so that the sand was squeezed out through the close lattices of his shaking fingers. "You want me to believe that to—to throw the blame on Louvaine . . .?"

"I only say," said Cockie, "that that may be a counter to your objection."

"But . . ." He shook his head impatiently. "Inspector, Helen simply isn't like that. I mean—well, you're insisting on facts, and it's a fact, a positive fact, that it's not in her character to do such a thing. You've got to take character into account: and it would be out of character for her to even think of an unworthy thing like that, and what's more, utterly out of character to have struck out and killed the girl. Why should she, to begin with? She had nothing against Miss Lane, there wasn't even anything against her in the blackmail book—on the contrary, there was a suggestion of wanting to be on her side, sneaking to her about Louvaine and me—at a price, it's true, but that's neither here nor there. Of course, you may say that Helen would be revolted, she might strike out at the creature; but I tell you, and it's true, it counts, she's just not that kind of person, she's not one to lash out if she's angry or insulted . . ."

"Or in danger?" said Cockie.

"But in danger of what?"

"Of losing what she most values," said Cockie. He extinguished his cigarette, grinding it with unnecessary violence into the sand between his bare feet. "Mr Rodd—Vanda Lane was in love with you. Everyone could see it; everyone could see her watching you, listening to you, skirmishing to be at the same table or in the same party, scheming to speak to you, even a few trivial words. One didn't catch Miss Barker doing these things; she was frank enough goodness knows, but not to all and sundry—she concealed the affair between you because there was something to conceal. Miss Lane didn't try to conceal it—because there was nothing to conceal. I've seen her myself, we've all seen her, those first evenings—slipping along after you, hoping, I suppose, to meet you somewhere 'by chance' and get some word or some sign from you." He looked at the battered stump of the cigarette, unseeingly, and tossed it away from him. "Vanda Lane was in love with you."

"Well, so what?" said Leo, impatiently. "It was Louvaine I was going to meet—not Vanda Lane."

"Are you so sure," said Cockie, and his voice was very grave, and very kind, "that your wife knew that?"

When at last they went up together to the hotel, they went in silence; what they had to say to one another had been said. At the door of his room, Leo paused. "Well— thank you, Inspector. I still don't believe it; but either way, you'll do your best for us?" He said again, "Thank you," and pushed open the door.

She made an instinctive movement warning him to silence, motioning him to close the door; but Inspector Cockrill had seen her standing there, deathly pale, with the red blood staining the white sleeve of her dressing-gown.

She must have moved in her sleep, half awakened perhaps by the softly-opening door. The knife had gone through the fleshy part of the right upper arm, pinning her in sickening helplessness to the bed. The room had been dimmed by the closed shutters for the siesta hour; startled into terrified awareness, she had seen nothing but the soft closing of the balcony door. She had struggled to release herself, fallen back fainting with the pain and horror of it, come-to again, and a second time fainted away. She could not tell how long she had lain there, how long ago the attack had been made; except that she had been still asleep, and it was not like her to have gone on sleeping for more than an hour or so. "On the other hand, it was hot, I'd been having bad nights; I might well have slept on." She dwelt upon the contradiction a little insistently, Inspector Cockrill thought; and for some reason avoided her husband's eye.

The wound had been made with a steel paper knife, identical with the one that had killed Vanda Lane. Cockie picked it up gingerly, handling the hilt with loving care. "I suppose, though, you've been handling it yourself?—trying to pull the thing out, poor girl!" He looked at her with kindness and with admiration. "You're a brave woman, Mrs Rodd." He thought of the fuss some women would have been making by now, and wondered what further reserves of courage might be there for him to draw upon.

The injury was not serious. Once she had got the knife out, she had staunched the bleeding effectively with cold water and he bound it up for her now with torn hotel towels. He seemed in no hurry to rush off and spread the glad tidings; and she said to him at last, hesitantly: "I suppose it wouldn't be possible to—to say nothing about it to the police here?"

It was what, above all things, he wished for; but he was startled into asking sharply: "Why?"

"Well, I don't know," she said, rather uncertainly. "I just hate—fuss." She leaned back against the pillows on the four-poster bed. "It doesn't hurt too much now; I could wear a long sleeve and I don't think anyone need know anything."

"Just go about as if nothing had happened?"

Leo Rodd sat perched against the dressing-table, his legs straight out in front of him, looking at the toes of his shoes. "Suppose they try again?"

She attempted a light shrug and desisted, wincing with the pain. "There can't be an unlimited supply of Toledo steel daggers. Miss Lane and I account for two."

"The Gerente has the one that killed Miss Lane," said Cockie. "This one . . ." He looked at it fondly. "If I could get it back to England, you see—we might yet find finger-prints. But if we tell them here, I shan't have a chance."

"Who else bought these knives?" said Leo Rodd.

"Just a minute," said Cockie. He left them but returned a couple of minutes later. "Miss Barker and Mr Cecil bought them at the same time as Miss Lane did. Their rooms are empty at the moment—so I just looked in. The knives are there."

"Of course other people may have bought them?"

"It's a little unlikely," said Cockie, "that they'd have concealed the fact after Miss Lane's death; unless of course they intended this second attack." He added thoughtfully that there would have been no opportunity to buy one since then, for no one had been let out of the hotel grounds.

"Until to-day," said Leo.

"To-day?"

"When we got back from the funeral."

When they got back from the funeral they had caused a sort of jolly havoc among their guards by dispersing about the little town, kicking their heels for a few minutes in the joy of freedom from surveillance. Mr Cecil had laid it on, darting about the deck of the vaporetto, all excitement and boyishness. "All split up and go different ways as soon as we get off the gangway, there are seven of us and only two of them and they won't know which to follow, it'll be too

amusing for *any!*" Mr Cockrill had complied by simply walking on doggedly up to the hotel which was the only place
he had any particular desire to go to, and he remembered
that at the time he had been a little surprised at the avidity
with which the rest had embarked upon so remarkably
childish a proceeding. But meanwhile it meant . . . It meant
that any of them might have been long enough alone to have
slipped into the shop that sold the Toledo steel knives.

He left Leo Rodd on guard over his wife and went down
to the shop, full of a tarradiddle about an Inglese who had
recommended him to buy a similar knife to one purchased
that day. The tarradiddle was not entirely lucid, since his
attempts at the Spanish-Italian argot of the island consisted
in speaking very loudly in pidgin-English and adding an
'a' after arbitrarily chosen syllables. A Juanese-speaking
customer clarified matters a little and went his way, leaving
the shopkeeper not much the wiser, but Inspector Cockrill
unhappily aware that there had apparently been a ceaseless traffic in the knives all day, and that they were all
identical anyway, so it did not matter what his friend had
recommended. He abandoned the tarradiddle and to the
measureless astonishment of the shopkeeper threw himself
into an impersonation of Miss Trapp. The shopkeeper,
unable to keep his good fortune to himself, went to his back
door and yelled for his esposa. Juanita took one look and
rushed off to fetch the children.

By the time two stout, brown little boys had appeared,
Inspector Cockrill had grown weary of Miss Trapp. His
first attempts at hugging an imaginary handbag up under
his chin had resulted only in a frantic search along the
shelves for the cardboard boot-box in which the safety-razors
were kept and a further demonstration with a bag borrowed
from the counter, in an unseemly tussle with the proprietor
who had evidently concluded that he must be a dangerous

kleptomaniac. He gave up Miss Trapp and turned his attention to Leo Rodd, raising his voice to a frustrated bellow and sawing away at his upper arm with great abandon, finally hitching up his shoulder so that his arm disappeared into the sleeve leaving it dangling, apparently empty. The proprietor, understanding English no better when it was shouted than when it was more moderately spoken, looked blankly on; but the little boys were enchanted and, taking off their jackets altogether, hung them over their shoulders and prowled about the shop, gorilla fashion, swinging the long, empty sleeves before them. Cockie, understandably irritated, gave up Leo Rodd also, and directed his powers to a verbal and visual description of Mr Fernando, alternately crying, "Senor! Gibraltar! Much gold!" baring his teeth in an ear-to-ear grin and pointing into his mouth. Juanita, delighted to make herself useful, produced a tin of denture fixitive.

And yet surely, if any of these three had been into the shop that afternoon and bought a knife, the man must have recognized the key to the whole absurd affair? Inspector Cockrill gritted his dentures, and went doggedly on. He could think of no more original way of explaining Louvaine than to waggle his hips and draw patterns in the air about his own meagre figure, emphasizing the higher lights of the well-developed female form. The armless wonders shuffled back quickly into their jackets, alert for business, for now the whole matter explained itself. "Jeeg-a-jeega? Senor want jeeg-a-jeega? Very pretty girl, big sister, I go fetch?" Not waiting for an answer, they dashed off in different directions, crying, "Maria! Marietta!" at the tops of shrill voices, their parents now wreathed in smiles at having so puzzling an episode happily settled to the profit and satisfaction of all.

Inspector Cockrill was horrified. "No, no (good gracious me, what people!), no, no, not jig-a-jig, all mistake, call boys back, come on, call the wretched kids back . . ." But it was hopeless. "Well, never mind the young lady. I said, never mind. Niente! No importa!" He lost patience. "Now, look. Listen. Try and use some sense if you've got any which I'm beginning to doubt." He looked despairingly into their happily smiling faces, picked up the knife from the counter and once again launched into the whole routine. "A knife-a. Like this-a. This afternoon, well, just before lunch, what the hell do you call it, collartsiony—you understand collartsiony? —no, no, no, I don't want something to eat, for goodness sake stay still for one minute and *listen!*" He raised his voice again speaking very slowly and patiently, clarifying the words with descriptive gestures worthy of Fernando himself. "Before—you understand 'before', m'm?—before —collartsiony—to-day—was a knife—knife-a, like this— bought by a senor?—very thin, thin like this; pale face— hair yellow, well, gold—look, hair like this picture frame here—very, er, very . . ." He broke off, exhausted. "Senor like senorita . . ."

"Si, si," said the shopkeeper eagerly. "Senor like senorita. Boys go fetch."

"No, no, I don't want any senorita, I tell you this senor, this senor who bought the knife, he is like a senorita, he look like senorita, understanda? Senor—looka—like senorita . . ." He pulled a lock of his grey hair as far down as it would go over his forehead, gave a pansy wriggle and turned out his hands in the immemorial gesture of the effeminate male.

Juanita simply could not wait to rush out and recall the little boys.

And yet he could not believe that, if in fact any of those five people had that day bought a knife, the whole episode, however ridiculous, could have failed to ring a bell. He went out into the steep, cobbled, sun-baked little street and down to the quay and bought a bag of peaches from an old woman, and sat there eating them, perched on a bollard, pitching the stones into the harbour between the close-packed prows of the fishing boats. Later he must pry and question, must sort out movements, alibis, all the rest of it. But he had little faith in anything of importance resulting. The hour after lunch was the hour, above all, when people were alone—unseen and unseeing, asleep after their heavy meal behind their closed shutters, true to the sacred tradition of the Spanish siesta. It had been about half-past three when Leo Rodd had left his wife sleeping, alone in their room; for an hour after that, anyone who had seen him pass across the sunlit slats of their own shutters, might have felt confident of creeping along, unobserved, to where she lay. And the question was—who? Who on earth could have wished to kill Helen Rodd? Why on earth should anyone have wished to kill Helen Rodd?

He could think of only one answer; and, chucking the last of the peach stones into the scummy water, he knew that it was not over-indulgence in fruit which was causing that uneasy feeling in the pit of his stomach. For Inspector Cockrill also had seen Leo Rodd move over to his wife that day, and hold out his injured hand to her like a troubled child.

He smoothed out the crumpled paper of the bag in which the peaches had been. He drew a potato-figure and clothed it in a large, triangular skirt. He divided the skirt into a maze of oddly-shaped pieces, and darkened some and left some plain. Outside the shop once more, he waylaid two day-trippers from the mainland, jabbering in mixed Italian and English as they strolled through the sunny street. He launched into another of his tarradiddles, this time more successfully. He had arranged to meet a young lady at the shop where the knives were sold. She had been wearing a skirt like this—a skirt of bold patchwork, a skirt you couldn't help seeing, an unmistakable skirt. Would the day-trippers, of their charity, go into the shop—without him, if they didn't mind—and ask the proprietor if a young lady had been there within the last three or four hours—wearing a patchwork skirt.

But it was odd, the day-trippers said to each other when, their errand of kindness concluded, they went on their way, that the gentleman should look so delighted when they told him that no such young lady had been to the shop.

CHAPTER TEN

LEO RODD received a summons next morning. He was to go up to the Palace of the Hereditary Grand Duke; the Grand Duke wished to see him. No, the Grand Duke did not wish to see Detective Inspector Cockrill, he did not wish to see Fernando Gomez, he wished to see nobody but the Senor Rodd. A carriage would be sent for Senor Rodd at midday, the Gerente would conduct him to the pallatio. Nothing was said about who would bring him back.

The palace on the hill was a fairy-tale thing, a cobweb of fretted white marble, glittering in the sunshine on its topmost tip of the pinnacle of the rock; but Leo Rodd remembered what happens to flies who venture upon cobwebs and his heart was sick within him as, abandoned at the gateway by the Gerente, he followed the cloaked and sabred guard alone —through the great archway and the lovely cloistered court-yards, up the wide stairways, past the pools and the fountains and many-flowered patios, over the great, broad pebbled pavements, intricately laid. There had been long and anxious discussion as to whether or not he should come: he knew and they all knew that there was very little that could be done about it, if he did not return. Oh, well, he thought, I'm here now so I'd better Be British and put a decent face on it, stiff upper lip and all. . . . But what in God's name could the spider want with this particular fly? He saw him in his mind's eye, El Exaltida, Gran Ducca del San Juan el Pirata —old and obese, crouching, a fat, hairy spider at the far-away end of some great, echoing, gilt and marble room, across which the poor fly must drag itself with that wrenching, shoulder-forward gait, under the scrutiny of cold eyes, greedy and malign. Oh, well—I'm here, and that's the end of it. . . .

There were sharp orders, the posse of guards reeled back against the wall on either side of a small, arched doorway, as though they had been flung there, their captain lifted aside the curtain with the point of his sword. The fly crept in.

It was a room about the size of a suburban bathroom, with just enough space to squeeze past the bath to the wash-basin at the far end. In the centre was a small, cheap wooden office desk and on a wooden chair, squeezed in between the desk and the wall, sat the most enormous young man Leo Rodd had ever seen. He wore a faultlessly-tailored dark-blue suit and an Old Wykhamist tie. His hands, ablaze with jewelled rings, were folded across the ends of the tie, his chin sunk on his breast; and under the hyacinthine, heavily-curling hair, the brooding face was so magnificently handsome as to be beautiful. He lifted his head for a moment and looked Leo Rodd up and down, and sunk his chin again upon his chest. A small grey man sitting at his left hand (where the wash-basin would have been) got up and placed a chair. Nobody spoke.

There was a miniature bird-cage on the desk, of gold, with a tiny humming bird in it, set with semi-precious stones, turquoise and topaz and tiny white seed pearls. The Grand Duke moved his hand; the door of the cage flew open, the humming bird stooped and pecked up a cigarette, civilly handed it to Leo Rodd and, enraptured with its own cleverness, burst into the tinkling strains of Au Clair de la Lune. The secretary came round with a lighter and squeezed back into his place again. He riffled through the pages of a notebook and said suddenly: "Mr Rodd?"

"None other," said Leo. Damn it all, he thought to himself, this is not going to get me down. He gestured with his cigarette. "And this gentleman would be El Exaltida?"

A very small quirk appeared at the corners of the secretary's grey mouth. He made a little bow. "None other." El Exaltida, unrelaxed, brooded over his tie. The secretary riffled the pages of his book again and began to speak.

El Exaltida, said the secretary in stiff but excellent English, was not pleased about the murder at the hotel. El Exaltida had read foreign press reports and these would be bad for the tourist trade. The matter must be settled at once and Odyssey Tours must remove their clients without any further delay.

Mr Rodd could assure El Exaltida that nothing would give Odyssey Tours more pleasure; to say nothing of the happiness of said clients.

"On the other hand, El Exaltida feels that we must retain —a hostage."

"I see," said Leo. "Well, I'm sure I shall be very comfortable." He did not, however, feel comfortable at all.

"El Exaltida has studied the matter. He thinks highly of some notes of Inspector Cockrill of Scotland Yard. It seems to El Exaltida that there can be only one answer to this crime."

"That makes it as good as answered, I'm sure," said Leo.

"Mr Rodd—it is understood that Inspector Cockrill claims to have seen you lying asleep on the beach during the hours when the murder would have been possible: half under the sun-shed, but with your head covered with a piece of paper. El Exaltida suggests that all the Inspector really saw was—a piece of paper."

Inspector Cockrill had suggested the same thing to Leo that afternoon. "Does the Exaltida suggest that I was not under the paper?"

"El Exaltida asks why anyone should lie underneath a sun-shed, which is expressly designed to give shade where it is needed, and then put his head out into the sun and cover it with a sort of cocked hat, made of paper."

"I am an Englishman," said Leo. "Let him be thankful that it wasn't a handkerchief, knotted at the four corners."

The jewels flashed sparks on El Exaltida's great hands, but no other spark appeared to be ignited. "El Exaltida suggests," said the secretary steadily, "that you were not under the sun-shed at all. That you waited until your wife slept and then went quietly across the beach and up to the hotel."

"Leaving the paper-cocked hat there, to deceive the more wakeful?"

The Grand Duke put out a hand and drew the secretary's note-pad towards him; the grey man waited alert and respectful while he unhurriedly wrote. He translated. "It is suggested that you would at that time have no particular wish to deceive anyone but your wife. Everyone else knew that you were conducting—I beg your pardon—an affair with Miss Barker. Miss Barker was not on the beach."

"She was with Inspector Cockrill."

"From your place under the sun-shed, you could not see that."

"I see. So I went up to the hotel to find her? I didn't find her—but I did find Miss Lane?"

The jewels flashed and sparkled but there was no sign of animation or understanding on the dark, brooding face. "El Exaltida suggests, Mr Rodd, that you went to the lady's room: perhaps spoke her name at the door. Miss Lane heard your voice—her room was next to Miss Barker's. She came into Miss Barker's room and found you there. You were holding . . ."

"Don't tell me, let me guess. I was holding Miss Barker's red shawl."

"That is the suggestion. You had picked up the shawl and you were standing holding it. Miss Lane was in love with you. She would not blackmail you for money, she could not hope to blackmail you into loving herself: but she was jealous and she might blackmail you out of loving someone else. She might threaten that if your affair with Miss Barker did not end, she would tell your wife."

"That wouldn't get her very far," said Leo. "My wife already knew."

"She knew that you were having a flirtation, no doubt. But did she realize that this time you were planning to leave her?"

"You know all about it, don't you?" said Leo. He leaned forward and jabbed out his cigarette in the carved jade ash-tray beside the golden cage.

"Everybody knew all about it, Mr Rodd—except your wife. Miss Barker told Mr Cecil, Mr Cockrill overheard her doing so—and there was another eavesdropper there. Long before you came, Miss Barker heard someone on the terrace above her: she said, 'Is this him coming now?'"

"Then everyone equally knows that, if I were going to leave my wife anyway, it would hardly be worth murder to keep the news from her for another week or so."

"Nobody suggests that you killed the woman for calcu-lated reasons. She threatened you. You followed her into her own room—pleading, arguing, quarrelling, we don't know. She had been writing at her table, the blackmail book and the knife were there. She resisted you, she said ugly things about Miss Barker, perhaps. You lost your temper, you picked up the knife and struck. You still held the shawl and her blood spurted on to it. You had to account for the blood on the shawl—on Miss Barker's shawl. You spread the shawl on the bed. The rest followed." He folded mouse-like grey paws. "That, Mr Rodd, is what the Grand Duke suggests."

"I see. And does he then suggest that I trotted back blithely to the beach and dived in under my cocked hat, to the amazement of all beholders?"

"El Exaltida suggests that if you trotted at all, you trotted as far as one or other of the terraces, hung about there and joined your wife when she drifted up with the rest. El Exaltida understands that Mrs Rodd is not a lady to broad-cast to the world that her husband had crept away from her side to an assignation with another woman. She would keep silence; at first from pride, and later on, when the murder was discovered, from . . ."

"From expedience?"

"From loyalty," said the grey secretary with a little bow. The Grand Duke moved his hand and the jewelled bird proffered another cigarette and burst again into self-congratulatory song. The secretary slid out of his place, held the enamelled lighter, and slid back. "You will have observed," said Leo Rodd, pleasantly, drawing on the cigarette, "that I have only one hand."

El Exaltida folded his own two hands back on his chest; but for the first time he lifted his head and looked Leo Rodd in the face. Leo stared back into the bold, dark eyes. "The Grand Duke has missed so little that it will not have escaped him that this was a right-handed blow. It came from above and went down from right to left. But I have no right hand." He glanced down at the empty, pinned-up sleeve. "I lost it falling off a bicycle in an English lane and for the first time since it happened, I can find it in my heart to be exceedingly glad that I did. So the whole thing falls through." He rose to his feet. "Well, I'll be going now. Tell the Exalted One that I have very much enjoyed our chat." He gestured to the golden bird-cage. "And tell him with my compliments that I wouldn't be surprised if this little number was dreamed up by a gentleman called Fabergé, in which case it would be of quite incalculable value. The ancestral loot, no doubt; but a charming thing."

"I am glad you like it," said the Grand Duke, and he added in a voice like poured black treacle: "Sit down!"

The treacle had steel filings in it. Leo sat down. "I perceive, Mr Rodd, that you share my interest in objets d'art?"

"I know practically nothing about them," said Leo, with truth. "But I hope I can recognize Fabergé when I see him."

"I hope you can. This piece, however, was made by a goldsmith in a shop in Barrequitas; he does them in silver gilt too—they come very much cheaper." He snapped thumb and finger at the secretary. "Take this thing down and put it in Mr Rodd's carriage. Come back when I send for you." To Leo's bewildered protests, he held up an enormous, jewelled, deprecatory hand. "You must indulge me, senor; it is the penalty of tyranny to be surrounded exclusively by people one cannot respect—I find it refreshing to meet someone I can."

"Even if you can't respect my knowledge of objets d'art," said Leo.

"I respect the fact that you are not afraid of me, Mr Rodd."

"Not of you personally," said Leo. "But afraid I certainly am. Frightened to death."

"There is nothing to be afraid of. You have your strong right arm to protect you—by its absence. You rightly count on that."

"Then why am I here?"

"Because I wish you elsewhere—you and your friends. But I must have a scapegoat. I care nothing for what

148

happens when you get back to England, but I must do the thing with some semblance of decency here. My people do not appreciate quixotic clemency; and we are sensitive to the foreign press." He leaned back against the flimsy rail of his little wooden chair and once more folded his hands upon his vast chest. "Now, Mr Rodd—you did go up to that room?"

"No, as a matter of fact," said Leo, "I did not."

"You didn't? A pity. I genuinely thought you might have. Then the paper-cocked hat . . .?"

"My wife and I were not on the happiest terms," said Leo. "We were obliged to share the same sun-shed, to keep up appearances—with one another as much as with anyone else; but we were not feeling what you might call chatty. Nothing was said, nothing was overt or even very positive; we just instinctively kept to ourselves, I think—she lay down at one end, with her legs out in the sun, I lay up at the other end. It got a bit hot and I got drowsy. I'd been holding the paper—a musical score it was—between my face and the sun, looking up at it. I let it fall and cover my face, and dozed off to sleep. It's very simple really, like all those things; and it happens to be true."

"A pity," said El Exaltida again. He brooded over it. "Still—for the sake of argument, Mr Rodd, say you *had* gone up. Miss Lane hears your voice, she goes into Miss Barker's room and finds you there, you follow her back to hers, still holding the shawl. She retreats behind her table; she has been sitting there looking through the blackmail book." He paused. "But the book, when it was found after her death, was turned the other way." The great dark eyes questioned Leo Rodd's face. "Does that suggest anything?"

"It suggests that I—since you're talking in terms of my being the man in the room—that I was looking at the book. Open at the page with Inspector Cockrill's name."

"Exactly. Which in turn suggests——?"

"It suggested before," said Leo dourly, "that the woman was answering my threats to kill her, with a reminder that we had a policeman handy."

"A ridiculous proposition," agreed the Grand Duke readily. "So much more likely . . ."

"That *I* would use it, to counter the threat of blackmail."

"Exactly," said El Exaltida again. He twiddled vast thumbs till they looked like revolving bananas, diamond studded. "And now, Mr Rodd, what have we? A woman at the uttermost end of her tether. She is in love and she knows her love is in vain: worse, she has just made a hideous scene which will alienate even such friendship as her lover has shown her. Moreover, she is by now that hopeless and helpless creature, a blackmailer whose own secret has been discovered—that she *is* a blackmailer. She has given herself away to this man, she has given herself away earlier, by her outburst on the terrace. What has she got left? She has lost her lover, she will lose such friends as she has, the police of England will now be warned, she has no other means of livelihood. She has nothing left to live for; and there is the knife on the table."

"I see," said Leo.

Round and round and round went the great jewelled thumbs. "You will find, Mr Rodd, that the Duke of San Juan el Pirata is an understanding man. He quite sees the awkwardness of the situation in which you would find yourself. Your would-be mistress dead in her bedroom at your feet with a knife-wound in her breast; your true mistress's shawl, blood-spattered, in your hands. That you should hastily fling the shawl on the bed, compose the poor creature upon it, sluice yourself down in her bathroom and go quietly about your business, would seem to the Grand Duke no reason to keep you in any kind of custody." He lumbered to his feet and his splendid bulk loomed like a navy-blue genie in the tiny room. "Well—she has been given Christian burial, poor lady, and that's more than most suicides get in San Juan el Pirata." He held out a great sparkling hand. "I should have liked to make your better acquaintance, Mr Rodd, but I quite understand that you feel you should all of you go back to England to-morrow. . . ." He moved to the archway and lifted the curtain for Leo to pass through, into the shimmering loveliness of the sunlit courts below. "I find all this orientalism very tedious. I like my little study, it reminds me of my toys at Winchester. But you, Mr Rodd, are an old Etonian?"

"Charterhouse," said Leo, fingering his open-necked shirt.

"I'm as bad as you with Fabergé," said the Grand Duke and went back into his little study and let the curtain fall.

Down at the hotel, the new courier had collected his Stainless Ones and got them off at last en route for the sights and scents of Venice; and there were new arrivals, a sort of vicious circle, or rather, said Mr Cecil, madly witty, a vicious square—a Belgian count of dubious sex in pursuit of an elderly gigolo in pursuit of a rich South American mama, in pursuit of her daughter who was in pursuit of the Belgian count. "The Battle of the Belge," said Cecil, gaily; but Louvaine only smiled at him vaguely and wondered for the millionth time when Leo would be back from that horrible palace; and really, she was becoming a bore with her Leo, Leo, Leo, morning, noon and night and moping round after him, losing her looks, silly thing, just when she needed them most, slapping on her make-up all anyhow, and honestly, that skirt with that top . . .! "Honestly, ducky, I *don't* think that skirt with that top, you won't mind my saying?"

"I know, but the other top's dirty."

"Well, but, my dear, one does know about soap and water?"

"I simply couldn't care," said Louli. She wandered away from him, up the wooden steps to the balcony where Mr Cockrill leaned with the rest of the party over the rail, staring, uneasily waiting, out to sea. "Don't you think it's time that Leo—um, Mr Rodd—came back?"

"It's a long way," said Fernando. "It's steep. The horse goes slowly."

"He's been gone for two hours."

Helen Rodd looked at the haunted face and stifled her own deep anxiety. "It always seems a long time when one's waiting. I don't think we need worry."

She stood clutching the rail with her narrow fingers, the red head bent, the heavy curled eyelashes shading the terrified blue eyes. Much you care! she thought. Standing there as cool as a cucumber in your beastly, neat print dress, much you care that he's up there in that white iceberg of a palace, kept there perhaps, not allowed to leave, taking the blame for all of us, getting trapped there, held there, never getting away. And she blurted out, suddenly and uncontrollably, that nobody cared, nobody thought about him, they were all thinking of their own beastly skins. . . .

Miss Trapp was scandalized. "As *Mrs* Rodd is present, Miss Barker——"

She knew that she was behaving badly, was being unjust, was being impolitic, was making a fool of herself; she knew that Leo would be angry, with that bitter, ruthless anger of his, when he came back. But he might not come back; and at the bare thought of his danger, the sick fear rose in her soul, she cried out through rising hysteria that they needn't worry about Mrs Rodd, Mrs Rodd was far too busy being elegant and cool and putting on her act, to worry about poor Leo. . . .

Helen, rather irritably, shook off Miss Trapp's protesting hand. "It's all right. She's upset, we're all upset, she doesn't know what she's saying."

"I know what I'm saying perfectly well," said Louli. "I'm saying that you don't care whether he's in danger or not, you don't care about him, you don't love him, you don't love anyone but yourself." And she spat out, beside herself with horror, with horror at the very words she was speaking at that moment, that that was all right too, because Leo didn't love Helen either, if he had ever loved her, he loved her no longer, he wanted to go away with her, with Louvaine, and be with her for the rest of his life . . .

Helen raised her head sharply. "That's not true."

"Of course it's true."

"Very well," said Helen, in the cool, proud, almost supercilious manner that masked the deep vulnerability of her heart, "very well, then, it's true. We won't discuss it here."

Inspector Cockrill looked on, much interested. Since his abortive visit to the Barrequitas shop, he had pursued his enquiries into the attack upon her, with complete unsuccess. Under oaths of secrecy—as far as outsiders to their own, increasingly desperate, little group were concerned—he had confided the history of the afternoon's events; with equally little result. Mr Cecil, Miss Trapp, Fernando had been alone in their respective rooms. Louvaine had left hers only to go to her assignation in the pinewoods with Leo; nor did this furnish any more of an alibi for her than the others had, for she had arrived rather later than he, leaving her ample time to have dropped in on Mrs Rodd, en route. Of all of them, she had had the most motive—or rather she had had some possible ostensible motive, while nobody else concerned had any at all; but several people could testify that she had bought only one knife on the original visit to the shop, she was hardly likely to have concealed a second purchase later on, unless some deep-laid plan had been in her mind; and she had certainly not been to the shop since the death of Miss Lane, nor could one buy the knives anywhere else in the town. It was exasperating to be able to do so little, to feel so hamstrung without his little black bag, the graphite and the foot-rule and the magnifying-glass and all the rest of it, backed up by the vast departments of Scotalanda Yarda. All one could do was to emulate M. Poirot, use the little grey cells and observe the psychological behaviour pattern of those concerned. In pursuance of this sport, he gave a little dig in the ribs to Helen Rodd's behaviour pattern. "Mrs Rodd has had a bad shock this afternoon, Miss Barker, and she's in some pain. You're distressing her."

"Don't worry about me, Inspector. I'm used to my husband's—flirtations," said Helen. She added with an air of superior pity, that she always liked to avoid scenes, if she could, with the current girl-friend.

"If you know who she is?"

"There hasn't been much doubt about this one," said Helen, looking Louvaine up and down, from the mop of red hair, by way of the ill-matching blouse and skirt, to the vividly manicured sandalled feet.

"Oh, no, of course you've known all along," said Louli, sarcastically.

"All along," agreed Helen, pleasantly. "I had a seat in the gallery—up above you—when you opened the attack that night in Rapallo. I thought you did it very well—and I've witnessed a variety of approaches, I assure you."

"You knew *then*, did you?" said Cockie; for if that were really so, what price his theory of this afternoon?

"I'm not deaf and blind," said Helen, still pleasantly smiling. "I know all the symptoms by now. I watched Miss Lane too—as far back as Milan, Miss Lane got it. Then for a moment in Siena I thought my husband was settling for her, but I soon knew that wasn't the way of it. If you'd seen your faces, you and Leo," she said to Louvaine, "that morning in the hall, when you realized you weren't the only two people staying back from the expedition! And Miss Lane came down all ready for departure, it wasn't till she knew Leo wasn't going that she suddenly developed her headache—those two hadn't planned anything; that was clear." She leaned with affected nonchalance on the rail, propped on the uninjured arm, and looked out over the bright sea, fighting to keep the pleasant smile. "Not that I cared. You could all go or stay, whichever you liked, and be hanged to the lot of you!"

"So Miss Lane stayed; and be hanged to somebody," said Inspector Cockrill. "We've yet to know who." But bang went another neat theory: Helen Rodd had not killed Vanda Lane because she believed in an affair between Vanda and Leo.

Mr Cecil appeared, making his graceful way up the wooden steps to the balcony, outwardly languid, inwardly agog with curiosity at the raised voices above him. He looked with arched eyebrows at the two tense faces. "My dears, how white you look and how cross! Like two Piccasso doves gone belligerent."

"Mrs Rodd is making a last dovecote stand," said Louli. She appealed to him, shaking hands clutching at the verandah rail, literally for support. "Cecil—Mrs Rodd won't believe that Leo and I were planning to go away together. But *you* know it's true, don't you? Didn't I tell you about it?—that night on the beach?"

He looked again at the two faces: the rouge-patched face of a girl on the edge of hysteria, the composed, set face of a woman in physical pain, fighting the impact of emotional pain as well. For once in his lifetime, he did the decent thing. "Did you, Louli? I can't say that I remember."

A breeze had blown up, a little warm breeze coming in from the west, bringing the scent of the pine trees, dark and dusty under the afternoon sun. It swept back the heavy, forward-falling red hair and once again there was a glimpse of that face that Leo Rodd had seen the day before: the once gay face drained of all gaiety, the face that till now had never known sorrow, grown heavy and ugly with pain. She left the rail and went slowly away from them to the door of her room. Just inside the room, she turned. She said to Helen: "If you think this has only been a flirtation— you're wrong."

" 'Has been'? " said Helen. "So you realize it's over?"

She was terrified; terrified at the implications of what, unconsciously, she had confessed. "It's not over. You'll soon find out—it's not over at all."

"Very well," said Helen. "I don't want to discuss it."

Mr Fernando was accustomed to scenes among his Odysseans, accustomed to pouring oil upon stormy seas. He said pacifically that they had all better wait until Mr Rodd came back. He looked like an owl, the yellow horn-rimmed sun-glasses ringing the bright eyes in the large round face.

"Yes," said Louli. "You'll wait, you'll all wait and do nothing; but supposing he doesn't come back?"

"Now, now, Miss Barker, of course Mr Rodd comes back."

"Well *I* won't wait," said Louli. "I'm going up to the palace. I'll give him a few minutes longer, and then I'm going up to the palace. You may all be willing to let him sacrifice himself, but I'm not. I'm going up there."

"You'd much better stay away," said Helen. She looked rather anxiously at Cockrill; God knew what mess this silly, hysterical female would make of things, her look unequivocally said.

"You can do no good at the palace," agreed Cockrill.

"It's better than staying doing nothing down here."

"Better for you perhaps," said Helen. "But not better for Leo. What can *you* do?"

"I shall see the Grand Duke, that's what I'll do . . ."

"You'll never get anywhere near him," said Helen, impatiently. "And if you do, what on earth can you say to him?"

Louvaine stared back into her face. "I can tell him the truth, Mrs Rodd."

"The truth," said Helen. "What truth?"

"The truth. The truth that he's gone up there to hide." She clutched at the lintel of the doorway with trembling hands, panic rose in her, a red mist rose before her eyes; she knew that what she was about to do was appalling, but she was driven forward by her own inward torment of terror and doubt, she was unable to stop herself. "Do you think I don't know why he's gone, do you think I don't see now why he's sacrificing himself? He knows, you see—he knows what I've known all along, he knows who the murderer was." She knew that she must not say it, she knew that the words should never be uttered, she knew that what she did was ignoble and yet she could not stifle the hatred in her soul against this woman who stood here, cold and sneering, a woman without heart, without warmth, without emotions, who yet could stand between herself and her love. She stared back into the cold, pale face: and screamed out suddenly: "He knew that it was—you!"

They all stood very still. It was as though a motion picture had broken down and left them all standing there, each in his characteristic attitude—alert, sceptical, fascinated, aghast. Helen Rodd broke the spell. She said with chill contempt: "You must doubt very much that Leo really loves you: if you're reduced to anything so—despicable—as this."

The desperate blue eyes fell before her own. "You think I'm using it to try to get you out of the way?"

"Yes," said Helen.

"If Leo comes safely back, I swear by all I hold sacred I shall not mention it again."

"You can never unsay what you've said in front of all these people."

"I've said nothing. If I happen to believe you're the murderer, what's that to do with them?"

"It's a great deal to do with *me*. I am not a murderer. I had no reason whatsoever to want to murder Miss Lane."

"I never thought for a moment," said Louli, "that you wanted to murder *Miss Lane*."

Silence again, up on the sunlit terrace; and that stillness —only the little warm breeze blowing in softly from over the scented pines. "It would be nice to know," said Helen Rodd, scornfully, "exactly what it is that you do think."

I must not say it, thought Louli. I must not say it. I'm saying it because I hate her, because I'm afraid of her, because I want to get her out of the way. I'm saying it for vile reasons, and if I say it now, God knows I'm damned for ever. But she said it. She said: "I think you wanted to kill—me. I think you went to the wrong room. I think you saw somebody that you thought was me." And she lifted up her arms, suddenly, and twisted her bright hair into a knot at the back of her head, sweeping it away from her face; and stood so for a moment and then released it. The red curls fell softly back round her face again.

Mr Fernando screeched out, one curious, high-pitched, chopped-off train-whistle of a scream; and crossed himself and burst into a mutter of prayer. And Leo Rodd, coming cheerfully up the wooden steps with the Gerente at his heels, stopped short and said: "Good lord, Louvaine—except for the colour of your hair as you stood there just then—I'd have thought you were Vanda Lane."

CHAPTER ELEVEN

Two cousins. Long, long ago, in the old hard-up, struggling days—two cousins, sharing a tiny flat: Louise Barr and Vanda Lane whose names had been woven at last into that lovely nom de guerre—Louvaine. Louvaine Barker: whose first brain child had been born in the long, sick, agonizing months of labour; to the cousin called—Vanda Lane.

"She was always the clever one, the writing one," said Louli, explaining it all over again to Inspector Cockrill behind the closed shutters of her little room. "I was the gay one, I loved people and parties and going around, but she hated it, she only wanted to stay at home and scribble away at her precious book. And then the book was accepted and she had to go and see the publisher and she was petrified, she loathed it, she sat there as mum as a mouse feeling more and more certain that she was mucking up all her chances; and then there was a film of the book and they said that she must appear at the première . . ."

And the arguments and the cajolements, the sick headaches, the sleepless nights, the despair, the dread . . . "Louise, I can't, I won't, everyone will talk to me and I shan't be able to think of a word to say, I shall make a fool of myself, I shall probably be sick in front of everybody, from sheer nerves." And the reluctant climbing, at last, into the specially bought dress, the tentative dabs with unaccustomed make-up, a sudden piercing stench of singeing hair. . . . "There, that's done it, now I really *can't* go, thank God for that!" And, close upon it, the breaking of the first glimmering dawn of the great inspiration. "Louise, you go, you can wear my dress, tell them I'm ill, tell them I'm dead, tell them you're representing me, tell them—my God, Louise! —tell them you're *me!*"

"We were both really quite alike in those days, Inspector. We were the same height and about the same figure, we both had sort of mud-brown hair and, which was the real thing, our features were alike—a sort of family likeness, you know, not identical at all, but enough to make us now and again mistaken for another by people who didn't know us well. And of course the people in the film world didn't know us at all, they'd seen her about once and me never, and the same applied to her publishers and any other people that were likely to be there. They'd all insisted that it was important for her to go, because of press photographs and publicity and so forth; and so we took a chance, and I went. I did my hair like hers and I wore no make-up and I talked in a low voice and said hardly anything, and it worked like a charm. Only at the end, I couldn't quite keep it up and I went a bit gay and made a few jokes and everybody muttered to each other that the Barker wasn't too bad at all when she got a bit of drink in her and livened up, poor little thing . . ."

Inspector Cockrill sat on her white-draped, four-poster catafalque of a bed and swung his short legs, absently knocking the ash from his cigarette with the nail of a nicotined finger. "And that was the beginning of it all?"

"Well, yes. Because the next time, she naturally said, 'You go again.' And it did make sense, because by that time I'd said things at the première which they might refer to and she wouldn't know what it all meant; and anyway, however mildly, I'd gone and set a standard which she swore she couldn't now live up to. Besides, she loathed it all and I adored it, and of course the joke of it made it all the more fun. So I let 'Louvaine Barker' blossom out, sort of gradually, over the weeks and months and they all thought that with the increasing success of the book, it was natural enough that I should get more and more gay and begin to use make-up and break out into real clothes instead of mouse coats and skirts. Vanda was only too pleased; she said it increased the difference between us, in case we should ever be seen together and she more and more toned herself down and I more and more dyed my hair and had red nails and generally gayed myself up. Of course by then her writing was earning money, real money, and she paid for things."

"I see," said Cockie. His hands dangled between his knees, the smoke of his cigarette drifted up between brown fingers. "And you were content to accept that?"

Louvaine sat with the legs of the wooden chair tilted till her bright head rested back against the wall. "Well, yes—why not? I made a little of the money myself: I used to do the odd bits and bobs, the reviews and articles—we can all write a bit in our family, it's just one of those things; and of course I made money by just being around, picking up commissions for work and so on, let alone leaving her free to get on with her writing; and I gave up my job and stayed at home and worked as a general secretary—dogsbody, coping with the letters and the telephone. But that was only while we were still sharing flats."

"You separated?"

"Yes." She tipped back the chair to its normal position and sat with her hands clasped on the little table before her. "We began to get worried about being discovered. Vanda worried more than I did. By that time she'd got a terrific following, the books meant a great deal to people, women especially: they used to write to her—they were attracted to some extent by her publicity, they thought it was wonderful that anyone who was outwardly worldly and gay, could write with so much depth and sincerity, could understand the problems of inarticulate people like themselves. If they'd ever found out that they were being deceived——"

"That would have been the end of Miss Barker?" said Cockie.

She raised her head sharply. He had never seen her so grave, for a moment she seemed far away in another world. "It was much more than that. They'd really have minded. They looked on me as—actually as a friend."

"And they'd have felt cheated if they'd discovered that the friend wasn't you at all?"

"They'd have thought we'd been making fools of them."

"So you took it very seriously?"

She shook off her absorption. "My dear, it would have been catastrophic. I mean, they used to write in and bare their *souls!* So we decided that we must be even more careful. We emphasized the differences between us more and more, she got more and more unobtrusive, I got more ob. We thought up all sorts of gags, we both learnt this eighteenth-century script stuff—everyone was writing books about it just then, so it came in quite naturally and so we could manage about our writing . . ."

"Yes," he said. "I noticed she used it, in the blackmail book."

". . . and then we thought we really ought not to share a home any more. Of course we had masses of money by then, we could afford to live as we liked."

"Miss Lane never grudged you your share?"

"Oh, no," said Louli. "Never for a moment. We got it very business-like in the end; a percentage of her earnings by way of a salary for the work I did, which was quite a lot, and then expenses—the expenses were the biggest item: after all, I had to live as Louvaine Barker was expected to live. It was Vanda who insisted on it, I was representing her. And as for grudging it, she always said that she'd never have been where she was without me—which I think was true; and that she certainly couldn't do without me now, which was also true. Anyway, she didn't miss it—there was lots for two."

Cockrill thought back to the contents of the room in which she had died, to the Stiebel coat that had cost 'fifty or sixty,' to the unobtrusive excellence of all her possessions. It was clear that in whatever luxury she had supported her alter ego, the true Louvaine Barker had had more than enough left over for herself. "And no doubt she would feel that you were being prevented from earning a living in some other way; you might even have written yourself, perhaps."

"Well, as to that I wouldn't know."

"But you did the articles and reviews?"

"Oh, well, those," she said. She shrugged them off. "I don't call that writing."

He turned the cigarette in his brown fingers and looked down at its glowing tip. "I was just thinking of something you said to Mr Cecil—that evening down on the beach."

"Something I said? What something?"

"Just something," he said. "It's puzzled me all along. Well, never mind. You took separate flats. And then?"

"And then we grew more and more careful about being seen together, or even appearing to know one another. It became—well, almost an obsession. Yes." She thought it over. "A game with me; an obsession with her. And the more elaborate the whole deception became, the more the danger grew. We just couldn't take risks."

"Of being recognized?"

"Of the likeness being recognized. Supposing a reporter, for example, had tumbled to what was happening."

"You were together all the time on this tour. Nobody noticed anything."

"Nobody was looking for anything," said Louli. She leaned forward across the small table, hands tightly clasped, blue eyes bright with the earnestness of her conviction. "In England, Louvaine Barker's news; I never know when I'm being watched, when I'm being followed about—I don't mean that I constantly am, but I never know. Wherever I'm recognized, people stare at me, they watch me, they talk about me. Magazine readers want to know about me, what does Louvaine Barker wear, what does Louvaine Barker eat, what does she read, what does she like, *who does she know?* Somebody notices that she knows one other girl particularly well, they spend a lot of time together; immediately that other girl becomes interesting, who is she, why are they friendly, how do they come to know one another?—she's approached for interviews, tell us what you know about Louvaine Barker. And then—somebody notices the likeness. But here, you see nobody would be interested in the other girl: everyone would know that she was nobody special, just someone else on a tour: if a likeness was noted, it would be purest coincidence, in two casual acquaintances. And anyway, we never did appear to become too friendly: we hardly spoke, we never sat near one another if we could help it so that people could make comparisons, we more and more exaggerated the differences in our appearance, it was easier abroad where one can wear such a variety of clothes. You see, these tours were one of our ways of spending some time together. We simply had to keep up with what we were each doing, I had to know what she was writing, she had to know what I was saying—it needed really constant discussion. But we didn't trust the telephone, it was too risky to put it all into writing, and anyway, as I say, discussion was part of it, and you've got to meet, to discuss. Of course we managed it quite a lot in England too: we used to go very occasionally to each other's flats, we used to stay in country hotels and meet outside and go for long walks; but, in the early summer, when Vanda was planning her new book, we got into the habit of coming abroad on these tours—we'd try to get rooms next to one another, and creep in silently at night and work and work and work, into the small hours . . ."

Inspector Cockrill recalled Vanda Lane's inexplicable preference for room number five, following Louvaine's apparently casual choice of number four. He reflected, however, that the ladies had done very little night work on the present tour: thanks to Leo Rodd.

And Leo Rodd. "Did Mr Rodd know about all this? What was to happen if either of you married?"

"Oh, well," she said, "we'd simply have told our husbands, I suppose. What had they got to lose?—they'd just have accepted it. I hadn't told Leo, because it was Vanda's secret too; but I would have. He wouldn't have cared."

He thought again over that odd remark, down on the beach that evening. But he put the thought aside. "And your families? What had you told them?"

She shrugged. "They believed what everyone else believed. I told my mother and father, under oaths of secrecy; but— I don't know—we've both rather grown away from home since all this began. Vanda told her father, but he's dead now. Her mother—well, she was away, she was ill."

"She never told her own mother?"

"Her mother was away," insisted Louvaine.

"What, away in hospital? All these years?"

She said rather defensively: "It's a sort of hospital. She's always there. She's—incurable."

"I see," he said. It accounted perhaps for odd things in Vanda Lane's character. The exaggerated dread of meeting strange people which had led her to sacrifice her very identity as a famous and much loved writer, the entire absorption in her work, the anxiety complex which had obviously arisen about keeping the secret of the change of identities. Certainly, once started, it would have seemed imperative to keep the deception alive, and Louvaine had evidently herself agreed wholeheartedly in going to the lengths they did; but with her it had been 'a sort of game'; with Vanda it had been an obsession.

And if the mother were mentally unhinged, had for many years been incurably insane, if there were that sort of instability in her family—might not this to some extent explain the business of the blackmail? After all, clearly enough there was no need for Vanda Lane to make money by this means. He remembered saying to Louvaine on the day of the murder, that Miss Lane had merely enjoyed seeing her victims wriggling on the hook; one might ascribe that to a not very pleasant human failing, but to go to the length of extorting money, or even only playing at extorting money that one could not possibly need, argued a mind surely not entirely sane?

It was the hour of the siesta. In and out of the long line of rooms, the new arrivals swarmed like a hive of bees through the sweltering heat of the afternoon, settling themselves in. In number two, Mr Cecil lay, unbeautiful in sleep, his pale mouth open, his pale hands flopping, his sunburnt arms flecked with delicate shavings of peeling skin, his doors fast bolted and locked against the prowler with the Toledo knife. In number four, Inspector Cockrill sat, short legs dangling, on Louli's white bed and thought and thought and thought. In number eight, Mr Fernando curved a heavy arm about the thin shoulders of his lady love and assured her that thus he would protect her from lurking danger, now and throughout their lives; and Miss Trapp, trembling in his embrace, reflected that this was the price one had to pay for the love of a good man, and wondered if, after all, it were not going to prove too high. In number seven . . .

In number seven, Helen Rodd picked up brushes and combs and mirrors and jars from the dressing-table and, with shaking hands, tossed them into her travelling case. Leo, sitting on the further of the two beds, struggling with his tie, looked up and said sharply: "What are you doing?"

She went on packing. "I'm taking my things. I've told them at the desk that I'll move into number five for to-night." She gave a small, cynical shrug of the unhurt shoulder; it was part of her make-up that when most her spirit cried out in pain, she must repel pity with a show of unfeelingness. "After all—it's vacant now."

He said stupidly: "Moving? Into number five?"

"It's only for to-night. We've all got to leave to-morrow."

He was absolutely still for a moment; then he lifted his hand again and continued to wrench at his tie. "I see. So this is It?"

She jerked open a drawer and began to lift out the contents, the nighties and the nylons and the hand-embroidered lingerie, intimate paraphernalia of a woman of wealth and taste. "It isn't anything. I don't know what's going to happen, we must discuss that afterwards. But I can't go on sharing a room with you, Leo: going to bed, getting up, dressing, undressing—all the time knowing that you're looking at me and cursing me in your heart for being me; wishing to God that I was—that I was Her." And she tumbled the lovely things into the case and blurted out suddenly, all defences down, that she had never in all her life known one moment of unkindness, of unlovingness, of humiliation—until she had known him; and she could bear no more. "Do what you like about it, Leo, leave me, marry her, cook up a divorce case, do what you damn well please about it: but do one thing or the other, don't keep me hanging around like a tiresome but necessary servant till it suits you both to dismiss me." She added, lifting her face and looking at him for a long moment: "Or get rid of me in some other way."

"What do you mean by that Helen?"

"I mean that I'm not going to share a room with you, that's all." She crushed the things down into the case and closed the lid. She said more quietly: "I'll see you through, I'll help you with your arm, I can come along any time you need me—I won't let you down. But I'm going to the other room."

He had pulled off the tie at last and he sat with it dangling in his hand across his knees. He had gone very white. "Well, I don't understand that last crack; it doesn't make sense. But anyway, why all this now? Because of what Louvaine said to-day?"

"She said that I killed Miss Lane—well, I don't care about that, I didn't and that's all. But she said other things that you weren't there to hear." She had fastened the case and now stood still, just balancing her finger-tips on it, looking him in the face. "She says that if you ever loved me, you no longer do. She says you two are planning to go away."

He said nothing, sitting looking down at the tie. "I've always known about your affairs, Leo: I'm not a fool, you know. But I've also always known that they were just affairs. If this one's different, why didn't you say so straight out?"

"How can I say anything straight out?" said Leo. "I don't know myself."

"She says it's all planned."

"Nothing's planned," he said wretchedly. "Damn it all, I've only known her a week."

"She says it *is* planned."

His face took on the old, familiar, impatient scowl. "Dear God—women!"

A sick hope rose within her, but she forced it down. "Don't try to be kind to me, Leo, don't 'let me down lightly.' I'd much rather be told." She added bitterly: "I assure you I shan't make a scene; *or* any objections."

He put his hand up to his head. "I don't know, Helen. This beastly murder's changed everything, everything seems different now, it's all sort of—well, I don't know, mixed up and ugly and distorted, it's as if the sunshine had suddenly gone out of the place." And he thought of Louvaine, Louvaine with her bright head and the gay, sweet smile, suddenly bursting out like a virago, with her accusations against Helen; of her repudiation, coming back from the funeral, of pity for the dead woman they had just left in a lonely grave: of the little jokes and absurdities that in the first days had held such tender charm for him and now seemed often only silly and unkind. "It's the murder," he said. "It colours everything." The night before it had happened, he had held her in his arms and thought the world well lost for her indeed; but now, if he could recapture the magic of that evening—would it be the same? "I'm not trying to deceive you, Helen. I don't understand it myself. I'd tell you if I knew." And yet, he thought, even as I say the words, I *am* deceiving her. For he knew, as he had known in the first moments of his surrender, that there in his arms he had held the one woman in the world for him, the true love of all the loves of a lifetime, the heart of his secret heart. "God help us, Helen, I just don't know how on earth it's going to end. I did love her; it was something real, that I couldn't help—people say that, but now and again it's true. It was true for me; and I can't pretend that when all this filthy business is over and we're back to normal, it won't be like that again. To be utterly honest with you—I hope it will; I can't help hoping it will—it was something so wonderful, you couldn't not want it again." He looked at her in pity and tenderness. "Try to understand, darling. It's not that I haven't loved you, I always have, even though I know I've been unkind. But I suppose there are degrees of love; and this other love was something different from yours and mine, something we just didn't know existed." He raised his head and looked into her bleak white face, so bemused with his own dreams that he did not see the draining away of the last dregs of her hope. "If it comes back—I just can't fight against it. Meanwhile, be patient with me and try not to mind too much." He gave her the most truly spontaneous affectionate smile that she had had from him for many days. "In my own way, if you can bear to accept it from me, I love you and need you as much as I always have. This other thing—if you'll try to understand that it's sort of over and above, it doesn't affect my loving you and needing you . . ."

"To do up your shoe-laces," she said.

He bowed his head. "Well—that I suppose I deserve. But in fact it's nothing to do with my bloody arm."

"Or *my* bloody money?" said Helen.

His face grew black as thunder. "Or with your money. After all," he said, with ugly self-mockery, matching his cynicism with her own, "Louvaine's rich. And you've got me conditioned to living on my wife's money, haven't you?"

"The only trouble with your wife's money this time is that it now appears that the goose that really laid the golden eggs is dead."

"Well, you needn't worry," he said. "We won't trouble *you*."

Her finger-tips whitened with the pressure as she steadied herself, half fainting, against the dressing-case. Then she lifted it off its chair, opened another and tumbled in the contents of another drawer. He bent to untie his shoe-laces, and she thought: When he comes to do them up again, he won't be able to. He could go to Louvaine; but Louvaine would not know the special way of doing them so that they could be easily untied with one hand. Never mind, she thought, bitterly, that'll be a happy excuse to go to Louvaine again. She closed the case and put it on the floor beside the other. "I'll leave the rest of my things; I take it you can bear to have them around till we leave to-morrow. If we leave to-morrow."

"Why shouldn't we leave to-morrow? The Grand Duke's arranged it."

"The Grand Duke hasn't yet had a chat with your girl friend."

"She was overwrought," said Leo, briefly. "She said what came into her head."

"She said it very convincingly. She said that I went up to the room that afternoon to have it out with her; and saw Vanda Lane standing in the doorway, and thought it was *her*."

"She couldn't see herself," said Leo. "She couldn't see her own hair. Even with it pulled back, you couldn't mistake the colour. You wouldn't really have been taken in for a minute. And anyway, as you rightly say, the Grand Duke has not had a chat with Louvaine about it; and can't wait to get rid of us all to-morrow morning. You are in no danger whatsoever." He flung himself back on the bed, put his arm over his face and composed himself to sleep. "Now, if you've finished your furniture removals I will take my siesta. I hope you'll be comfortable in number five. Au revoir."

She picked up the cases and went into the little passage leading past the bathroom to the corridor. After a moment she returned, still carrying them. She opened the balcony door and looked out, but she did not go. He roused himself to say, with calculated irritability: "Well, what is it now?"

She had put the cases down, one on either side of her, and she stood very still. The light from the half-closed shutters threw narrow lines of shadow across the white dress and the set white face; and for a moment he had the ugly fancy that it looked as though she stood behind prison bars.

And outside the door, open upon freedom—shiny black hat, dark cape, gleam of silver inlay on old black steel, drowsing at his post in the heat of the afternoon sun, stood a guard of the San Juanese politio—caging her in.

CHAPTER TWELVE

INSPECTOR COCKRILL, with Fernando as interpreter, rushed up to the prison. The Gerente, a sick and sorry man, turfed Lollita off his knee and held out the hand of fellowship to his blood brother. For now, said the Gerente, things were very bad for them all, they were all at the mercy of El Exaltida and who could fathom the capricious vagaries of the great ones of the earth? Two days ago he, the Gerente, had been under orders, upon pain of God knew what appalling penalties peculiar to San Juan el Pirata, to produce from among the Inglese a subject suitable for immediate execution upon not too outrageously inadequate grounds; to-day he had presented himself, a-quiver with excitement, before the Exalted One and confided all he had seen and heard as he followed Senor Rodd up the steps to the balcony on their return from the palace. And behold!— were there thanks, was there praise, had there been perhaps a hint or two of splendid decorations to follow?—no, indeed, cried the Gerente, hammering himself upon the forehead and chest with such knock-out blows that he was obliged to resort to reviving sips of arguardiente, no indeed! El Exaltida it seemed, had meanwhile made other arrangements. Was he, was the Gerente, a magician that he should see through walls, listen across the vast acres of the Grand Ducal palace, read himself into the secret mind of authority?—or what mystical attribute was to divine for him the reasons why Senor Rodd had looked pleased with himself as, nursing his golden bird-cage, he had sat silent through the homeward drive. For the senor could speak no Juanese, as they all knew, and the Gerente no English, and nothing had therefore been explained to El Gerente of the plot hatched up in the Grand Duke's room. What more natural therefore than that, ceaselessly alert in the service of the Politio, the Gerente should seize upon the proof of guilt exposed before his very eyes at the moment of their return to the hotel, and, pausing only to share it with such friends and members of his family as he encountered upon the way, rush up to the Palace with the news. But, El Exaltida . . . He shuddered at the bare memory of the great jewelled fists raised above the splendid head and brought crashing down among pens and papers and exquisite bric-à-brac on the wooden desk. "He says El Exaltida was angry," translated Fernando, en précis, for the Inspector. "He says that he smashed a golden bird-cage like the one Senor Rodd had. He says El Exaltida keeps a stock of bird-cages, to hand out as favours to visiting foreigners. He says some are gold and some are silver gilt, according to the status of the expected visitor. He says . . ."

"What did the Exleteeder say, that's all *I* care," said Cockie.

"He says El Exaltida said that he must tell no one about the Senora Rodd being the murderer, that if nobody knew, they could keep to the suicide theory still, and let us all go."

Cockrill raised his head with the light of hope in his eye. "Well, then, what's he worrying about? Let him tell no one."

"He says he's already told everyone," said Fernando simply.

The Grand Duke, upon hearing this had, it appeared, sworn for ten full minutes by the Gerente's own watch, reaching such heights of inventive invective as had made the blood run cold; had thrown a blotter, an inkwell and a carved jade ash-tray at the Gerente's head and, scoring a near miss with this last, had suddenly recovered his temper and lapsed into a sort of bland affability which for some reason had been far more frightening. Very well then, said the Grand Duke, let the Gerente continue with the affair of the Senora Rodd. True, a reason had been found for letting the Inglesi go, an outwardly tenable solution had presented itself and he, the Grand Duke, had taken advantage of it to rid the island of a troublesome business which might interfere with the tourist, and so indirectly with the smuggling, trade. But now, thanks to the—initiative—of el Gerente, said the Grand Duke, smiling terribly upon his hapless servant, this solution was no longer useful. San Juan had her reputation to uphold, she was not to be presented in the world's press as a poor little backward island, unable to manage her own legal and criminal affairs, permitting the escape of a murderer through over-long adhering to a suicide theory which—through el Gerente's initiative, repeated the Grand Duke, smiling again into the Gerente's bleached face —everyone now knew to be nonsense. Let the Gerente handle the affair in his own way as he had taken it upon himself to interfere—er, to intervene. And this time, *let there be no mistake*. Let the Gerente walk carefully until he had arranged for such proofs as would satisfy any future enquiries from abroad; let a guard be set over them all, until the woman could reasonably be arrested and thrown into prison and the rest be packed off home. In due course, they would hang her or, if the British wished otherwise, simply forget her and let her die a natural death—they never lasted long under prison conditions, said the Grand Duke comfortably, especially the women; and thus the whole wearisome business would be closed, and demonstration made to the outside world that here in San Juan el Pirata, they were not barbarians. . . .

"You are going to arrest Mrs Rodd?" said Cockrill, horror-stricken.

Fernando translated. The Gerente shrugged helplessly. Orders was orders, Fernando translated back.

"But the whole thing is nonsense." He pursued, with elaborations, the argument Leo Rodd had put before Helen earlier that afternoon. "Tell him Mrs Rodd couldn't possibly have mistaken Miss Lane for Miss Barker. Point out to him about the colour of the hair. The conditions were the same on each occasion, there was strong sunlight, if Miss Lane had answered her door, she would have been standing just as Louvaine Barker was standing to-day. She wore her hair scraped back into a bun as a rule, you might not have seen much of it; though even when Miss Barker pulled hers back, you could still clearly see its colour. But Miss Lane had been bathing, she'd pulled off her bathing cap, her hair was all about her shoulders, the Gerente saw it for himself when she lay on the bed; and all the darker for being wet—you couldn't in that light, even in the light of the room, have mistaken it for red hair. And Mrs Rodd would be looking for a girl whose most noticeable feature is a thick head of flaming red hair."

Mr Fernando looked down uncomfortably at the stolid gold rings on his fingers with their diamond and ruby chips. "I confess, Inspector—this morning, *I* thought she was Miss Lane. *I* did not observe the colour of the hair."

"Then you must be colour-blind," said Cockie, coldly.

"Perhaps Mrs Rodd is colour-blind?"

"Women are never colour-blind," said Cockrill. "Or practically never. It's a rule of nature. And anyway, Mrs Rodd isn't: I've checked."

The Gerente spoke in Juanese. Cockrill said quickly: "Anyway, say nothing about it to him. It won't help in getting Mrs Rodd out of this mess and that's all we want for the moment. Just say what I told you."

Fernando translated obediently in his stumbling Juanese, the Gerente replied, Fernando gabbled back excitedly, the Gerente flung helpless hands wide and shrugged hopeless shoulders. "He says, Inspector, that he cares nothing for red hair or dark hair, he saw for himself that Miss Lane looked like Miss Barker, he saw that Miss Barker was accusing Mrs Rodd, he has orders to arrange the whole thing by day after to-morrow." The Gerente spoke again and he translated solemnly: "He asks me to request you not to make things more difficult for him, by bringing forward these facts which do not fit in with his case." He too shrugged helplessly. "I'm afraid they have quite decided it shall be Mrs Rodd."

"Well, I've quite decided it shall not be Mrs Rodd," said Cockie. He thought it over unhappily. "Of course he doesn't know . . . I suppose we'd better. . . . Yes: tell him, Mr Fernando, tell him about the attack yesterday, on Mrs Rodd."

The Gerente was perfectly delighted with the story of the attack on Mrs Rodd. He listened with unimpaired gravity to the account of Inspector Cockrill's investigations at the shop and scribbled a hasty note to the proprietor informing him that a tall, slim, English lady had on the afternoon of the funeral purchased a Toledo steel knife there, and that he would be required to remember the incident when called upon and to have witnesses ready. "A pity the poor lady did not succeed," he said to Fernando. "It would have put an end to her troubles and ours, with one blow." Why Mrs Rodd should have aimed a suicidal blow at her right shoulder, or how, having aimed it at her heart, she could have missed that fairly easily located organ by about eighteen inches, need not concern him, for El Exaltida was predisposed to theories of suicide and certainly would not enquire. As far as he was concerned, said the Gerente, contentedly smiling, this evidence of the murderer's remorse and fear, rounded off the whole business. Meanwhile, if the Inspector would be so good as to hand over the dagger . . .?

"Very well," said Cockie. "You can send down a man for it." He slammed his white hat on his head and marched off out of the prison without farewell. The Gerente looked sorrowfully after one who, as a brother, must hereafter be lost to him, and sent for a selection of witnesses who might be persuaded to have seen Mrs Rodd creep up to the balcony on the afternoon of the murder and come away afterwards, wiping a bloodstained knife. . . . But no, no, the knife had been still in the body. He amended his notes on the subject. One must walk with extraordinary care in a matter like this: it was one thing to have proof of things which might not have happened, but to prove things that *could* not have happened might well, with the Grand Duke in his present mood, be a foolish mistake. After all, as El Exaltida had said, here in San Juan they were not barbarians.

Down at the hotel, Miss Trapp had made her diffident way to room number five, and there offered comfort. She knew Mrs Rodd was alone; for, after begging in vain to be allowed to come in and speak to her, Leo Rodd had flung away from the locked door and down the curved steps to the terrace; Miss Trapp had seen him there later, talking to Louli, he with a face of set, cold anger, she with the new look of terror and dread which now came all too often to those blue eyes that had once been so blithely gay. "You will not think I am intruding, Mrs Rodd?" said Miss Trapp nervously, sitting on the little wooden chair, hugging the bag. "I thought, perhaps, another woman . . ."

"It's very kind of you, Miss Trapp," said Helen, longing only to be left alone.

"You won't misunderstand me?" pleaded Miss Trapp humbly. "I didn't come to interfere or to ask impertinent questions or to seek any confidence from you. It was only that—it's a dreadful thing, Mrs Rodd, not to know who are one's true friends: nobody knows that better than I do; and though, of course, I wouldn't presume to consider myself a friend of yours, I would just like to tell you that if—if you should need a friend, and, since you have no one else here, I—I am quite at your service."

Helen Rodd looked at the scraggy figure perched uneasily on the little chair, the pinched, pale face bent over the brown bag. "It's very, very kind of you, Miss Trapp. Thank you."

"And I'll just add," said Miss Trapp, clutching still more tightly at the leather handles, "that of course I don't for one moment believe that you killed that woman."

"Well, thank you for that too," said Helen. "Though I don't know why you should be so definite about it. After all, one of us did kill her: doesn't it sound extraordinary, Miss Trapp?—'one of us did kill her.' But it's true: one of us, one of seven people—six if you exclude Inspector Cockrill, which we surely must, and only five if we leave out Miss Barker too, because she certainly was with him. But even counting her in, that's only six—Miss Barker, Mr Cecil, Mr Fernando, my husband, and you and me. And after all, more than all of us I may be said to have had—provocation."

"Not to kill Miss Lane," said Miss Trapp.

"They suggest that it wasn't Miss Lane I intended to kill."

"You would not have killed the other one either," said Miss Trapp, firmly. "It would not be your way."

"It hasn't been my way so far," agreed Helen. She sat back against the high bed, her hand on the wooden poster, her weary head resting against her upraised arm. "But then, this time was different. This time I was being betrayed."

"You must have faith," said Miss Trapp. She remembered the two faces staring at one another down on the terrace below the bougainvillea boughs, the angry face and the frightened face. "You must have faith. He will come back to you."

"Faith isn't a thing you can switch on and off like a light," said Helen. "It requires some—co-operation on the other person's part."

"Do you think so?" said Miss Trapp. She relaxed her grip a little on the handles of the brown bag, gradually it slid into her lap and she let it lie there, only fiddling with the straps. "I think that that's the very quality of faith, you know—that it grows of itself: it's almost a definition to say that to have faith is to believe without a reason." She paused, toying with the brown straps. "If—if I might intrude my personal affairs for a moment, Mrs Rodd—you know that I and Mr Fernando . . .?"

Helen looked up quickly, impetuously protesting. "Oh, Miss Trapp—no!" She added, as quickly: "Well, forgive me, I ought not to say that."

Miss Trapp smiled a little sadly, a little ruefully. "You think Mr Fernando is—an adventurer?"

"I like Mr Fernando, Miss Trapp. But I do think that you—that you don't know him very well yet."

"All the more reason to have faith," said Miss Trapp. She smiled again. "I thought I would tell you, as a sort of example of what I mean, you know—that everything I have in the world, I am making over to Mr Fernando."

Helen bowed her head. "I can only say that you must be very much in love."

"Well, no," said Miss Trapp, "I am not in love, Mrs Rodd. And so you see, as I can't offer love, I think that I must offer perfect trust, perfect faith. One must give something when one is receiving so much."

"But what can you be receiving, Miss Trapp; I mean, what is there that Mr Fernando can offer *you?*"

"Only not to be lonely any more," said Miss Trapp.

"But with a man you hardly know, a man you can't know anything about yet, a man of his—well, of his type . . . Supposing it doesn't last? Then you'll be lonely again, and poor into the bargain."

"Well, I shall have had something," said Miss Trapp. "Up to now, I've had nothing. Mr Fernando you know is not just entirely what he appears to be; any more, Mrs Rodd, than any of the rest of us are. And, for the moment at any rate, he has need of me; materially, yes, but, I flatter myself, in other ways too—he really, he actually has need of me. Nobody has ever needed me before in all my life and if I were to lose all I have and suffer for the rest of my days, this one little hour of being necessary to somebody will have been worth it to me. But I shan't lose and I shan't suffer. He'll repay me—in other ways, perhaps, but anyway in happiness. If I didn't have faith in that, I'd have no right to be accepting what he is offering me."

The thin hands had relinquished altogether their grasp on the handbag, they lay in her lap, palms up, fingers crooked, a little pathetically, like the claws of a dead bird. But for once they were still, relaxed and still. Helen thought: She means what she says. She's got faith in him. She said: "I can only say that I hope you'll be very happy; and that you deserve to be."

"You'll be happy too," said Miss Trapp. "He'll come back to you."

"I don't think so," said Helen. "You see, this is something different. He really loves her."

"He hates her," said Miss Trapp. "He's talking to her

now, down on the terrace; and there's hate in his face." She gathered up the brown bag and began to fiddle with the handles again. "She's done you an injury, you see, she's placed you in danger and now all his love for you comes back, he wants only to protect you, he's afraid for you." The old, nervous grip on the handles reinforced itself, she hugged the bag up under her chin as though to preserve it from a world full of villainy. "She thought that by getting you out of the way, she could have him for herself. But she was wrong. Through this one action, she's lost him for ever." And she smiled a strange smile, oddly exalted, oddly at peace. "You're like me, Mrs Rodd—you may suffer, you may have lost everything, you may even lose your liberty or your life. But you haven't lost in the end. She's lost. You've won."

Louvaine Barker met Cockrill at the gate when, with Fernando, he got back to the Bellomare Hotel. She had been hanging about there awaiting his return and now intercepted him with a casual air which ill masked some deep and desperate inner resolve. Fernando, all regretful excitement, poured out the history of their unsuccess and hurried forward to meet his beloved, agog with sensational bad news. Cockrill slowed down his pace to Louli's since she was obviously anxious to talk to him. She said: "So you think it's pretty hopeless?"

"We are at the mercy of unreason," said Cockrill.

"Leo will have to have another try with the ineffable boy friend." She spoke lightly but he knew that she hung on his answer with desperate anxiety. "After all, he *is* an Old Wykhamist or something."

"The veneer appears to crack rather readily," said

Cockrill, dryly (for he is not, himself, a public school man), "under pressure from several centuries of depravity and rape. The Hereditary Grand Pirate is reverting quite simply to the code of his forefathers which is to say to a hereditary conviction that everything in life can be settled very nicely if someone can be found to walk a plank."

They turned a corner that brought them within sight of the great, ever-open front doors of the hotel. A line of battered carriages was drawn up there, the horses, with their long sad faces beneath shabby straw sun hats, looking as though at any moment they would catch up trugs and secateurs and wander off into the gardens remarking that the oleanders were far better two or three days ago if only one had been there then. . . . The succeeding wave of tourists was frothing about them, the Battle of the Belge raging round a question of amatory precedence, the new guide darting hither and thither like a Cardiganshire corgi nipping at the heels of a herd of refractory cows. "History is repeating itself," said Louli. "Not even giving themselves time to murder one another, Odyssey Tours is off on an expedition round the island." She added, carelessly, "So we have the place to ourselves."

"What for?" said Cockie.

"What for?"

"What is this leading up to, Miss Barker?"

"Oh, do you still call me Miss Barker?" said Louli. "People never do." All she was leading up to, she said, was wouldn't it be a good idea to have a reconstruction of the crime, people always did in detective stories and why not they?

"In order that you shall make a dramatic appearance as Miss Lane?" said Cockie. "And demonstrate that you murdered her yourself, stabbing her in the few moments that you were together alone, up at the top of the rock: but only sufficiently for her to be able to stagger up to her room, lay herself down on the bed and there die with her characteristic decorum."

"What, *me?*" protested Louli, laughing.

"And thus offering yourself, a willing sacrifice, to save the life of the wife of the Man you Love, and win back his devotion and respect: even if you're no longer in a position to benefit by it."

She was silent for a moment. Then she said lightly, "That phrase about the life of the wife is tricky to say."

"The life of the wife will not be saved this way," said Cockie. "Because I shall not permit it."

But public opinion was against him. Leo Rodd, frantic with anxiety about Helen, cut off from her by a barrier of resentful reserve, was crazy for action, for anything to vary the endless round of discussion and argument and guesswork and surmise, the ceaseless inward gnawing of self-questioning and self-reproach. "It can't do any harm. Something may come of it." And Helen would perforce be winkled out from her self-imposed solitude, must surely be broken down into some sort of responsiveness, must at least be made aware of, if she still would not accept, his agony of protectiveness, of pity, of pain. "For God's sake, let's get on with it, let's do it, what harm can there be?"

"Who is to play the part of Miss Lane?" said Cockie bleakly.

"Well, we thought that Louli . . ."

"I am not staging any theatrical entertainment for the exhibition of Miss Barker's talents."

Leo flushed an angry red. "It's nothing of the sort."

"Are you telling me that this is not Miss Barker's idea, from beginning to end?"

"She suggested it, certainly. Good God, she's only trying to make up for some of the harm she's done. If she doubles the two parts, we may, at least, prove that no one could really have mistaken her for La Lane."

"We are already all convinced of that," said Cockie. He was fed up with the lot of them. "Your proposal then is that you should run through the events of that afternoon, so as to demonstrate when and how and of course by whom the murder was committed?"

"To try to demonstrate it," said Leo, sullenly.

"Under the eyes of the two members of the Politio now guarding Mrs Rodd's every movement: and only too eager to dash off back to the Gerente with news of anything new."

They had forgotten the guards. "Oh, well—they won't understand what they hear and they probably won't know enough to be able to draw any reasonable conclusions from what they see."

"The Gerente is not interested in reasonable conclusions," said Cockie.

"The Gerente wants to get my wife into his filthy prison," said Leo, impatiently, "and if you can think of a better plan to find out the truth and keep her out of it, we'll try it. If you can't, we'll go ahead with this."

"Very well," said Cockie. But he did not like it. "On your heads be it." He gathered them all together on the verandah outside the line of rooms. "You will all do exactly what you did on that afternoon, timing it as nearly as you can. Miss Barker can play her own part up to the time she joined me on the lower terrace; after that, she was under my eye for the rest of the afternoon, so she can be counted out; and she can proceed up to Miss Lane's room and we'll act out the various theories. I'll walk through Miss Lane's part to the time she was last seen alive—which was at the top of the rock, going back to her room to lie down after her second dive." He added without humour that he would omit the actual diving, and further added that if they cared to include him with the suspects, which they were at liberty to do, it could all be acted over again later with someone else walking through Miss Lane's part. And having himself now wasted half an hour in vain argument, he adjured them all to stop hanging about and get a move on with their precious demonstration or the Odysseans would be back and the place cluttered up with people before they had even begun.

They went off to change.

It was half-past four. In the sky the sun was high, glittering down upon the curly blue-green tiles of the hotel roofs, on the long lines of the walls, studded like a dove-cot with rounded arches of windows and doorways, facing out over the sea. Behind the white buildings, the chill pines whispered together, mourning their lack of the colour and scent of the rose and geranium, the jasmine and myrtle, massed on the many-coloured, pebble-patterned terraces below: and it seemed to Inspector Cockrill, who on the whole is not given to fancies, that something of its cold breath struck through the windless heat of the afternoon. Despite his mistrust of the forthcoming performance, he found he could not stifle a rising excitement oddly at war with a sense of foreboding and dread. He wished he had fought harder against it, forbidden it altogether; but they would have acted without him anyway, and it was best that at least he should be there. As the minute hand of his watch touched the half hour, he took up his position at the rail of the balcony and called out, ungraciously: "All right. You can begin." The die was cast.

Helen Rodd had changed in her new room and walked along the inner corridor to join Leo, followed at a respectful distance by her guard. In obedience to the summons, they emerged, doll's-house figures walking out, mechanical and stiff, from a doll's-house door. She wore her neat, dark bathing dress, he carried the frogman's outfit and wore as usual a folded towel, thrown across his maimed shoulder. A little self-conscious, not speaking to one another, they crossed to the steps that led from the balcony to the terrace and went quietly down. He saw them turn left and pass under the bougainvillea creeper that roofed the terrace in, en route for the jasmine-covered steps leading down to the end of the lower terrace and the cabins at the top of the diving rock. Louvaine came out of number four.

"Right," said Cockie. "You came over to me and spoke." She crossed and stood before him in the red and white Bikini, swinging the gay red plastic bag. "You'd broken the strap of your bathing costume."

"Well, actually I'd split the bra part."

"I've wondered since—we've got time, you stopped a minute to speak to me—why you hadn't mended it before you left your room?"

"Well, it didn't split till after I came out. It must have just started, but I hadn't noticed it—then you said something when I was fiddling with it, and I gave a jerk and it started to really split. It was when you told me that Mrs Rodd had gone on with Leo."

"I see."

"I'd been hoping to catch him alone for a second, you see. Not for anything; we'd just had a sort of optimistic date. In those days, the chance of just one word . . ." She broke off sadly. "Well, so I'd better go on now?"

"All right," he said. She was terribly white; for once she wore no rouge and he was suddenly smitten with pity for her, pity and fear. He remembered that first meeting which now seemed so fantastically long ago, when she had clung to him, green to the gills, because the aeroplane was descending, had 'moulted all over him like a red setter . . .' As she turned, he said on an impulse: "You really intend to go on?"

She looked at him blankly. "Go on?"

"We could stop this whole business here and now."

"I don't think we could," she said. "We have to think of 'the life of the wife,' don't we?" And she gave him a smile, whose helplessness and hopelessness smote at his heartstrings. "But thank you." She went off down the steps and he saw again the flicker of the red and white suit, passing beneath the bougainvillea boughs.

Miss Trapp and Fernando had been peering out of their respective doors, awaiting their cue. They advanced, he in his orange satin trunks, she a near-Victorian figure, in saggy stockinette, and went on down the steps and along the terrace. Mr Cecil appeared in his turn and came and leaned with the Inspector on the rail. Under his reedy arm with its sunburned front and lily white back he carried the red attaché case. "What now?"

"I'll go into number five and come out as though I were Miss Lane. You must stay here and be yourself and me. I'll come over to you and we can stand here for a bit and then I'll go off down to the rock as she did, and you remain here. Watch carefully to see exactly what we saw from here when we looked down at the rock. Now—I'm Miss Lane."

He turned towards the closed door of number five; and the door of number five opened and Louvaine, who a moment before had passed out of sight beneath the bougainvillea boughs—stepped out of the room and walked quietly towards them.

Close cap, tight, satiny, blue-black bathing dress, black rubber beach shoes, roll of white towelling startling against the swallow-wing sheen of the black. Pale face, devoid of make-up. Hooded blue eyes. No touch of colour—none;

189

save for one red curl, escaped from the hard ridge of the black bathing cap, straying across the pale cheek. She put up her hand and pushed it back; and they saw the bright red of the painted nails. She came across to them.

Below them and to their left, Fernando and Miss Trapp emerged from the jasmine tunnel and out on to the lower terrace, where the Rodds stood silently with their guard, at the top of the rock. Inspector Cockrill said: "So bang go all the alibis, all the witnesses, all the rest of it. She was dead before any of you ever came out of your rooms?"

"Yes," said Louvaine. "She had been dead for an hour. She came to my room during the siesta time, to work. I killed her then."

Mr Cecil stood staring as though his pale eyes would start out from his ash-pale face. He stammered: "But how could ... You've just ... But Louvaine ..."

"Louvaine Barker's just passed you and gone on down the steps in a very, very small Bikini," said Louli. "I've got it on under this." She pulled aside the strap of her bathing dress and showed the gleam of white satin underneath. "Make-up off—just the lipstick really, you were so used to Louvaine being painted up that you wouldn't notice, you'd take it for granted she was made-up like a clown. Bathing cap over red hair. Rubber shoes over painted toenails." She gave a grotesque little bow. "Miss Vanda Lane."

"And hands curled up into fists," said Cockie, "while you talked to us here on the rail: to hide your manicure. Nail varnish, I take it, doesn't go on and off as easily as lipstick?"

"Not varnish," she said. "Long nails. To have them varnished would really have been too risky." She gave him a wry smile. "If you remember, Inspector, I applied the varnish as I sat at your feet later on!"

"So you did," agreed Cockie, equably. He did not appear immoderately surprised. "A quick change artist indeed!"

"I had it all ready. I simply went down the steps and in through the doors, which are always open, of the salons under the balcony, and nipped through into the main hall and up the stairs and so along the corridor to my room." She unrolled a corner of the white towel and they caught a glimpse of glossy red plastic. "I chucked all this into the bathing hut, the one next to where Louli Barker was supposed to be lurking—nobody'd seen her go in there, by the way, but I could say I'd slipped round unobtrusively because of my split brassiere. When I got back from the dive—everyone had gone on down to the beach by then, I'd seen to that—I went in and stripped off this black and was back in the Bikini. Slapped some lipstick on my face, stuffed all this wet stuff into the plastic bag, and dashed down to the beach to join in the jolly fun." She said to Inspector Cockrill: "I don't believe you're surprised?"

"No," said Cockie. "Not very."

"You mean you knew?"

"There was one fact," said Inspector Cockrill, "that didn't fit in; one brick that hadn't got a place in any other explanation I built up." He had placed the brick under their noses long ago, on the evening of the murder, when he had described the dead girl's bathing things, rolled up in the towel, slung across the verandah rail. "She was supposed to have just got back from a bathe and taken them off. Why should she have rolled them up in the towel, shoes and rubber cap and all? You hang out a wet bathing dress to dry, you don't roll it up." He had a sudden memory of Louvaine—leaning casually back on her elbows against the verandah rail while the rest clustered, with increasing anxiety, round the door of the room where the girl lay dead. "You put them there then?"

"Of course," said Louli. "You were all milling around the door. I fished them out of the bag, sort of behind my back, and just humped them over the rail. Nobody would notice; the rail was festooned with things hanging out to dry."

"*I* noticed," said Cockie, austerely. "These things were, in fact, not hanging out to dry."

There was a hail from the rock. Leo Rodd was waving to them and shouting. "We're getting behind-hand with the schedule," said Louli. "I'd better go on."

"Surely . . ." protested Cecil.

But she broke from his outflung hand and ran off down the steps and this time they watched her to the end of the terrace. "Let her go on with it," said Cockrill. "She is, 'not only letting justice be done, but letting it be seen to be done'—as long as it is seen by Leo Rodd. For that, I take it, is the object of this exercise."

"It's a strange way to go about winning back a man's love," said Mr Cecil.

"Not if you love him as she loves Leo Rodd," said Cockie, soberly. He thought it all over for a moment. "I think perhaps, though, we'd better go down to the rock. No use our staying here now. We've seen—what we were brought here to see."

Down the wooden steps, along the terrace past open doors leading into the great cool salons, down shallow steps tunnelled over with jasmine, out on to the far end of the lower of the two terraces, where the bathing huts clustered at the level of the top of the diving rock, with its path to the board. They watched the slender figure, unhurried, emerge from the cool darkness of the tunnel, into the sunlight; they saw the four startled faces suddenly blanching, the uncomprehending stares of the guard. Again there came into Mr Fernando's eyes the look that had come there when she had stood, hair pulled back, in the doorway of the little room; he burst into a Spanish gabble of imprecation or of prayer, which broke off abruptly as she walked quietly past him and up to Leo Rodd. The red curl had escaped again and was blown softly by the scented breeze across her white face. She brushed it away with the back of her hand and instantly it was blown forward again. She said to Leo Rodd: "So now you know it all."

It was terrible to see a man in such an agony of pain—of bewilderment and doubt and pain. He turned his head from side to side, away from the thought of it, from the knowledge of it, beads of sweat gathered on his forehead and trickled unheeded down his face. He kept saying, "Not that . . .! Not that . . .!"

She closed her blue eyes against the pain of witnessing his pain. "It was because of you, Leo. Both of us were in love with you; from the first moment we saw you, both of us were in love with you. We quarrelled, she threatened me, the knife was there . . ." He made a movement away from her. "Don't turn away from me, don't look at me as though you loathed me, Leo. It was because I love you: and because I love you, I'm doing this." She lifted her head and looked across at Helen, standing incredulous and appalled, a little apart from them. "I'm doing it to save *her*."

Miss Trapp's eyes were nearly falling out of her head. "She was dead there, dead in her room—and you—you staged this masquerade?"

"I took her place, that's all," said Louvaine, impatiently. She gave a wan smile. "After all, we'd both acted parts for most of our grown-up lives, we'd both lived in a sort of private-theatricals world of interchange; and as for the rest, fiction was our business, the whole thing unfolded itself as I went along like the plot of a story." She looked up, pleadingly, to Leo. "Well—the story's come to an end now, though I doubt that I shall 'live happy ever after'—if I live at all."

He did not speak. She turned away from him and now he moved swiftly, he caught her by the wrist. "For God's sake —where are you going, what are you going to do?"

She said wearily, "Well—just give myself up. What else? These men can take me, and then you can all get out of this horrible place and go home." She said to Helen: "The worst thing I did was accusing you, letting you suffer in my place. That really was the worst thing of all. But I won't let you suffer any more." And she lifted her head and went if possible a shade more pitifully pale. "There's the Gerente himself, up by the hotel. He's coming down here; so I can just tell him now."

The little cold wind sighed through the pine trees, the sea below them flickered and shimmered with a million, million, million dancing lights. Up on the terrace by the diving rock, nobody stirred. The uniformed figure was passing, blue cloak flying, under the twisted grey boughs, plunging down the tunnel of jasmine and the shallow steps. And Helen Rodd said suddenly: "Quick! In here!" and, seizing Louvaine by the forearm, thrust her into one of the bathing cabins and, crowding in after her, closed the door.

The Gerente, emerging from the jasmine tunnel, was met by an eager jabbering from the guard. "They can't make it out," said Fernando, uncertainly translating. "They say we all started off to bathe and then stood and talked instead. They say we all seemed much upset. They say the two ladies have just bolted into the cabina, apparently at sight of him." The Gerente spoke and he added unhappily: "He now asks why."

"Tell him. . . . Tell him," said Leo, inspired, "that it was Miss Barker who took my wife there. Tell him that my wife was—was naturally afraid that he had come to arrest her."

Miss Trapp was distressed and uncertain. "Is this right? What would Mrs Rodd feel?"

"Mrs Rodd has just deliberately saved Miss Barker from being arrested," said Inspector Cockrill. "If *she* can do that, we had better just try to follow her lead."

"But if he really has come to arrest Mrs Rodd . . .?"

"If he has, we can reconsider the matter," said Cockie.

Fernando translated. The Gerente, terribly frowning, spoke at some length. "He says . . . He demands to know what is going on. Why are we pale and anxious-looking, why has Miss Barker been speaking strangely to Mr Rodd, why have we all changed into bathing things and come down here to the diving rock? Why have none of us dived?"

"We didn't come to dive," said Leo. "Just to bathe."

"He says that if we want to bathe, the way to the beach is down the central steps. He says this is the place where the girl was last seen alive. He says again, what is going on, if we came here to dive, why haven't we dived?"

"Tell him to mind his own bloody business," said Leo. "Why the hell should we dive if we don't want to? We don't like diving, we don't want to dive, none of us *can* dive; we just like this way to the beach, that's all, we've got a Thing against the central steps."

"He says again then, what were we speaking of, what is going on? He says," stammered Fernando wretchedly, "that if he gets no explanation, he will arrest Mrs Rodd this moment and take her back to gaol."

The door of the little cabin opened and Helen Rodd came out; and, clad in the poppy-starred white Bikini, red hair blazing, white face painted to a travesty at least of the gay, painted face of other days—Louvaine followed her and stood with smiling mouth and unsmiling eyes, blinking at the Gerente in the sun. Leo took one step towards them. He stammered: "Louvaine . . ." and then broke off. He said to Helen: "I will love you and thank you for ever—for doing this to save Louvaine."

The Gerente looked at the guards and looked at Louvaine and looked at Helen: ominously. Inspector Cockrill moved forward. He held up his small brown, nicotined-stained hand for silence. He said quietly: "Mr Fernando—tell the Gerente that the guards have misunderstood. We've all been talking about the murder, naturally; we've all been discussing ways and means, making up theories, making up stories to fit with our theories. As for Miss Barker and Mr Rodd—Miss Barker has been telling Mr Rodd a story and naturally, she being a writer of fiction, her story has been the best of all. And as to the diving—what Mr Rodd says is true: none of us can dive. It just so happens that none of us here can dive. I can't, Mr Cecil can't, you yourself can't, or anyway you don't. Mr Rodd can't because of his arm, Mrs Rodd can't because she dislikes it, Miss Trapp can't because she can't swim. And Miss Barker can't—Miss Barker least of all. Miss Lane could: Miss Lane could run out along a razor-backed ridge high over the sea, she could stand teetering at the tip of a diving board, twenty-five feet up. But Miss Barker can't." And he plucked an imaginary auburn hair from the sleeve of his jacket. "One thing one literally cannot control," said Inspector Cockrill, "is a horror of heights. And I happen to know that Miss Louvaine Barker has an almost pathological horror of heights."

But Miss Louvaine Barker was already lying in a dead faint at the feet of Leo Rodd.

CHAPTER THIRTEEN

MR CECIL assisted at the ritual of Louli's return to consciousness and life. She had been carried up to her room and there laid, propped against white pillows, on the four-poster bed. He trotted between bed and dressing-table, laden with pots and bottles and mirrors and powder puffs and bursting with expert advice. "A thorough good strip down with the cleansing cream, ducky, there's nothing like it after a scene: and then lots and lots and lots of astringent lotion patted well in, we don't want crows' feet by the time we're thirty, dear, *do* we?" She was so right always to wear huge hats. "Honestly, one was mad, my dear, ever to have come to this terrible climate, ruination to the skin, we shall all look like alligators by the time it's over, I wouldn't be surprised." And talking about being surprised, he added, honestly one had been utterly, but utterly boulversé'd by all this business about the heights. . . .

"Me too," said Louli, ruefully.

"But had you forgotten?"

"No, I just thought I never would get to the diving. I thought I'd appear before you all and you'd say, 'Oh, that's how it was done?' and it would never occur to anyone that I couldn't have gone on and dived, to save my life. Because of course, that's true—I've got this Thing, I just can't bear heights."

"*If* that's true," said Cecil, cautiously.

197

She laughed. "Oh, it's true enough. I mean, old Cockrill saw me on the 'plane."

And it was true. He too had seen for himself how green she had gone—she had been all right while they were flying at height, when there had been nothing to suggest, as it were, a drop; but as they descended, as the little houses and fields came up to meet them, she had shuddered and turned pale, her hands had shaken as she clung to the little man. You couldn't counterfeit that, and anyway, why should she have done so? She could have had no intention then of murdering her cousin, neither of them had yet had time— surely?—to fall in love with Leo Rodd; nor, supposing the remote likelihood of an earlier motive, of a preconceived plan, could she have anticipated the lay-out at the hotel, the open salon doors leading into the hall and stairs, the cabins at the diving rock, the diving board? Unless of course . . . "You didn't know this place before?" he said casually.

She laughed. "No, no. Never even been into Italy. You can see from my passport. Doubting Thomas!" she added.

All the same, he thought, the whole masquerade had fitted in with the facts remarkably snugly. He passed her the mascara brush. "Just a weeny bit *up* at the ends of the eyebrows, ducky, yes, that's wonderful, too Après Midi d'un Faune for any!" He looked into the hand mirror; a touch of Après Midi wouldn't do his own face any harm either, and he applied it with little expert sweeps of the brush. "Quite too perfect, we look like a couple of dear little Bambis, all wide-eyed wonder, just out of the wood."

"Are we out of the wood?" said Louli.

"You are. I mean, I do think this fabrication of yours does utterly blow up over the diving business. After all, having this Thing, you wouldn't ever have learnt to dive, would you? So even if you'd conquered it for the moment and driven yourself to go out along the board—well, one can't just hold one's nose and jump off that sort of height, can one? One comes a belly-flopper and it does one no good at all, and the thing is that *nobody* mistakes one for La Lane, who was quite too terrific." But the eyebrows would not do, alas, and he dabbed them off with spit on a piece of cotton wool. Some of his sun-tan came too. "My dear, I look quite leprous, Max Factor pancake this *min*ute, where can I find it?" Somewhat to her horror, he rubbed the cotton wool on the surface of the pancake. "But what I want to know is, what were you going to do next?"

"I've told you," said Louli. "I was going to give myself up. You see, I thought . . ." She looked down at her hands and Cecil saw that they were actually trembling. "I thought Leo hated me—because of what I'd said about Helen, getting her into all this trouble and danger. I thought it had made him realize that it was really her he loved. And if that was so, I simply didn't care what happened to me, I thought I might at least reinstate myself in his eyes by giving myself up to save her."

"Greater love hath no man than this," said Cecil, "that he lay down his life for his friend—to impress someone else." He suggested delicately that, anyway, it had worked and without going to all those lengths either.

"I'd got it all wrong," she said. "He was angry with me, yes—but that's different, that's not hating. And he was sorry for her and anxious about her—but that's not loving. You heard what he said—after she'd hidden me from the Gerente in my Vanda Lane get-up: he said, 'I'll thank you for ever—for doing this for Louvaine. For *Louvaine*." She closed her lids over the blue blaze of her eyes. "You'll never know, nobody will ever know, what those words meant to me."

"So you decided not to go on with the act?"

She shrugged against the white pillows. "Inspector

Cockrill decided for me. I was flat out by then. But I couldn't go on with it: he'd shown it was all a nonsense—which it was."

"Was it?" said Doubting Thomas.

She couldn't help laughing. "No use hoping, ducky! I know it would be more exciting if it could be true, but I'm afraid Mum's Out. I can't dive and I couldn't have dived: but that day she died, Vanda executed two beautiful dives." She acknowledged that for the rest it had all fitted in absurdly well. It had been like planning a story in the old days, with poor Vanda. "You settle on the main plot, what the book's about; and having done so, you usually find that you're stuck with certain 'constants' and you have to weave your story so as to take those constants in. In my case, the main plot was simply that I look like Vanda and I could have impersonated her. The constants were things like the lay-out of the hotel, the timing, that thing about the rolled-up bathing towel and so forth. I had to work them all in and it was really almost exciting if it hadn't been so horrible and frightening, to find how it all fell into place. I mean, what a bit of luck, for instance, that Vanda wore bathing shoes. And that business about her clenching her hands on the rail: I couldn't know that, I just relied on taking off the varnish and hoping you wouldn't see that my nails were long while hers were always short." She laughed again. "And meanwhile, clever old Inspector Cockrill had had it worked out, and discarded it, long ago. I wonder how he's feeling about it now?"

Inspector Cockrill in fact was feeling exceedingly relieved in his mind—or in his heart, rather, for his brain, he admitted crossly to himself, had little to do with it—at the escape of his pet from the noose which her own folly had set for herself: from that dark threat which in his anxiety for her, he had permitted to overhang his heart at the initiation of her experiment. It was better to let it go through, he said to himself; she had to do her piece for him, and I could always save her in the end. Why he should care about it all, he hardly knew; like Leo himself, he found her nowadays often only tiresome and silly and ill-behaved and certainly her accusation of Helen, however much the outcome of shock and hysteria, had been an unendearing episode. And yet— he looked back upon the line of pretty girls who, in his crabbed old age, had made his own arid heart beat for a little while a little more warmly: and thought that of them all, not least had been Louvaine—Louvaine as she had been in those first few sunny days, so gay and so honest, so hopelessly lost in love.

Meanwhile, however . . .

Leo Rodd came out of the hotel and across the terrace to his table and pulled up one of the scrubbed wooden chairs and sat down. He sent a waiter scurrying for a Bitter Campari and when the man had gone, hit the table with a triumphant hand and said, "Yes. You were right. Bills everywhere."

Cockie sipped calmly at his Juanello. "Has he paid now?"

"Not yet," said Leo. "But promised—and with chapter and verse, apparently, they're all quite satisfied. Camillo— that's this new guide who's brought on his party from Venice —passed through Florence and Siena and they were full of it. I rang up Rapallo and the Flora in Rome, and by a miracle somehow got through. Odyssey Tours have never stayed at the Flora before, but we were booked in there as you know. He owes at the two hotels I rang up in Rapallo and everywhere in Siena—you remember that ghastly albergo in Siena?"

The waiter came scooting back with the Bitter Campari, scooped up his money and departed at his own more accustomed stroll. Leo said eagerly, "How did you guess?"

"I don't guess," said Cockie, irritably. "I deduce. We'd been promised in the prospectus, 'first-class hotels.' Well, that means good second-class—we all know that. But what did we get? We got tip-top luxury in Rapallo, we got the lowest kind of pension in Siena, we were due for tip-top class again in Rome. So there was some reason why he couldn't take us to the intermediate ones and one good reason could be that he hadn't paid his bills there on previous tours. He's been using Odyssey funds for his own purposes."

"Would the hotels give him credit?"

"I suppose so. Odyssey's a big firm, they'd know that they'd get their money in the end and there must be lots of reasonable excuses for a courier not paying on the nail—money not arrived from England, that kind of thing. An awful lot of fiddling goes on no doubt, with currency; he'd spin some yarn."

"And of course he's actually a director; or so I believe."

"Do you indeed?" said Cockie, with ferocious pity.

"Well, isn't he?"

"All talk. He's a courier, my dear fellow, no more, no less. Mind you, these chaps have responsibility—they handle a lot of money, thirty or forty people travelling through the continent for two or three weeks, that costs money; and then no sooner have they got rid of one lot than they pick up another. Fernando's probably been this way several times already this season. And he'd have a lot of freedom too, with the arrangements—bookings and so on, why arrange it from England when you've got people actually on the spot . . .?"

The new courier appeared upon the terrace and sat down rather furtively all by himself, only to be besieged a moment later by his eager flock. It was pitiful to see the interested smile switched on, the listening ear inclined to recitals of Mrs A's pleasure in this afternoon's excursion, Mrs B's dissatisfaction with it, Mrs C's loss of a bracelet of exclusively sentimental value and her evident confidence that he would rush off forthwith and comb the unsavoury streets of Barrequitas for it; to watch the guarded skirmishings to avoid a jolly old glass of Jewanello with Mr D in favour of Hoowarne-ellyo with refined Miss E. Leo Rodd said—reluctantly, for hope was rising within him like yeast and he was loath to pick holes in a case which might even yet shift the load of suspicion from Helen: "Wouldn't the hotels confide in the courier who followed him on these trips?"

"I don't suppose couriers do follow each other. This would be Fernando's beat, the others would be conducting tours taking in other places. This business has thrown them all out, probably Camillo would never have come through Siena and Florence otherwise, they've had to reorganize because of Fernando being out of commission."

"Yes, of course," said Leo. He sat twiddling his glass in his one hand and tried not to be glad that suspicion was shifting to Fernando, who after all was a good enough fellow, a rogue if you liked, but a cheerful, well-meaning rogue. And yet—there was Miss Trapp; that didn't seem quite so well-meaning and jolly. "I'm sorry for the old girl," he said.

"Foolish woman. He's obviously getting money out of her."

"Yes. Hence the promises to the hotels."

"They didn't say what form the promises took?"

Leo laughed. "No. They were startlingly frank about the rest, but they got a bit cagey at that stage: both to

Camillo apparently from what he's just told me, and to me on the telephone. I dare say they think it's coming from illegal sources and the less they know about it at this stage the better."

"She couldn't have got money from England so soon."

"If at all, surely?"

"If at all." He sat musing for a little while. "Unless, of course—I wonder what's the position if she marries him?"

"Oh, good God—no!" protested Leo, as only a little while earlier, Helen had said before him.

"He comes from Gibraltar," said Cockrill. "That's a sterling area. Easy enough for him to bring it over from there. You convert it into Gibraltar pounds and then buy pesetas and then, I suppose, buy lire with the pesetas."

Leo was not interested in the economics of Mr Fernando's jugglings with the existing currency regulations. The thing is—how does this affect the murder? I mean, surely it must?"

"It might well affect the blackmail business," said Cockie.

"Well, of course. She could threaten to expose him to the company. You've never been able to get hold of the book?"

"No," said Cockie. He, Inspector Cockrill of Scotalanda Yarrda had asked in vain for a look at the bloodstained book; it was a sore point.

"Or she could threaten to expose him to Miss Trapp. Only how could she have known?—La Lane, I mean."

"She was observant," said Cockie. "It was her job to be—like mine: and after all, *I* knew. And she was a student of human nature."

"*And* she was a goddam bitch."

"She had a cruel streak. She didn't need the money and, in fact, she never asked for any. She just liked torturing people, that was all."

"Louvaine—though she was her cousin—had no idea of it."

"Miss Lane would hardly be proud of it, I suppose."

"Of course Louli knew that she kept books of notes: she thought they were just for people, to base characters on and so forth. She nearly passed out when the Gerente produced that one."

"She behaved very foolishly—and worse than foolishly—in not telling me at once the true state of affairs."

"Yes, of course," said Leo. He deflected this uncomfortable offshoot of the conversation. "If Miss Trapp had promised Fernando money . . ."

"We don't know that she had," said Cockie. "Only that he expected to get it. In either case, she doubtless won't have known what it was for." He pinched out the untidy end of his cigarette and pitched the butt over the balustrade into the oleander bushes below. "He was certainly ripe for blackmail. If marriage was really in the air, he had a lot more to lose than just his job."

"It does constitute quite a hefty motive for murder?" suggested Leo, deprecatingly, fighting down the optimism rising again within him. "The only thing is—how? We now know for certain that it really was Vanda Lane who came out alive and dived and went back to her room that afternoon, don't we? Or don't we?"

"Yes," said Cockie. "I think we do."

"I mean, I was a fool ever to doubt it for a second, even without having had time to reason. You see—I *know* it was La Lane diving. I saw her dive at Rapallo. She was magnificent, Louli would have had to be exhibition standard to have copied her; but what's more to the point, she had a certain style, sort of mannerisms—I'd recognize her just as I'd recognize a batsman or a bowler or a runner."

"All right, all right," said Cockie, "I know, I'm convinced, I knew it long before you did. That was Vanda Lane diving; so, definitely, she was still alive at half-past four that afternoon, when we all gathered on the beach to bathe. She was murdered between that time, and the time she was found in her room. But as for Fernando . . ." He sat leaning forward in his chair, his knees apart, his hands between them, looking down, rolling a new cigarette; and shook his grey head. "I just don't see how the chap could have done it. He makes a great play about swimming but he can't swim really: it was all he could do to go porpoising out to the raft and he could no more have swum back without attracting attention than he could have flown. And he'd have to do it there and back. As for under water . . ."

"I asked Camillo that too," said Leo. "Not letting on, of course, just casual chat about Fernando, following on the revelations—about which he's in a great state of pleasurable excitement—regarding the hotels. He says Fernando's a bit of a joke at the swimming club, can't swim for toffee, let alone under water; and you can't learn that sort of thing all in a day, it's true. I suppose he *was* on the raft?"

"Oh, yes, he was on the raft," said Cockie. "I watched him go out there, splashing and gasping and I saw him there, on and off when I glanced up from my book; and when we all started moving in, I watched him swim back. And in the interval—the woman was murdered." He licked the edge of the cigarette paper and gummed it down with neat, accustomed fingers. "*I* don't know."

Hope died a little in Leo Rodd's heart. "I can't pretend, Inspector, that I wouldn't—well, rather have it this way." He thought it all over. "There's only one other curious thing—if it amounts to anything. Both times that Louvaine's appeared in the Vanda Lane transformation—the only person who's really been deceived, has been Fernando. I noticed both times. He went an awful colour and muttered and crossed himself, or whatever it is these heathens do."

"I noticed it too," said Cockie. He shrugged. "Superstition, probably."

"Or a bad conscience," said Leo; and once again could not keep the rising optimism out of his voice.

For the hours were passing by, passing by: and with every moment, the time crept nearer when the great hand would stretch out over the chessboard of their little lives and gather up the chosen pawn, the randomly-chosen pawn, and with one great sweep tumble the rest of them, helpless, out of the way. Leo craving audience with the Old Wykhamist pal, received in return an ominous invitation for the party to see over the Grand Ducal palace the following afternoon. They had missed it on an earlier occasion, suggested the El Exaltida's message, delicately, and no doubt would like to remedy the omission *before their early departure the following morning.* A car, by the way, had been laid on to take them from Piombino to the airfield, the vaporetto leaving at 8.15 a.m. would probably suit them best. If, during their visit to the palatio, he found himself at liberty, said the Grand Duke, he would send a messenger for Mr Rodd; if, as unfortunately was probable, he was too much occupied, he must content himself with making his adieux herewith, trusting that *such of the party as were leaving* would have a pleasant and uneventful journey. It was evident that the public school veneer, though restored, was spread very thinly across the volcano within.

They all sat uneasily at dinner under the bougainvillea and the swinging lanterns, wretchedly toying with the savoury mess of rice and pimento, artichoke and olive, heaped on the plates before them. "I don't think we should go near this terrible palace . . ."

"But, ducky, if we don't and he sends for Mr Rodd, he'll be so *cross*."

"I could go alone," said Leo.

"No, Leo, don't!" said Helen, but she cut it off short and amended indifferently: "Well—perhaps."

"Suppose he sends for *Mrs* Rodd," said Miss Trapp. She looked about her, into their faces, cold with fear and dread. "I think we should speak of it outright. We haven't got much more time. Suppose while we are at the palace to-morrow, he sends for Mrs Rodd."

"It won't make any difference where I am," said Helen. "If they want me, they've only to make me come. Here at the hotel or anywhere. If I was at the palace, anyway I might get a chance to see him and talk to him—he must be more rational than the Gerente. If they make me go straight to the prison, I'm nothing to him, just an impersonal speck of dust to be got rid of." She spoke very calmly but her voice shook. "I don't see anything to be gained by not going to the palace."

Mr Cecil was of opinion that they should all make a mad dash for it away from San Juan altogether. "That has been considered," said Cockie. "It won't work. Mrs Rodd is guarded day and night by two men; even if we could get rid of them, we'd have to get away from Barrequitas by boat, and even then we'd only get to Italy and Italy would quite certainly pack us straight back again." He had given it far more serious thought than appeared from the way he spoke; but he knew that to fail in an escape plan would make their last case far, far worse than their first. He voiced for the first time an intention which he thought it might not be easy to put across. "Not only must we not try to get away to-day—but we must not get away at all." He said to Helen: "You needn't think that we shall all go off and leave you here."

"But we've got orders to go," said Mr Cecil, paling.

"We aren't going."

"But I mean, they'll *send* us, ducky . . ."

Inspector Cockrill did not care for being called ducky by Mr Cecil. In revenge he, for the first time, included him in the proposal. "You and I and Mr Fernando, and Mr Rodd of course, are staying here on the island. The ladies, perhaps, had better go; but the men will stay. All the men."

"Of course," said Mr Fernando, bowing gallantly to Helen; but his soft brown eyes filled with tears of apprehension as he looked at Miss Trapp.

"I should not dream of going," said Miss Trapp.

"Of course not," said Louli. "After all, we've paid! Odyssey would never refund the money, we must simply work it off in San Juan."

"But, Louli . . ." Mr Cecil wrung his white hands at this wholesale defection. "But, Inspector . . . But one's *got* to get back, my dears. . . ." He brushed back the golden forelock and threw out a shapely hand to Helen. "You *will* understand, my dear, how one longs, but longs, to stay on and sympathize, buns through the bars, and the lute played quite ceaselessly outside the little cell window; but there *is* the business to consider, so much hanging on one, and after all, dear, buns aside, what actually could one *do*?" And what was more, he added, calming down, if that wicked old Exaltida didn't want them on his island, he'd surely have ways of simply making them go? "They just wouldn't keep us in the hotel. So then?"

"It's nice and warm," said Cockrill. "We can sleep in the pinewoods. But it won't come to that. They're within their rights in keeping—one of us—as a hostage if they can really pretend to think they're the guilty party; but they'd make themselves unpopular among the British tourists if they used force to make us go, and that wouldn't be good for business —as Mr Cecil would say."

"I don't see what good you can do by staying," said Helen steadily. "The Grand Duke has said that you must all go by day after to-morrow, yes; but he's also said that by day after to-morrow I must be in custody with a good case cooked up against me. Whatever is happening to all of you, it won't stop that happening to me. And once I'm there . . ." And she burst out suddenly that the minutes were passing and there they all sat eating and drinking and not being able to *do* anything: and that once she was there in that ghastly place, they would all be helpless wherever they were, in England, in San Juan, it wouldn't matter, they could kill her, they probably would kill her, and nobody would even know. . . .

Miss Trapp sat silent, watching her: the caged and the free. For she, Miss Trapp, was free. In thirty-six hours she could leave this place, could go away to where these hideous things did not happen, could there in quietness and peace, await the new happiness that was to come into her life. To be needed—she had said to Helen Rodd that only to be needed was happiness to her, was happiness enough. And now she was needed. Fernando might turn anxious eyes to Miss Trapp at the perils of separation, but Miss Trapp knew that it held no perils for her: as soon as he might, he would follow her—because he had need of her. The knowledge was very sweet to her; and to keep it safe, she had only to go away from this island, as she was free to do, and embroil herself no more in all this uncertainty and dread. It is my first, my only chance of happiness, she thought: the only happiness I have ever known. To keep it safe, I have only to keep silent now.

And she looked into Helen Rodd's face, sick with a sort of dry-eyed desperation, and said deliberately:

"I think there *is* something, after all, that we could do."

The waiters had cleared the half-empty places, had put little bowls of wild strawberries, with bottles of the thick, sweet raisin wine to be poured over them, and pots of sour white cream. Their table was in a corner of the terrace, away from the curious eyes and ears of the other guests. She pushed aside her bowl and leaned forward, her elbows on the table, her thin hands cupped about her plain face. "I think," said Miss Trapp, "that we must all stop trying to seem innocent: and all try to seem guilty."

Mr Cecil had never heard, but never heard, of a more repellent idea. "Just try to be quiet for a moment," she said to him as though speaking to a child. She went on: "The Inspector used a phrase just now: he said these people wanted 'someone they could pretend to think was guilty.' I think we should all make it impossible for them even to pretend to think that any one person is guilty."

"You mean we should all con*fess?*"

"Not all confess," said Miss Trapp. "That would make the whole thing ridiculous."

"Unless," said Louli, "we could confess to a sort of mass slaying, I mean not a mass of people being slain by one person, but one person being slain by a mass. *You* know—there was some hold she had over all of us so we banded together . . ." She slapped her hands down suddenly upon the table. "And there was some hold she had over all of us. The blackmail book!"

There was some magic in Miss Trapp this evening, that they should all turn respectful eyes to her, to await her reaction to this proposition. "If we all confessed, we should all be thrown into prison," said Miss Trapp, "and seven people would suffer instead of one. We must not confess about ourselves—we must accuse one another. But the blackmail book . . ." She broke off. She took her hands away from her face, they began their automatic groping for the handles of the brown bag. "We must help build up cases against ourselves," she said. "We must each tell what there was against us, in the blackmail book."

The blackmail book had remained with the Gerente and not all Inspector Cockrill's efforts had induced him to part with it even for an hour. He retained, regarding it, a passionate curiosity, that curious, curious, blackmail book with its jottings about each one of them and at the end of each page a figure ringed in ink. He knew what was written on his own page—that page now flecked with its tadpole shapes of dried blood. That he was a Det. Inspec., that he was small of stature, that he looked like an English country sparrow that had somehow got into the blaring sunshine of Abroad, the more absurd because he had tried to adjust his plumage, poor ruffled little brown bird. Etcetera, etcetera. Nothing surely, worthy of blackmail in that?—and yet, at the foot of the page, had been written £50, ringed about. He said, smiling: "I can only suppose that Miss Lane thought I was only masquerading as a policeman: I think her suggestion in the book is that I'm not tall enough, that I'm not the regulation height. In fact, I'm five foot eight, which is the minimum, but I stoop badly and I lose a lot that way." He thought it necessary to add that she had also said that he looked like a sparrow, mumbled when he talked and had floating false teeth. "Anyway, they have a case against me, because the book is known to have been turned on the table to face the murderer, and open at my page. I don't know what it's supposed to indicate, but after all they did take me into custody and they've never actually said they were satisfied that I didn't do it."

"And there's a case against me," said Louli. "We can always tell them about the impersonation—I could even do my act for them again. We needn't mention the business about the diving."

"We can't use that," said Cecil. "Without the diving thing, it's much too convincing."

"Well, not tell them about that till the last minute."

"In face of all this magnanimity," said Leo, "it's humiliating for me to have to face the fact that there's no case against *me*. Nothing against me in the book, and only the one bloody hand to have done the deed with. Of course we could always cook up the Grand Duke's suicide thing again, with me as the villain behind the scenes."

Fernando sat with his heavy ringed hands drumming nervously on the table edge. "For me it is, alas, proved that I cannot have swum from the raft. So no use to confide what was in the book. If anything was in the book," he added and shrugged enormously. "As to this—who can say?"

"Well, as to this, the Inspector and I can say," said Leo, cheerfully. "We could rake up a case against *you*, old boy, don't worry." He explained to the others: "After all, it's not watertight stuff we want, not real cases—only a lot of suspicions that will confuse the issue, as good as the case against Helen anyway." He looked expectantly at Mr Cecil.

Mr Cecil's strawberries lay untouched before him, the lanterns gently swinging threw splashes of light and shadow across his pale face. "What, my turn? Well, actually, my dears, madly eager, of course, to join in, but what is one to say? I mean, there one was in one's rubber duck, paddling up and down, fast asleep most of the time and cooking to a *turn;* but *not* up in the hotel murdering that poor harmless Lane."

"Harmless?" said Cockrill.

"Well, harmless to me."

"Not according to the blackmail book. There was some reference to your 'work'; and the sum to be demanded was a hundred pounds."

"It never was demanded, that's all I can say."

"No," said Inspector Cockrill. "She was killed instead."

"Not by me," said Mr Cecil shrilly. His shirt this evening was of lavender silk to tone with his lavender flannels and he wore a coloured hankie tied round his neck like a cowboy's, the knot to one side. It was all very chic: and yet, thought Cockrill, beadily watching him, if the knot had been only a bit further back it would have come where another knot comes, just behind the ear—the knot of a noose. And of them all, he reflected, the world could perhaps best spare Mr Cecil. Leo Rodd, Helen Rodd, Louvaine —they had their faults no doubt, but they were people, real people with hearts and minds to think and feel. Fernando, no doubt, was a rogue, but as Leo Rodd had said a cheerful rogue; and as for Miss Trapp—Miss Trapp to-night was lit with a sort of glory, she took in her ugly hands not just the burden of life but the promise of happiness never before enjoyed—and laid it down for a friend. And not merely 'to impress someone else,' either. "Perhaps we need not trouble Mr Cecil," said Miss Trapp with kindly pity, "as he is not quite willing to add his mite. It's true that Mr Cecil could not have killed Miss Lane. He was in the rubber boat and he was within our sight, or the Inspector's sight, for most of the time. The Inspector may have missed him perhaps for some little while, ten minutes, Inspector?—or even twenty? But surely not as long as an hour? And, Inspector, you will correct me if I am wrong in suggesting that it must have taken at least an hour to do—all that was done—up in that room that day?"

Cockie thought it over as he had so often done before: the preceding interview, the actual killing, the arrangement of the dead girl on the bed, the washing of the room, the cleansing in the little bathroom. "If not an hour, the best part of an hour," he agreed. "Say three-quarters."

"Well, I couldn't possibly have been gone all that time without your noticing it."

"No," said Cockrill reluctantly. "I don't think you could."

"So there!" said Mr Cecil triumphantly.

"So we will leave Mr Cecil out," continued Miss Trapp blandly. "Each of us has some sort of accusation that can be made against him by another party—later contradicted, perhaps, proved untrue: but enough to unsettle the case against Mrs Rodd, and enough to force them to keep us here on the island while it is sorted out. All except Mr Cecil. We'll leave him out."

"You seem to be leaving yourself out too," said Mr Cecil. He pushed back the lank hair, he bent forward across the big table, his face narrowed down by the lantern shadows to a sort of pale wedge, his lips curled back from his slightly prominent front teeth. He looks like a rat, thought Cockrill: and like a rat cornered, he struck back viciously for his life. "*You* were being blackmailed, Miss Trapp, what about 'the turn of the tide,' eh, what about that? And what about the book? You, Fernando, you know what there was in the book about her, the Gerente read it out to you."

"Yes," said Fernando. "I know what was in the book."

"Fifty pounds she was going to get out of you, Miss Trapp, fifty pounds . . ."

"Rather a small sum to demand," said Inspector Cockrill, "from one so rich."

Miss Trapp began to speak. Fernando put out his big hand and caught at hers. "Say nothing!"

"Perhaps what she was blackmailing Miss Trapp about wasn't worth more than fifty pounds."

"Then it wasn't worth murder," suggested Inspector Cockrill.

"Miss Lane may not have realized how much Mr Fernando's attentions meant to Miss Trapp."

"But nothing Miss Lane could tell Mr Fernando would alter his attentions. Mr Fernando already knew whatever the secret is."

"He knows now," said Cecil. "Because he saw it in the blackmail book. But he didn't know till after she was killed." The rat face swung round upon Miss Trapp. "You could have gone up to her room and killed her. You were there in your idiotic tent, you could have crept out and up the little path where the rock joins the rise of the land, the terraces; and up the jasmine steps to the hotel. Why," he cried excitedly, "why have we lost sight of this, why haven't we thought of it before? She could have done it, she could have done it easily. All she needs is a motive, and the motive's there."

"To prevent me from knowing this secret?" said Mr Fernando.

"It meant a lot to her," said Cecil. In face of their stony unresponse, the excitement died out of him a little, the lantern swung in the breeze and its shadows swung with it, leaving the narrowed face wedge-shaped and rat-like no longer, but only rather mean, rather cowardly, a little ashamed. "We are all supposed to be making up cases against each other. It was you that suggested it, Miss Trapp." He forced a tinkle of deprecatory laughter. "Well, this is my case against you!"

"It's a very good case," said Miss Trapp. She looked round the table into their watching eyes, eyes that had been so kind, so grateful, so appreciative, so suddenly friendly— now gone wary. "An almost perfect case."

"It might be," said Fernando. "But I knew already the secret. Long before the blackmail book appeared, I knew it. So there is no case at all."

"*If* you knew it," said Cecil.

Helen Rodd leaned forward across the table. "Miss Trapp

—you started all this to save me. Couldn't you—couldn't you somehow prove that Mr Fernando knew? Do think, do try and tell us something that will prove it. *I* believe you. If you could just convince these others . . ."

"Yes," said Fernando. "You're right. We must prove it." And suddenly he lifted his head. "Mrs Rodd—you are the very person. You can prove it yourself." He shot out a hand across the table and caught at her hand, clutching it so that his rings bit hard into the bone of her thin fingers. "In Siena—that evening, in Siena, try to remember, Mrs Rodd. You walked round by the Duomo, Miss Trapp and I were sitting there by the wall, looking at the old Duomo with its striped leg stuck up in the air. You passed us there, Mrs Rodd, you said, 'Good evening,' we said 'Good evening,' but perhaps not attending very much; for at that moment, Miss Trapp took something from her handbag and passed it over to me. A letter. You saw that letter, Mrs Rodd?"

"In Siena? Up by the cathedral . . .? Oh, well, yes, I remember seeing you there," said Helen, uncertainly. "But a letter . . ." She was silent. "Yes, I do remember now. You were leaning against the wall and Miss Trapp had her handbag open. I think—yes, I think I do remember that there was something white in her hand."

"The envelope. She passed the envelope to me."

"Yes, she passed it to you. It was a little dark," said Helen to the others, intently listening, "but it could well have been an envelope I saw."

Fernando released her hand. "I thank you, señora." He gave her one of his florid bows, but his brown eyes were filled with those foolish tears that came so easily and might mean so little and on this occasion at least, meant so much. "My dear," he said to Miss Trapp, very gently, "I think now you show these ladies and gentlemen the envelope?"

"Yes," said Miss Trapp. She took it out of the handbag

and held it in her hand—the good white envelope with the crest embossed on its flap. "We had been talking about—about friendship," she said. "I said that the tragedy of being rich is that one does not know who one's true friends are. I knew, because I had lost a friend that way—several friends, indeed, in the course of my life. While I spoke, I was clutching my bag—it is a habit of mine I know, a very bad habit. He asked me what was in my bag that made me hug it so closely, and I told him that it held the most precious possession I had. And then, suddenly, in view of our late conversation, I decided to show my treasure to him. This was my secret which, thanks to Mrs Rodd, you now know was no secret from him: no matter for blackmail and murder, anyway!" And she took out the white sheet of crested writing paper and spread out the few lines before them. It was headed with a Park Lane address.

Lady Bale herewith confirms that Miss Edith Trapp has been for the past seven years her companion help. . . .

CHAPTER FOURTEEN

THE last day. The last hours of their last day on the island of San Juan el Pirata. Perched on the rocky spire of the island, the many-fountained patios of the white palace, fretted to a lacework of marble, dreamed in the sunshine, the cypresses brooded, dark and melancholy, over the pink-starred blue satin of the water-lily pools; and through the courts and the scented gardens they wandered, unhappy and ill at ease, seven heart-sick people, conscious that time was slipping away, slipping away, that nothing was being done and that all too soon it would be too late.

Leo Rodd walked with his wife, restless and unhappy. If only I could see him. . . . Why doesn't he send for me. . . .? He said at last: "I'll go up to the patio where his office is, I'll see if I can't intercept him somehow—this doing nothing is more than I can bear." He walked off, a sombre figure among the massed bright flowers, in flannels and dark-blue blazer, the right sleeve pinned up flat to be out of his way. She looked after him with grey foreboding; but whether for herself or for him, she was too dazed with sorrow and dread combined to know.

Miss Trapp caught up with her. "Dear Mrs Rodd—once again I intrude upon your solitude."

"That's all right, Miss Trapp," said Helen listlessly.

"I left the others, to say a word to you. Just to thank you—for what you did last night."

She gave a bleak smile. "It was the least I could do to repay you for being such a champion of my rights."

"Of course it is true that Mr Fernando did see the letter then. You do believe that?"

"Yes, I do," said Helen. She smiled again, more whole-heartedly. "Even though I never went near the Duomo that night!"

"I had no idea, you see that people took me for a rich woman. My clothes, of course, are what one might call cast-offs, Mrs Rodd, from my kind employers; I'm not ashamed of that. I'd rather have good things that have been bought for others than the quality I could afford for myself. But of course I don't care to broadcast the fact among strangers; I admit it was embarrassing that day that Mr Cecil commented upon my hat. My last lady had several things from Christophe et Cie." She gave a sad little reminiscent smile. "She was very good to me, most generous and kind. This very handbag, Mrs Rodd, was one of hers, and not at all worn when she gave it to me. These are her initials, in gold, actually in gold. I thought I should remove them but, 'no don't, Miss Trapp,' she said, 'it would leave a mark on the leather, and monograms are always quite indecipherable, no one will notice that they aren't yours.' So considerate; she was always considerate."

"Always?" said Helen.

"Till towards the end. It is as I say, Mrs Rodd, it's hard for rich people to know who are truly their friends. I am sure Lady Bale had no more devoted and loyal friend—or servant, if you prefer—than I: and for nearly seven years. But—somebody spoke a word perhaps, or somebody else let her down and she grew suspicious of everyone about her: I don't know. Anyway, she began to—to question my intentions, Mrs Rodd. She suggested that I was faithful only because I hoped for something from her will. 'Can you tell me, Miss Trapp,' she said, 'that no such thought has ever entered your head?' Mrs Rodd—how could I say that now and again I had not wondered if, with so much herself and with no one to leave it to, she would not perhaps do something to make my old age just a little easier. God knows, I did not look for anything considerable or even really believe it possible: it was just a little dream I toyed with sometimes when I was weary and depressed. But I couldn't answer her question with a downright denial: and in the end, well, she decided to 'rearrange her household.' But she gave me a most generous reference, I must be grateful for that: more than I've had upon similar occasions."

"This wasn't the first time then, poor Miss Trapp?"

"I have been going out as governess and companion for thirty years," said Miss Trapp simply.

"And so you decided to go a little bust and cheer yourself up, before you started again?"

"It was Lady Bale who suggested it," said Miss Trapp, eagerly. "You see, Mrs Rodd—how truly kind she was, left to herself. She gave me a cheque, a most handsome cheque, and said I should take a short holiday abroad, and meanwhile I might leave my things at Park Lane until I had somewhere to move them to. And she actually suggested that I might have the use of her crocodile leather suitcase as I had not much of my own. She never uses it herself now, it is so much too heavy. So you see she was really kind and considerate to the end. It was only that she was too rich to know whom she might trust."

Her ladyship's heart, thought Helen, had evidently smitten her when it came to the parting with one so patently, so patiently true. No doubt if one could tolerate her oddities of manner, Miss Trapp would be an excellent servant. I remember now, thought Helen, the way she automatically switched to a sort of sickroom attendant manner, after

Vanda Lane hurt herself diving; impersonal yet firm, insisting on her lying down and relaxing, taking aspirin or brandy, all the rest of it: the complete companion-help to a rich old woman, probably a good old hypochondriac into the bargain. She said, gently probing: "Then this material help to Mr Fernando, Miss Trapp . . .?"

"He needed some financial assistance," said Miss Trapp. She added, gently smiling: "I told you I was making over to him everything I possessed in the world. You just didn't understand that it wasn't very much." And she added with happy simplicity that it had been just enough.

Mr Fernando, sent ahead by his lady while she engaged Mrs Rodd, caught up with the others as they trailed, gloomy and motiveless, along the tiled pathways and pebble-patterned steps that led up through courts and gardens to the tall central tower. Miss Trapp's plan for universal acceptance of suspicion, had turned out only a qualified success. Faced with half a dozen alternatives, the Gerente had said simply that he had had instructions from the palace to perfect a case against Mrs Rodd; nothing had been said about anybody else and it was as much as his life was worth at this stage to introduce conflicting suppositions. Cockrill and Leo had in vain banged down exasperated fists until the hospitable glasses jumped on his great, dirty office table; in vain had argued, reasoned, threatened, implored. The Senora Rodd had killed the Senorita Lane, said the Gerente, hands outflung, shoulders up to his shiny hat brim with the excess of his sympathy and regret, and he had orders to take the senora into custody as soon as the case was complete. At sundown that evening, the case would be complete; for sundown that evening was the hour appointed by the Grand Duke. At that hour, witnesses would be in attendance who had seen with their own eyes, the senora creep up to the balcony and creep away again with the bloodstained knife.

. . . No, no, not with the knife, simply with blood on her dress. Very well, then, on her bathing suit, he must make a note of that, the senora had not been wearing a dress, she had had on a bathing suit; he thanked them with perfect sincerity for calling his attention to it, and made another note in his book. Meanwhile, he must positively get down to the quay, there was some difficulty with the Interpol anti-smuggling people and unless he was there to mete out justice in person, one of his own boats was likely to suffer. Sick with frustration and despair, they had crept away. It was incredible, it was intolerable, it was indefensible, it was insane: but as Cockie had said, they were at the mercy of unreason and there was nothing more they could do.

Lost in miserable argument, they found themselves at last in the highest gallery of the tower. Roofed in with a myriad mosaics of azure and gold, its high arched windows looking out over the sun-gilt gardens, it formed the very topmost tip of the spire of the great cathedral rising out of the sea, that is the island of San Juan; and here, upon benches of mosaic and marble, they sat down to rest, wearily, acrimoniously wrangling, blind in their dread and frustration to the matchless loveliness all about them. Louvaine had developed a theory that Inspector Cockrill might have, unknown to himself, dropped off to sleep and so missed Fernando's return from the raft. . . . "All the new lot of tourists are saying that you hadn't paid the bills for the last lot of tourists you took to Siena."

"There was a misunderstanding," said Fernando with dignity. "All is now arranged."

"With Miss Trapp's money," said Mr Cecil, nastily.

"Miss Trapp and I will be married," said Fernando, his round brown face flushing beneath the layers of sun-tan, his eyes moist with wounded pride behind the yellow circles of his sun-glasses.

"Yes. On account of her money," insisted Cecil.

"Her money will all be gone by then," said Fernando. He held his stubby hands clasped together between his knees, looking down at the ruby and diamond chips a-glitter in his fat gold rings. "You think that I am—adventurer. Well, perhaps so. But I tell you—Miss Trapp is not one to make bargains, if Miss Trapp gives to her friend, she gives and asks not return. Miss Trapp would give me her all, which is not very great, but enough to help me out; and accept my thanks and no more and go on her way." The soft big brown eyes stared back into Mr Cecil's mean little grey ones. "I marry Miss Trapp because she is kind and true and will keep me in future from being what—and I say, perhaps you are right—you call adventurer. I marry her when she is penniless. Thanks to me that she is penniless, yes—but I offer her not only gratitude, not only some recompense. I offer my heart." He placed his hand upon the plump bosom covering that organ with a gesture oddly moving and dignified; and spoilt it with a second gesture, addressed to Mr Cecil, not dignified at all.

Mr Cecil after last night's exhibition had been almost back to his sunny self, allowing only for the gloom cast by Helen Rodd's predicament; which, however, could not but be mitigated by the knowledge of his own limpid freedom from suspicion. Diverted by Mr Fernando's simple red herring, he applied his recurrent spiteful irritability to his dear friend Louvaine. "One must remark, ducky, that if as you suggest Mr Cockrill was too sleepy to have observed Fernando's goings-on, ditto applies to you. Up to the verandah in a trice, dear, not nearly so far to go as the rest of us; do the horrid deed and down again, the Inspector still snoring. I mean, it cuts both ways, doesn't it?"

"It cuts three ways," said Louvaine. "Positively minces

your alibi, for example. Because if he was asleep, so could you have gone up."

"But he says he wasn't asleep," said Mr Cecil hastily. "That's my point."

"Which I was not," said Cockrill. "Things are bad enough. Stick to what Miss Barker would call 'the constants.' I did not go to sleep."

"So *I* could not have left the terrace. . . ."

"And *I* could not have left the raft. . . ."

"And *I* could not have left my rubber duck for a whole hour. . . ."

"Well, and Mrs Rodd couldn't have left her sun-shed," added Louli.

"Yes, she could," said Inspector Cockrill. "That's another constant, and we must not evade the constants. She could, in fact, have passed under the terrace, and, wide awake as I was, I need not have seen her."

"Anyway she's out because she had no reason to kill Vanda, and she couldn't really have mistaken Vanda for me."

"Mr Fernando mistook you for Vanda," said Cecil significantly. "He mistook you both times."

"What then?" said Fernando. "What if I did mistake her? What has this to do with the murder? The Inspector himself says, once and for all, that I cannot have got from that raft." The swimmy brown eyes behind the yellow lenses, turned upon Cecil, heavy with sarcasm. "Did I have perhaps a diving suit concealed in the pocket of my trunks, so that I could walk to and fro along the ocean bed?"

Far, far below them, two doll figures strolling along a flower-bordered terrace, deep in conversation, Helen Rodd and Miss Trapp appeared in sight. But Inspector Cockrill if, leaning in the arched white window of the tower gallery, he saw them, did not observe them. A diving suit! Had Mr Fernando then had a diving suit concealed in the pocket of his bright satin trunks, that he could have 'walked to and fro upon the ocean bed' . . .? A diving suit!

". . . and anyway, I could not have left my rubber duck for an hour, the Inspector says so himself. . . ."

"You could have, for a few minutes at a time," said Louli. "The Inspector says that too."

"Up to twenty minutes perhaps, he says. But the murder could not have been done in twenty minutes, not with all that laying out and tidying up. . . ."

"Well, perhaps," said Louli casually, "you did it by instalments."

Instalments! Perhaps you did it by instalments! Cockie looked down unseeingly at the two little doll-like figures far below and his mind was a reeling kaleidoscope of thought. Mr Fernando could have come ashore 'in a diving suit.' Mr Cecil could have committed the crime 'by instalments.' Mr Fernando, wallowing along beneath the surface of the water with the rubber frog-feet and the rubber under-water mask that Leo Rodd was 'always leaving on the raft'; Mr Cecil, creeping up at the far side of the diving rock to commit murder—reappearing in his rubber boat, paddling idly along the shore with slowly reddening arms, paddling back round the rock to creep up once more, twice more perhaps, and cover up the outward signs of his guilt; never out of sight for more than a few minutes at a time. And Mr Cecil had been in some way under a blackmail threat concerning his 'work'; and Mr Fernando had so bad a conscience that twice he had been ready to believe in ghosts: despite the unmissable, unmistakable blaze of the bright red hair. Nothing surely but a bad conscience could have taken the colour from that flaming red hair. . . .

Two cases, two real, positive possibilities at last: no 'cooking up' of cases to match against the case of Helen Rodd, but two genuine possibilities, however bizarre, however absurd, in this whole bizarre, absurd affair; two cases either of which must surely triumph over the feeble, the impossible case against Helen Rodd. For Helen Rodd had not figured in the blackmail book, had had no reason on earth to wish to murder Vanda Lane: and though she might well, as Louvaine had just hinted, have wished to murder Louvaine, she could not have failed to recognize that hair. Helen Rodd could not have mistaken Vanda Lane for Louvaine. Only Mr Fernando had ever for a moment been taken in, only Mr Fernando had failed to see the bright red flame of the hair. . . .

He looked into the round brown face, the round brown eyes swimming moistly behind round yellow sun-glasses: and far, far away at the far, far back of his mind, stirred a memory: something about rose-buds, something about the brussels-sprouts, something about a hat. . . .

Below them the white courts gleamed, the gardens glowed, the little town huddled pink and white and dustily brown, tumbling down to the blue of the sea; beyond, the dark patch of the pines was threaded through with the cool white lines of the Bellomare Hotel. Inspector Cockrill saw none of it; he stood staring, staring, staring sightlessly down to where two figures walked, deep in their conversation on the terrace below. Yet he must have uttered some sort of involuntary exclamation, for they came and stood beside him, looking down also, Fernando and Mr Cecil and Louvaine, leaning upon the low white parapet under the delicately pointed curve of the arch. He put out his hand, wordlessly, and took Mr Fernando's glasses from him and held them for a moment before his own eyes, and handed them back; no need to look twice—for, sure enough, one glance down through those yellowy lenses into the rose-red gardens, and the colour was gone; scarlet and crimson and damask, geranium, oleander, bougainvillea, rose, hazed into a sort of Technicolor brightness of indeterminate yellows and greens and blues. He said quietly to Mr Cecil: "Try the glasses, too. Do you see what I see?"

Mr Fernando had put the glasses away in his left breast pocket of his linen holiday suit. Mr Cecil, the precious red attaché case tucked under his right arm, reached out with his left over Fernando's left shoulder and down towards the pocket. The movement perhaps attracted the attention of the two women walking below; for they glanced up and Cecil, fishing out the sun-glasses, said casually: "These are the same as Mrs Rodd is wearing."

"Mrs Rodd!" said Fernando. He jerked round upon Cockrill, "Mrs Rodd! She was . . . That day . . ." But in jerking, he had knocked against Mr Cecil. "Oh, sorry, I beg your pardon, the attaché case . . ."

With a cry of horror, Mr Cecil grabbed wildly at it as it fell; but, soft and slithery, it skated across the smooth marble of the parapet's edge and hung for a moment, teetering, over space. Louvaine lunged after it and, perilously balancing, just managed to clutch at the tab of the metal zip; but in doing so, hauling the case triumphantly up, ripped open the zip. A shower of white sheets of drawing paper belched out in one conglomerate mass and, slowly drifting apart, in ones and twos and threes, fluttered down to the gardens far below.

Slowly, slowly, into the breathless afternoon sunshine, hanging and fluttering like tiny white gliders launched on a windless day—the priceless store of pencil sketches, the hastily scribbled, secret sketches that, perfected when one was in reach of easels and paints and varnishes once more, were to take the world of fashion by storm. . . .

White sheets of paper, lazily fluttering, lazily turning, lazily drifting down to the flowers, the fountains, the lily-pools below. White sheets of paper that should have held hurriedly-scribbled pencil sketches—each with its finished design, inked, painted, varnished, all the rest of it—as, ready completed (by somebody else), Mr Cecil had brought them with him from home.

He gave one choking, chopped-off, terrible cry; and fell in a dead faint on the blue-glazed tiles of the floor.

Inspector Cockrill did not even glance his way. A face raised to look up from the terrace below them; an arm stretched forth to take a pair of sun-glasses from a breast-pocket; a hand flung out to catch a falling case that showered gay paintings upon the gay gardens below. . . . Fool, fool, fool that I've all this time been, thought Inspector Cockrill, fools, fools, fools that we've all of us been. . . .!

For now he knew.

CHAPTER FIFTEEN

THE Gerente came that evening for Helen Rodd and she went with him, very pale, saying nothing, making no demur. Inspector Cockrill apparently did not oppose her going. To the others, clamorous with horrified uncertainty, he refused to comment. "You had better all of you get packed to-night. We leave to-morrow morning."

Leo Rodd came out of his room and walked across the balcony and down the wooden steps; they approached him diffidently, trying to offer some word of sympathy, something to express the horror in their breasts, but he merely said, Thank you, thank you, in a toneless voice and went on; Louvaine's outstretched hands he utterly ignored, almost literally shouldering her aside, walking on, threading his way through the tables of the other tourists on the upper terrace and down the long flight of steps; they saw him emerge, a sombre figure in the failing twilight and move with bent head across the lonely beach, to sit down at last, very still, on a hump of rock close to the edge of the sea. After a while, Inspector Cockrill followed him there.

Nobody obeyed the instruction to go and pack. Wretched and bewildered, reunited by their common unease, they huddled together at the balcony rail, looking over the heads of the carefree tourists sipping at their Juanellos and Americanes on the terrace below, and away to the two lonely figures, dark against the evening sky. Mr Fernando held Miss Trapp's crabbed hand in his strong, protective grasp and she, in an agony of anxious and indecisive sympathy with the absent Helen, was content to leave it there. Louvaine leaned with her elbows on the rail, silent, her face in her hands. Mr Cecil, the ormolu lock casting a strange, hollow shadow in the middle of his forehead, tried to cheer them up with promises of unsolicited favours to come when they should all, please God, be home again and under the civilized wing of Christophe et Cie. Miss Trapp should have her wedding costume made for her there, a present from himself with extravagant good wishes; yes, and a hat too, madly becoming, he had just the thing in mind, a little nest of lilies and roses to perch on the bridal head. . . . "And no brussels-sprouts?" said Mr Fernando, wanly joking. But there they were back with it all again: the yellow sun-glasses that had taken the red from the wreath of rosebuds and turned them into brussels-sprouts, that for him had taken the colour from a stray curl of red hair. Could it be true, could it honestly be true that Mrs Rodd, deceived by those horrible glasses . . .? Yet apparently the Inspector was content to let her go with the politio, no more had been said of their refusal to abandon her in San Juan. . . . The poor lady . . .

"On the other hand—if she really did kill Miss Lane," faltered Miss Trapp wretchedly, "should one sympathize?" It was all so terrible, one didn't know what to think. She tailed off into indeterminate whimperings.

"And me, Cecil, will you design a dress for me too? San Juan inspired?"

Now, horrid thing, *not* to be catty about poor Mr Cecil and his designs! "I do take home ideas, lots of them, you've seen me doing the very sketches."

"But not the ones you'll show to Christophe et Cie? Come on, now, tell—who really does them?"

"Well, a girl called Jane Woods if you must know," said

Cecil, shamefacedly. "Only *ab*solutely not to tell, any of you: you do swear?"

"Oh, we won't tell," said Louli.

"It's what that bitch said that day up here, right here on this very spot. Old Bevan, you know, who owns Christophe's, I met him abroad—years ago it was now, of course; and perhaps one did show off a little, one was so young then, I mean really quite a child. But he suddenly showed a bit of interest and I was caught on the hop, I happened to have some sketches of Jane's with me that I'd been cop—er— that'd I'd been sort of modelling my work on; and on an impulse—I let him think they were mine. He was impressed and, on the strength of them, he opened Christophe et Cie. So—well, there you are, my dears, it suits Jane, she gets the money, I get the credit, she wouldn't get as much for them without me behind her, I wouldn't be where I am without her. And the two of us rolled together, well—genius," said Mr Cecil modestly; but the idea of being rolled together with large, plushy Jane, who was quite too dreadfully feminine, was a little embarrassing, and he gave a small private shudder.

"And the 'inspiration'?"

"Well, we work it all out of course, sometimes she takes her holiday early and goes to wherever we've decided to be inspired by, sometimes we just cook it up out of books. Then she does the designs and I bring them away with me and come back with them. I always have a studio booked somewhere, you see," explained Cecil, "where I'm supposed to finish them off. Then they appear in all their glory. Rome, it was supposed to have been this time." He spoke with a simplicity that suddenly made him almost human.

"And Vanda had found this out?"

"She was a devil," said Cecil. "I'm sorry if she was your

cousin, ducky, and all the rest of it; but she was a devil. Though how she could have found out . . ."

"She watched people, that's all," said Louli. "It was her job." She added pleasantly, "So you up and slew her—to keep your ghastly secret?"

Mr Cecil's voice took on once again its shrill note. The secret, he said, and not unreasonably perhaps, would have caused unpleasantness if it had come out, if Mr Bevan had got to know of it. But no more than that. The business was established now, it would have been all Mr Bevan's loss to have discredited one, to have dispensed with one's services for so trivial a reason. What did Mr Bevan care, who it was who actually did the designs? It was Mr Cecil who put them across, Mr Cecil who had cultivated acquaintance with half the fashionable women of London and New York, who called duchesses by their pet names and had actually come by a glossy magazine in which, against an article by himself on Designing for Our Fairy Tale Princess, someone had scribbled in pencil, 'But he never has designed for me!' At least Mr Cecil swore that it was 'for me'; of course it *might* have been 'for her.' But honestly, duckies, horrid and mortifying, of course and *not* to tell, like pets and angels as they were!—but really not something to murder a person about.

"And yet you fainted when we saw the drawings!"

"I faint very easily," said Mr Cecil growing pink.

"I see. So we're back to the dear old mix-up, then," said Louli. "You thought she was me."

"Why should I have wanted to murder *you?*" said Mr Cecil, looking, however, not disinclined for it now.

"Lots do," said Louli, cheerfully.

"And anyway I do not wear sun-glasses; and it does seem quite obvious, my dears, that the sun-glasses do take all the red out of Louli's hair and that if anyone killed La Lane in mistake for her, it was because they had sun-glasses. Like you," he said sweetly to Fernando.

"I had no cause to kill either of these ladies," said Fernando. "All this is settled now, surely? Your secret is out, Mr Cecil—mine too. And neither had anything to do with the murder." He made apologetic movements with his hands. "I do not like to say it at this time; but if we are to regard the evidence of the sun-glasses—there is only one other person who wears them. And that is Mrs Rodd."

"Poor Mrs Rodd," said Miss Trapp. "Where is she now? One can't help wondering and worrying. Such a fastidious person, always so elegant and correct—not used to roughness and ugliness! What is she doing?—now, at this moment, while we stand here on this pleasant balcony looking out at the lights of the fishing boats beginning to twinkle on the water. What is she doing now? Where is she now?"

"Not where she will need sun-glasses," agreed Fernando, glancing back over his shoulder to where the dank prison loomed over its rocky foundation, falling away steep and sheer to the sea.

"Not that she always wore them by any means," went on Miss Trapp, unhappily twittering. "I think, on the whole, *Mr* Rodd had the use of them more often than she did. I remember particularly on that afternoon . . ." And suddenly her hand tightened on Fernando's warm grasp, she stammered out: "That afternoon . . . That afternoon . . ."

"You are right," said Fernando. "That afternoon—the one who had on the sun-glasses—was Mr Rodd."

As though he had heard the words, far away down on the beach, Leo Rodd rose suddenly to his feet. They watched him stand there, quietly, beside the little hunched figure perched like a gnome on the hump of the rock, not looking up at him, staring out to sea. And then . . . The slow inching round, the almost imperceptible, stealthy, crab-like movement that was bringing him round behind the rock. Inspector Cockrill sat on; did not move, did not look up, seemed utterly unaware that behind him there stood now a figure, silent and motionless, with upraised hand. But suddenly, swiftly, he turned: and the arm came down, came forward and down with a jabbing, thrusting, stabbing movement that, if the hand had held a knife, must surely have found the heart.

If the hand held a knife.

Miss Trapp screamed, one short, sharp squeal of horror and buried her face in Mr Fernando's shoulder. Louvaine cried out, "No! No! *No!*" on a rising note of terrified repudiation. Mr Cecil caught at her wrist and, immobilized by shock and horror, they stood there, staring down. On the terrace below them, attracted by the sound of Miss Trapp's scream, the hotel guests looked up and, following their panic-stricken gaze, away to the beach; and, with a concerted upsurge of movement, crowded forward to the balustrade. It was as though at the rail of a ship's deck, impotent to assist, they watched the death-throes far away down in the water, of a drowning man.

And away on the beach, in the gathering dusk, the dark figures moved again and fell apart. The one sitting on, hunched and, after that one shifting jerk, motionless: the other—the other without a backward glance, running out over the sand, with that familiar, sideways lurching gait, out across the sand, into the ripples at the edge of the shore, running, running, splashing out into the sea, throwing itself full-length into the waves, swimming, first jerkily, splashily and then with a rhythm of swift, strong strokes, steadily away and away from them, swimming out to sea.

Louvaine broke from Cecil's immobilizing hand. "Leo! *Leo!*" She flung herself down the wooden steps and across the terrace, thrusting through the gaping crowd. "Get out of my way, get out of my way, let me through . . ." Down the long central flight of steps, down through the scented gardens, across the lower terrace, down pebbled steps again, out across the sand. Mr Cecil followed close at her heels, Mr Fernando with feverish impatience had caught Miss Trapp by her upper arm and was hurrying her, clutching and falling, down the steps after them. The crowd on the terrace, stunned by the shock and inexplicability of it all, had not yet sufficiently found its wits to follow.

Across the white sand, sick and sobbing with terror and pain, Louvaine came stumbling at last to the edge of the sea. "Leo! Leo! Leo, for God's sake come back . . .!" Her throat was harsh with the terrible gasping for breath after her flight down the steps but she forced it to shrillness, screaming out over the gentle lisp of the waves. "Leo, Leo— for God's sake, Leo come back! Come back!" But the dark head, glimpsed only now and again in the trough of the night-dark waves, moved steadily on and on, away from her. She began to tear off her frock, wading out into the sea, floundering in after him. "Leo, Leo! Leo, come back, come back!" Mr Cecil rushed after her and catching her by the arm, pulled her back out of the water. "Don't be a fool, Louvaine, what good can you do?" But she struggled with him, "Let me go, let me go after him, I must get him back, can't you see he's—he's swimming away, he's not coming back!" She collapsed to her knees in the water, supported only by his grip under her arm. "For God's sake do something, isn't there someone who can swim after him, isn't there a boat . . .?"

"There's no boat, Louli, no one can swim." He hauled her up to her feet. "Come on, come back." Wet and exhausted, she let him lead her, still half supporting her, back to the sandy beach and the hump of rock.

Fernando and Miss Trapp arrived, running stumblingly towards them across the sand. "He's gone," said Cecil.

"He's miles out." He swung round to the quiet figure on the rock. "But the Inspector?"

Like children afraid to approach some expected horror, they crept, massed together for proof against shock, up to the rock and, massed together, stood silently regarding the hunched-up form. Miss Trapp said, on a note of high terror: "Is he dead?"

"No," said Inspector Cockrill. "I'm not dead."

Louvaine thrust through them, throwing herself half kneeling on the sand at his feet. "Inspector, do something—he's gone, he's swum out to sea, he's never coming back. Can't you *do* something?"

"No," said Cockie, very quietly. "What is there to do?"

Fernando too threw himself on his knees beside the low rock. "Has he hurt you?"

"No," said Cockie again. "Why should you think he had?"

"But we saw him. He came round behind you. He stabbed down at you, we were up on the verandah, we saw him."

"A demonstration," said Cockrill.

"A demonstration?"

"The wound in Miss Lane's breast," said Cockie, "went from right to left, in a downwards direction. It must therefore have been made by someone right-handed, standing in front of her. Or so one assumed. Mr Rodd kindly demonstrated to me how it could have been done by a left-handed man."

Louvaine had subsided almost full-length on the sand, dreadfully sobbing, dreadfully gasping for her agonized, labouring breath. She half raised herself now on one elbow, gazing up at him imploringly. "Don't sit here talking. Can't you *do* something?"

"What do you want me to do?" said Cockie.

"Get a boat, get something, get someone who can swim—go out and rescue him." The rest of the hotel guests were coming now, streaming down the steps, with one or two of the waiters, white-coated, in their midst. She dragged herself to her feet. "Ask them. Perhaps someone can swim. They'll know where there's a boat." She started running towards them.

"Yes," said Cockie at once and more briskly. "A good idea. We'll ask them. Fernando—you go: tell them what's happened, tell them you think he's not going to try to get back. Ask the waiters if they can get hold of a boat." As Fernando, still rather dazed, lumbered up to his feet, he added: "Put on an air of hurry, look as if this is what we've all been trying to arrange." To Louvaine, turning back as Fernando rushed past her towards the crowd, he said: "They can hurry as much as they like now. It's too late."

And indeed the dark head was to be seen no more. Standing craning their eyes into the rapidly falling dusk, they did think that they saw for a moment a hand thrown up, and Louvaine screamed and hid her eyes. "It's for the best," said Cockrill, doggedly. "It's what he wanted, it's for the best."

She tore herself away from them and fled back down to the sea. "Leo! Leo!" Her despairing cry rent through the hush-shush-shush of the waves, she stumbled in through them again, flinging out helpless arms to where, for a moment, they had thought that they glimpsed that helpless arm. "Leo! Leo!" But there was no answer; only the slap and sigh of the waves on the cooling sand. She stumbled back again and, flinging herself down on the damp sand at the water's edge, abandoned herself to grief.

Fernando returned with the crowd loping at his heels. "All get back to the hotel," said Cockie fiercely to them. "Back to the hotel!" He climbed up on the rock and addressed them and, for a moment, was Mr Cockrill on holiday no longer, but Detective Inspector Cockrill, the

Terror of Kent, whose voice was the voice of accustomed authority backed by the law of the land. "You must leave the beach at once. If you want to know what has happened —well, a man has swum out to sea, intending to drown himself. The—inference—is that he was responsible for the murder committed here the other day. There is no use now in anyone swimming out after him, he's got too far and he had every intention of letting himself drown. None of us could swim, so we had to let him go. We've been wondering where we could get hold of a boat." Fernando said something. "Oh. I understand that the manager, the Dirrytory, whatever he calls himself, has gone off to ring the police; and there's a boat in the next bay, he's getting that sent out. A pity," said Detective Inspector Cockrill coolly, "that we didn't know about it before. Now—there's nothing else to be seen here; you will help everyone by simply going back to the terrace and getting on with your drinks." He added, with a glance at the moaning, shuddering figure prostrate on the sand, "Including this poor girl."

Their chivalry thus appealed to, and seeing, furthermore, that there was indeed nothing at all on the beach worth staring at, they drifted, gabbling with excitement, back to the hotel. Cockrill went and crouched on the sand close to Louvaine, and the others, helpless and compassionate, followed him. He did not touch her but he began quietly to talk and he talked only to her. After a little while, she raised her head. She said: "He did this for me."

"He did it because he was afraid to face the San Juan gaol," said Cockie. "And I would have done the same."

"He did it for me." She said imploringly, tears pouring down her face: "Don't take that, at least, away from me. He did it for me." And she dragged herself up once more and stumbled forward into the waves again, screaming his name, Leo, Leo, Leo, come back, come back . . .

No answering cry from the sea. She turned back to them, frantic with helplessness. "Where's the boat, why don't they get the boat? Is there nothing we can do?"

"Nothing," said Cockrill. "They'll bring the boat, but anyway, it'll be too late. That's how he wants it to be." And he took her by the arm and forced her back up the beach to the drier sand and she collapsed once again and lay there sobbing; but she struggled no more. He said again, solemnly: "You must make up your mind to it. Leo Rodd was a murderer, he has done this because he has been found out; and that's all there is to it."

Miss Trapp stood between Fernando and Mr Cecil, three huddled figures looking down with anxious eyes at the shuddering figure at their feet, and away to the unbroken monotony of the wind-ruffled sea. She said: "May we not hope at least that he did it to save Mrs Rodd?"

"No," said Inspector Cockrill. He shrugged. "You can say, if you like, that he has done it because Mrs Rodd would no longer save *him*."

"But Mrs Rodd . . ."

"Mrs Rodd is a very gallant woman," said Inspector Cockrill, "and very loyal too. And she is one of those people who give their hearts away just once in a lifetime; and never get them back however unworthy the beloved turns out to be and however clearly they see that he is unworthy. And protecting her husband had become second nature to her. But there must be a limit, even for the Mrs Rodds of this world, there must be a breaking point; and I thought that a night in the San Juan prison might bring her to it—facing a future of utter hopelessness, locked up all alone in a prison cell with no light but a star outside the little barred window and no sound except the sea against the rocks hundreds of feet below, and no movement but the trickle of moisture down the slimy walls; and no prospect of ever leaving it except to be not very expertly hanged in a public square. And all for a man like Leo Rodd."

A man like Leo Rodd. A man used from boyhood to wealth and comfort earned by his own great gifts, a man accustomed to flattery and adulation, a man who had known nothing but the good life. Suddenly bereft of it all, forced to live upon the bounty of one woman, the woman he had married and whom he no longer loved—having for so long frittered away his heart upon other women. "He no longer had a heart to love with at all."

"He loved *me*," said Louvaine.

"Oh, yes," said Cockrill. "While he thought you were rich."

She shook her head drearily. "No, no, you're wrong, you've got it all wrong, it's utterly untrue. He loved me, he'd have loved me if I hadn't had a penny, he was going to leave a rich wife and run away with me. . . ."

"Until he found out," said Cockrill steadily, "that you were not rich after all."

There was a commotion on the rough little beach the other side of the diving rock, a small boat nosed its way off the dry sand and was hauled by two bare-chested fishermen into the sea. Mr Fernando rushed down to the water's edge and hallooed to them, pointing out to where that terrible upflung white arm had been. They leaned on their oars, pointing, gesticulating, arguing, and at last rowed off obliquely across the bay. Louvaine dragged herself up to her knees to watch them, clasping her thin hands in an agony of subconscious prayer. Miss Trapp said to Cockrill: "All this is so dreadful for her. Don't you think . . .?" She could not approve Miss Barker's passion for a married man —but you could see that her heart was smitten at the sight of that bleak despair. "Don't you think she should be taken up to the hotel?"

"I shall stay here," said Louvaine.

"But if anything . . . If they should. . . It will be very painful for her," said Miss Trapp to Cockrill.

"You can tie me with ropes and cart me away," said Louvaine, "but I'll drag myself back. I'm staying here."

"Then, Inspector, do you not think that this distressing story . . .?"

"This distressing story must be told some time," said Inspector Cockrill. "It will be better for her if she can believe the truth."

"There's only one truth," said Louvaine. "He loved me. Even—even after the murder, he still loved me, he still wanted to marry me." She knelt, hands clasped on her breast, her gaze riveted upon the little boat toiling out across the bay. The brief twilight was over, it was growing dark, the men had lighted their lantern and it swung at the boat's prow, a twinkling beacon, inappropriately gay, throwing its pale gold disc of light down upon the heaving waters. She prayed: "Perhaps he's still safe, perhaps they can find him in time."

"He's dead," said Cockrill. "He swam out there intending to die. He told me what he'd done and he showed me how he'd done it and then he told me what he meant to do: and in that very moment, it was too late to do anything to stop him. He was gone." He shrugged. "No use flapping about like a fool at the water's edge, and I can't swim. He'd gone. I, for one, hope for his sake that when the boat finds him, he's dead."

The breeze blew the red hair, dark now in the evening dark, back and away from the sorrowful face, wrapped the soft dress close about the lovely body that Leo had held in his arms. She said, "None of it's true. None of it's true."

"It's true," said Cockie.

Fernando and Mr Cecil and Miss Trapp stood wretchedly

by them, their anxious eyes on the boat. Miss Trapp said, miserably: "But why, Inspector, should Mr Rodd kill poor Miss Lane?"

"Poor Miss Lane was a blackmailer," said Cockie, sourly. "She blackmailed other people for the power it gave her over them, for the pleasure of seeing them wriggle on the hook. She blackmailed Mr Rodd for something different— she blackmailed him for love."

Louvaine shrugged her shoulders with a weary, derisive movement, looking away out to sea where the little boat crept across the waters, her attention only half with him. Miss Trapp said, "For love?"

"Or if not exactly that, to prevent his love from being given somewhere else. She told him that if he would not give up Louvaine, she would tell his wife that he had been planning to leave her.

"Mrs Rodd is a very patient woman," said Cockie, "and loyal. She had put up with innumerable flirtations because she believed that they gave her husband some comfort in his grief and frustration at the loss of his arm. She knew that he needed her, she knew that he always came back to her, she knew that even while they were going on, he himself never believed these affairs to be more than affairs. Mrs Rodd thought the thing with Louvaine was just an affair."

"And Miss Lane . . .?"

"Miss Lane knew that it was not just an affair. That night down here on the beach," said Cockie to Cecil, "when you and Miss Barker walked here talking, she told you all about their plans to run away together. I know, because I overheard you. And somebody else overheard you. Miss Barker said suddenly, 'Here he comes!' but it was several minutes before Mr Rodd came. Somebody else had been moving down there, listening to the conversation—and that somebody else was Miss Lane.

"The next afternoon, the afternoon of the murder, Mr Rodd lay on the beach and pretended to sleep. I said to-day that Mrs Rodd could have passed along under the terrace and I need not have seen her. The same applied to him. Not troubling, perhaps, a very great deal as to whether or not he was seen, Mr Rodd passed along under the terrace and up the little path in the corner of the diving rock and up the jasmine tunnel to the hotel. He was looking for Miss Barker. Miss Barker was with me on the terrace, but he didn't know that. You couldn't see the terrace from the sun-shed where he lay.

"He'd missed seeing you before the bathe, Miss Barker— you told me you'd had a vague 'date' but Mrs Rodd went with him and then your bathing dress tore and, one way and another, you weren't able to meet. So he went up to your room—I'm telling you now what *he* told *me*. You were not there. Your red shawl was over the back of the chair and he picked it up and held it against his cheek for a moment because it smelt of your perfume and reminded him of you. He was standing there with it in his hands, when Miss Lane came into the room.

"She had heard a movement there, I suppose, and she thought it was you—come up to do some work, perhaps, in the quiet hour before drinks on the terrace. But it wasn't you; it was Leo Rodd, standing there in your room with your shawl held against his cheek. She couldn't bear it, she started to rail at him, she said that if *she* couldn't have him, nobody else should and that she would tell his wife and put an end to it all. She rushed into her room, and slammed the door. He followed her there, arguing with her, trying to persuade her to keep her mouth shut. His wife had to be told some time; but not this way."

The little boat ploughed on over the waters and now it had begun to cast about, the voices of the men in argument and speculation carried to them clearly across the water in the still evening air. Louvaine crouched, head turned seawards, gazing after them with straining eyes, paying no further heed to his words, given up to the pitiful remnants of her hope. Fernando said: "But, Inspector—does Mr Rodd kill this woman, only to prevent his wife from knowing his plan too soon? And then—the blackmail book?"

"Ah, yes," said Inspector Cockrill. "The blackmail book. The blackmail book was lying on the table. She went and stood at the table with her back to him—not in the corner where the chair was, but looking across the table at the chair, with her back to the room. She turned over the pages of the blackmail book. He stood just behind her shoulder, looking down at the book and she showed him what she had written about him and about his wife and about his mistress. He saw it all written there and he saw also what she had meant him to see, that she was a blackmailer, an accustomed blackmailer, and that she meant what she said. When she came to the page with my name on it, he stopped her hand, he saw that he could play the same game, he reminded her that I was a policeman and threatened that, if she told his wife what she knew about himself and Louvaine, he would tell me, in his turn, that she was a blackmailer. That was how the book came to be open at that page. She said in reply that he could prove nothing; and then he lost his temper and told her to go ahead and tell his wife, it would hurt his wife but it would hurt nobody else—it could do no real harm to himself and Louvaine. . . ."

Louvaine had been listening after all, or at least half listening, for she lifted her head a little and said: "You see—he loved me, he was going to run away with me."

"Oh, yes," agreed Cockie readily. "Of course he was. He was going to run off with Louvaine Barker, the famous writer, who was rich."

She dropped her head again. She said, very quietly: "Yes, I see now. She told him then that I was not Louvaine Barker, I was not the famous writer—and I was not rich." But she did not seem really interested at all; the men shouted to one another across the length of their little boat, and she craned forward peering through the deepening dark. "Did they say . . .? Can you hear . . .?"

"It was nothing," said Fernando. "A false alarm." He said to Cockrill: "And the knife?"

"The knife was there," said Cockie. "Lying on the table beside the book. He says the whole thing flashed upon him in one blinding blaze of realization of what it all meant to him, and of rage with her. She would tell his wife that he had been planning to betray her; and his wife would not forgive that; and he would be left with a love affair on his hands with a girl who in actual fact was penniless. He snatched up the knife hardly knowing what he was doing and, with his left hand, his only hand, standing there behind her, he leaned forward over her left shoulder and stabbed down into her breast. Seen from in front, the wound ran from right to left: from in front, it could only have been done by a right-handed man. But it was done from behind."

The ring of light bobbed and swayed upon the water, the men's hunched bodies were silhouetted against the evening sky as they leaned over the gunwales, anxiously scanning the water. "It is all a make-believe," said Louli. "It's all lies." But she spoke now only with a sort of dreary refusal to believe, the fire had long gone from her denials, the faith was spent. She stared across at the light on the surface of the water. "It's all stupid lies."

"It's what he told me himself," said Cockie. "He told me how he dragged the body to the bed. He'd flung the shawl there when he first came into the room, finding that he had, not thinking, still got it over his arm. The shawl played no part in the murder, he needed no protection from spurting blood because he'd stabbed the girl from behind. The shawl was already on the bed. With God knows what vague idea of seeing if she was still alive, of saving her, perhaps, if he could—he hadn't meant to kill her, after all, the whole thing was simply a hideous impulse—he laid her on the bed. But she was dead. He was filled with horror at what he had done. He laid her out as well as he could, from a sort of—well, a sort of remorseful pity and respect for her, now that she was dead. He straightened the shawl, he got a towel to staunch the blood, he folded her hands on her breast. With only a very vague idea of protecting himself, he cleaned up the rest of the room as best he could and washed himself down in the bathroom; at the last moment, he thrust the blackmail book out of sight, but he really doesn't know why, just a general idea of confusing the issue, I suppose. He thought he had barely a chance of getting back unseen to the sun-shed, but luck was with him: his wife was still asleep as she had been when he went, Miss Trapp was in her 'modesty tent' as Mr Cecil calls it, Mr Cecil himself was out of sight round the other side of the diving rock, Mr Fernando on the raft was asleep or quite simply not looking towards the shore. While he walked under the terrace, he was invisible to Miss Barker and me—Miss Barker, anyway, was asleep. During the very short dash to the sun-shed, he had to chance my having my eyes on my book—which it seems I had: I've never claimed to have been watching the beach the whole time. It was a matter of luck and he had luck: murderer's luck! And from then on, he's been free from suspicion because none of us thought of that over-the-shoulder thrust."

He was silent. There was no sound but the grey monotony of the splash of the waves, the voices of the fishermen reaching them faintly across the dark heave of the water. Louvaine said at last: "But you say you knew?"

"I knew this afternoon," said Cockie. "I knew up on the tower when Mr Cecil reached over Fernando's shoulder and lifted the sun-glasses from his pocket. I knew when I saw how for a minute they slanted from left to right—as a dagger might slant. The sun-glasses play no part in it, none at all: whether Mr or Mrs Rodd was wearing them that day doesn't matter. Nothing matters except that I saw them this afternoon, lifted out of Mr Fernando's pocket—slanting from left to right: as a dagger might slant."

"And so you told him that you'd found out? You drove him to his death?"

"I told him, yes. He said . . ."

"He said what?"

"He said," said Cockie slowly, "that it didn't matter what I knew. Nobody would believe me: nobody here in San Juan, I mean. They didn't want to believe me. They had—he said that they had already made their choice."

"But their choice was Mrs Rodd," cried Miss Trapp, gooseberry-eyed. "And now, if she was innocent . . ."

"After all," said Cockie, reasonably, "he'd known all along that she was innocent. Yet he'd allowed her to be 'chosen'."

Louvaine said nothing, kneeling there on the sand, red hair blown back from the high cheekbones, pale face smirched with tears, staring out to sea. Miss Trapp stammered out that surely, surely—surely, at the end, it had been this that had made him act at last; could not Inspector Cockrill confirm—could he not just—just tell them that at the last moment this repentance had come, Mr Rodd had taken this terrible step to save his wife . . ."

"I've told you," said Cockie, bleakly. "He's killed himself because his wife will not save *him*."

"But what can she tell that they will listen to?" said Fernando; and at the same time, Miss Trapp cried out: "Do you mean to say that all this time she's known that it was her husband who killed Vanda Lane?"

Inspector Cockrill answered them both. He said: "Mrs Rodd could tell nothing about the murder of Vanda Lane. She knows nothing about the murder of Vanda Lane."

"But then . . .?"

"Leo Rodd killed Vanda Lane to prevent his wife's discovering the truth about his affair with Miss Barker," said Cockie. "And then what happened? As a result of the murder, everything came out about the affair with Miss Barker. I don't know that Mrs Rodd actually said anything to her husband: but I do know that this was something she would not accept. She is a patient person, she dislikes scenes: she would wait quietly, putting up with things until she could act; and then she would act. Leo Rodd knew that as soon as they got back to England, Mrs Rodd would leave him: whether he went off with Miss Barker or not, his marriage was over. But he had to have money; with or without Miss Barker, he had to have money. And Mrs Rodd had made her will leaving everything to him." There was a shout from the boat again and he lifted his head and looked keenly out to sea. He did not comment on any increase of activity there but he a little accelerated his speech. "There's a great deal still to be told, a lot to be cleared up. I will tell it all later. But to round off the story for now—you have forgotten, haven't you? the attack on Mrs Rodd. A clumsy attack— a thrust with a knife so ill-aimed that it struck the right shoulder, fifteen inches or so away from the heart." Louvaine looked up sharply and he said: "Do you remember Leo Rodd once saying to his wife: 'Your heart's in the right place, whatever they may say'? '*Whatever they may say*'!" He got to his feet and, standing watching the boat, said quietly:

"Do you think Mrs Rodd is such a fool that she wouldn't reflect that out of all the possible suspects, her husband was the only one who could know that she is one of those people whose organs are reversed: that her heart was not on her left side but her right . . .?"

There was a cry from the boat, a flurry of activity, the men leaned over, their silhouettes moved and changed, were humped, were elongated, flattened themselves almost to the water's edge. Louvaine cried out, "Oh, God!" and stumbled once again down the beach, standing knee-deep in the unregarded waves with outstretched, horribly shaking hands. The men called again and Fernando translated. "They have found him." He added gently: "He's dead."

They brought him ashore, covered with a huddle of dirty sailcloth, in the bottom of the boat. Mr Cecil held Louvaine back by the arms. Inspector Cockrill went forward and lifted the cloth and looked down quietly at the still figure. They had a glimpse of a white hand, hanging with lax, crook'd fingers at the end of a boneless arm, and then he stooped and lifted the hand and laid it upon the still breast. He let the cloth fall back and returned to them. He said in his expressionless, grumbling voice: "Yes. Dead."

Mr Fernando, backed up by weeping Miss Trapp, began anxiously to bumble. Could not something perhaps even yet be done? Artificial respiration . . .?

"He wanted to die," said Cockie crossly. "Why do you want him to live?" But he said to Cecil: "You come with me and see for yourself. I don't want any trouble about this when we get home." Mr Cecil, making no outcry, went forward and knelt with him beside the body and put out his hand and felt the heart beneath the dank clothes and laid his knuckles against the lips. He came back to Louvaine. He said, not meeting her eyes: "Go to your room now, there's no more to be done. Let Miss Trapp take you." As galvanized into action, she took a tottering step towards the boat, he caught her by the arm. "Don't go there. If you want to remember him—remember him as he was. Go to your room." His grip on her arm redirected her steps and she went obediently, moving up the long, shallow, central flight between the scented gardens, like a dead creature whose muscles continue to move automatically, after heart and brain are stilled.

The Gerente appeared with two of his henchmen, swarthy and glittering in the light of the rising moon. He spoke rapidly to Fernando. "He says they will take the body, Inspector. He says they will let Mrs Rodd come back to-night and we must all clear out first thing in the morning. It is all arranged, anyway, the flights are booked, he says that we must go. We shall be in London to-morrow evening. I come with you, Inspector, I must see my company and explain all to them." He added, his easy emotionalism beaten down for a moment by the acuteness of his curiosity: "And meanwhile, Inspector, you have promised to explain all to us? There remain many little things . . ."

"Yes, yes," said Cockie. "I'll clear it up for you. We must get a call through to the Yard to-night, they'll want to see us all and you'll hear it all then." To Miss Trapp, creeping up the steps after the reeling Louvaine, he called out: "You hear that? They'll let Mrs Rodd out to-night and we leave first thing in the morning. Get your things packed."

Louvaine stopped dead, turning her white face to stare down at them. "We can't leave before—before . . ."

"We go to-morrow," said Cockie.

"*I* won't go," she said flatly. "I won't leave him here . . ."

"There's nothing you can do. The police will take everything over, you'll know nothing about it. You must come with us."

"Nobody can make me go," she said. "I shall stay here."

Fernando spoke to the Gerente. "El Gerente says that he will let Mrs Rodd go free to-night—on condition that we all leave to-morrow." He repeated: "On condition."

She hesitated a moment longer and then turned and dragged herself on up the steps. Fernando said, swaying a little, very pale, "The Gerente did not say this, Inspector. What he said was that the ladies should as soon as possible be taken home. He says—he says that the funeral rites accorded to criminals in San Juan el Pirata are not—are not . . ."

"Are not very pretty," said Cockrill. "That's all right; we're going." He made a sign to the Gerente and the Gerente made a sign to his men; and the men stooped and, grunting, hoisted up the long bundle of sailcloth on to their shoulders. Their feet shuffled softly in the sand against the gentle shuff-shuff-shuff of the waves on the shore. The Gerente came forward and taking Inspector Cockrill in his arms, kissed him roundly upon both cheeks, fell back and, clasping his shoulders with outstretched arms, made him a long and fervid speech. Tears came into his eyes, he clapped the Inspector's sagging shoulder with a hand like a ham baked in brown sugar, released him and stalked away, cape flying, sabre rattling, round black mackintosh hat a-gleam in the moonlight, in the wake of his men. Inspector Cockrill watched him out of sight before he started the long toil up the steps with Fernando and Mr Cecil. As he went he said: "What was that about?"

"Just saying good-bye," said Mr Fernando, surprised.

CHAPTER SIXTEEN

"FASTEN your safety belts, please," said the air hostess. "We're coming in to land." The green fields surged up towards them, the long, low sheds of the airport buildings stood relentlessly waiting to be hit, the aeroplane was so extravagantly tilted that it would quite certainly meet the ground at too steep an angle, stand on its nose, turn turtle and go up in flames. . . . "All come this way, please," said the air hostess, standing at the open door. Inspector Cockrill was Home.

The telephone call had, with sufficient difficulty, been put through and they were met and personally conducted through the airport routine: a sad little group among all the gay amateur smugglers, furtively limpid-eyed. "Nothing to declare," said their guide, sweeping a gesture over the long line of luggage so hastily packed the night before. The customs officer sketched a salute and scribbled with his coloured chalk. "I've arranged for a room to be put aside for you," said the official, and to Cockie: "The C.I.D. want to sort things out, before you all leave the airport and disperse. You can interview them there." He led the way briskly. Transport had been laid on for them and would afterwards take them to their homes. . . .

Helen Rodd had not spoken during the voyage. She wore a thick veil after the fashion of mourning in San Juan and behind it her face was quiet and pale. Miss Trapp, repulsed in her efforts to offer comfort, had gone back to her ceaselessly clucking, kindly care of Louvaine. Louvaine wore no veil. Oblivious of care and curiosity alike, she walked with the rest of them like an automaton, Miss Trapp's hand on her arm. Her eyes were bright and dry, tearlessly blue, her hair hung heavy and out of curl about a face so colourless that the crude make-up, left over from last night, or this morning carelessly applied, stood out in painted patches like a clown's. They followed an official along narrow corridors. He opened a door and stood aside for them. Two police officers rose and came forward to meet them.

A man was sitting in a far corner of the room. He did not move until, the tiny crowd parting a little to make way for her, Louvaine, walking in her dream of pain, came wandering blindly in. Then he got up and went and stood before her. She took one tottering step towards him, hands outflung. He raised his own one hand and struck them down.

"Don't touch me, Vanda Lane," said Leo Rodd.

A door slammed in her mind, slammed-to with a crash and a clatter that shattered the last vestiges of her tormented self-control: and she was on the floor at his feet, weeping and gibbering, sobbing, shivering, whimpering, at last falling silent, crouched there at his feet in the stony ring of their horror and recoil. And the door blew open again and with its opening a silence fell and she was sitting again at the little table in the room at the Bellomare Hotel, with the sky and the sunshine for a moment blocked out because her cousin Louise had come in through the open door and was standing there smiling: her cousin Louise who through all the years of adventure and success had been 'Louvaine Barker,' her partner and her friend. Louli—standing there in her white Bikini suit while the rest of the hotel slumbered away the long, drowsy, hot hour of the siesta; Louli—her partner and friend, standing there smiling, a little diffidently, speaking the words that meant that the friendship was over, the partnership dissolved: that she was going to start life all over again—with Leo Rodd.

But she had known all that; had known it and was prepared. "I am not going to let you do it."

"You and I can go on, Vanda, just as before."

Just as before—watching them together, watching Louvaine and Leo as she had watched them and spied upon them through this past week of hell: watching Louvaine enjoy with casual happiness the rapture of love and belonging that she, Vanda, would have given her soul to possess. "I won't let you do it, Louvaine; that's all."

Louvaine had been astonished, had been hurt and bewildered: had been adamant. "Nothing matters to me except Leo. If you won't agree . . ."

"If I don't agree you're penniless, and you and Leo can do nothing. You'll have no job, you're not trained to anything, and he'll never work again, he hasn't a farthing of his own . . ."

But Louvaine had said, as she had said on the beach that night: "I'll make the farthings." Had added, as she had added, unthinking, then: "You think I can't, but I can; you'll see."

"You!" she said, coldly sneering, standing there balancing the knife in her hand, the knife of Toledo steel that she had been idly playing with when her cousin came in. "You! What can you do? You're nothing without me." And to prevent this, to prevent Louvaine from having him, she would end it all, would smash up the partnership, expose 'Louvaine Barker,' face disgrace and ruin, sacrifice it all. "I'm rich enough, Louvaine, if I never write a word again, I shall be all right. But you—what can *you* do?"

"I can write," said Louvaine.

"You write? Write what?"

"Write a novel," said Louvaine.

"You write a novel! My poor girl—wait till you try."

"I have tried," said Louvaine.

"And tried to find a publisher?"

"I've got a publisher." She said: "I did it for fun at first, Vanda, to see if I could. And then it seemed too good just to chuck it away. But I knew you wouldn't like it, you'd think it was dangerous, you've got such a bee in your bonnet about this exchange of ours. So I didn't tell you; and, besides, it was nice to have a little secret money, all of my own. Quite a lot of money, actually. So you see, you can do nothing: and Leo and I . . ."

The knife flashed out and down and into her breast, slitting through the flowered white satin Bikini top. Blood spurted over the table between them and on to her own white kimono. The chair fell with a clatter behind her and she grabbed at it automatically and righted it with a blood-smeared hand; and crept out from behind the table and looked down at what lay on the white, scrubbed floor.

How long she crouched there, she did not afterwards know: motionless, petrified with horror by the side of the still body sprawled in the poppy-starred white Bikini on the white wooden floor; staring down at the painted face that, robbed of its smiling vivacity, was so very much like her own . . .

So much like her own.

A girl called Vanda Lane dies: a quiet girl, without friends, without family save for a lunatic mother wearing away her sad life in a half-world of unreality and doubt. A girl called Louvaine Barker lives on and is reborn—reborn with all her own great gifts, with Vanda Lane's own gifts, and with so much more: a ready-made reputation for looks and charm, a ready-made character for gaiety and dash and a high self-confidence, a ready-made host of friends: a ready-made love.

A ready-made love. Leo Rodd is in love with Louvaine and how many thousand thousand times have I wished that I were Louvaine. And now . . . If I could be Louvaine . . .

Her mind, trained to action, took over from her heart, banished emotion, banished fear and dread, began very coolly and clearly to sketch out a plot. And at hand were all the accessories of a plot: the paints, the dyes, the false eyelashes, the padded brassieres, the plastic nails, all the paraphernalia of an imposition that now needed only to be destroyed—destroyed and re-created anew, with a double twist. If I were Louvaine, and Louvaine were me . . .

She dragged the poor, gangling body through into the little bathroom and set to work, wiping away rouge and lipstick and eye-shadow and eyebrow-pencil, loosening the fixative from eyelashes and nails, thrusting the bright head under the shower to rinse out the famous yolk-of-egg hair-dye washing away in rivulets of rusty red. It was gruesome to hold the lax hand in her own and cut and file at such of the long nails as had been Louli's own; but there was no time now for sensibility. She wiped them free of varnish and turned her attention to the manicured toes. Stripped of her gay artificialities, stripped of the flutter of gesture, the easy laughter, the beating of the loving and generous heart, it was a poor thing, after all, that lay here at her mercy in its puddle of blood and water on the bathroom floor. It gave her courage to see it lying there, inert and helpless and unlovely in death: courage and strength to drag it through to the bedroom again, to strip off the bathing costume and wrap the body in her own blood-stained kimono. The wound had long ceased to pulse out blood but the movements of the body jerked the knife so that it horribly sucked and shifted in its sheath of flesh and bone; she folded about it a towel from the bathroom while she set about drying the hair.

But the hair would not dry; and the terrible wobbling of the lolling head made her feel sick, she was afraid she might fail altogether if so early in her vast undertaking she put too great a strain on her physical endurance. Moreover, the dye had not been altogether washed away, it was coming out, a reddy-brown stain on the hotel towel. She took the towel through to Louvaine's own bathroom where a stain of hair-dye would excite no comment; and, returning with a dry towel, noticed the shawl.

It lay across the back of a chair: Louli's red shawl. A red shawl—that was the point: a red shawl. The damp head would make a dark stain on the red shawl, but if the stain were darker with the stain of the hair-dye it would not show on the shawl—because the shawl was red. And to account for the shawl—a pretence at some sort of ceremonial, some sort of laying-out, a disposing of the body in a formal way. She spread the shawl on the bed, heaved up the slight form grown in death to a sickening weight, composed feet and hands, spread out the damp hair so that as much as possible it would dry, took away the folded towel from the hilt of the knife. The blue eyes stared up into her own: she turned her head from the horror of their witless, unwinking reproach. Will anyone pause to wonder, she thought, resolutely forcing her mind to material things, will anyone pause to wonder how her hair—my hair—could have got wet all over, under the tight black rubber cap?

She rinsed the blood from the satin Bikini and mopped up the floor of the room. The chair remained thrust back from the table, smeared with blood; but she left it alone. After all, it is I who am supposed to have been attacked. I would have been sitting there, Vanda Lane, the occupant of the room, sitting there at the table. The attacker is the other one, the one who has come in and is standing on the other side of the table with his back to the door. It is Vanda Lane who is killed, sitting here at the table, getting up to face the intruder, pushing back the chair; tumbling, bleeding, against the chair.

But sitting there doing—what? Scribbling in her book, as it happened—in her 'character book,' the book she kept of jottings about people she met who might one day serve as pegs to hang her fictional characters on. That belonged in Louvaine's room (with the pencils and notebooks and scribbling-pads, she must remember those)—in Louvaine's room with all the impedimenta of a writer. But the book was bloodstained: and how to dispose—when there was so much else to be done—of a give-away bloodstained book?

Where would you hide a leaf? In the forest. Where hide a bloodstained object? Where there is already blood. The book must remain then, with undisguised bloodstains upon it: but how disguise the book?

She picked up her pen which had rolled to the floor, and at the bottom of each page wrote a figure and drew a ring round it. She collected pens, pencils, papers, and took them through to the other room. The book she tucked under the lining-paper in a drawer, as though it had been hurriedly thrust out of sight. In so much that was furtive, there was something more furtive than all in the sly, quick thrusting out of sight of the book; she glanced over guiltily at the bed and the dead girl was watching her, lying there softly on the crimson shawl, with wide, unwinking blue eyes.

The dead girl. Louvaine had been a great one for actual physical rehearsals. 'Let's run through it, Vanda, let's do that scene ourselves, let's see that you've really got it true to life.' O.K., she thought, I'll run through it, if it'll please you, since you're taking such a kind interest in it all. . . .

She took up her place behind the table. This is Vanda Lane who's lying dead on the bed, it was Vanda Lane who was murdered. So here I am, Vanda Lane, sitting in the corner, hemmed in by the oblong table. Someone comes in, there's a quarrel, the intruder attacks: that's the point, it's Vanda Lane who is attacked and Vanda Lane is the person who belongs in the room. So it's the intruder who attacks. The knife's on the table, he picks it up, he strikes, the blood spurts across the table . . .

Can they tell from the shape of the bloodstains on the table which side the victim stood when the blow was struck? For if so—then they'll know that it was the murderer who stood in the corner behind the table: and into their minds will come the first moment of doubt.

She stood for a long time, staring down at the tell-tale stains: and then she picked up the little table and turned it round. And she made a little bow to the body lying quietly on the bed. "Thank you, Louvaine: you were right to insist," she said.

And, through in Louvaine's room which was now to be hers, everything at hand to rebuild the imposture which now had been destroyed—rebuild it on a new foundation not too impossibly unlike the old. The destruction was completed: she had closed the door upon the dead body of Vanda Lane, that friendless, loveless, secret creature who had not known how to use her life: here, in this room, filled with a sense of suddenly triumphant power, she laid hands upon the materials that were to build up the new. The hair-dye first, the wonderful quick-drying hair-dye that could be changed half a dozen times a day, 'only the egg part was so revolting.' She rubbed the stuff in and rolled up into tight curls the mouse-brown locks that for so long had been ruthlessly brushed flat, manicured her toenails, stuck on with their own adhesive the long plastic nails that Louli wore whenever, as all too frequently happened, she broke her own. But she dared not paint them: I must make an opportunity to do that later, bang out in front of them all, if possible—Louli was always doing that kind of thing.

I will walk out among them all as Louvaine. I will say— I'll say that I've split the brassiere of my bathing suit, that'll account for the cut where the knife went through and at the same time give me an excuse for 'disappearing'—hiding away in one of the bathing huts will be best—while Vanda Lane makes 'positively her last public appearance.' I can dodge up through the salons, up the stairs, into the other room, into Vanda Lane's room: wipe off the make-up, put on the black suit over the Bikini, roll up the red plastic bag with the make-up things in a towel and carry it with me. Reappear again as soon as I possibly can, as Vanda Lane; talk to people, to anyone who happens to be at hand, it doesn't matter who, say something that'll lay a trail to the 'characters book,' prepare their minds for the idea that Vanda Lane was one of those people who make capital out of other people's weaknesses. . . . Yes, and that'll provide an ostensible motive for the murder, it all works in marvellously, marvellously, it's like one of my own plots. . . .

Excitement rose in her again, excitement and that sense of power. Down to the rock, and dive. Get them all collected together on the beach, dive again, dive a little crookedly. I can fake that all right, make an excuse to retire. With them all safely down on the beach, I'll be free to nip into a bathing hut—I must leave the towel with the red bag there —strip off the black bathing things, dab on a lot of make-up, fluff out my red hair and dash down to the beach all gay and Loulified. But in case that should fail, in case she should falter in this her first major appearance as the new Louvaine—a word, perhaps, with blackmailing Vanda Lane as they 'meet' at the top of the diving rock, dark hints afterwards to account for any possible oddness of manner, a pale face, a tense expression. Not that she was really afraid: I can do it, it'll work, it's all fitting in too marvellously for it not to work—and look how cool I am, how controlled, look how completely I've taken the whole thing in hand! And after all, I'm used to acting a part, I've been acting a part for ten years, every moment of my life. As for 'being' Louvaine —these people have known her a week, casually, impersonally—except for Leo and he's mostly seen her in the evenings, in the half darkness: for the rest of the time he's been busy pretending to ignore her. Louvaine and I were so much alike, really, alike with that family likeness of walk and voice and figure, far more than of face: in the old days I had to practise lowering my voice to a different pitch, I can go back to our 'family voice' soon enough—and as for the walk, I've deliberately got into the habit of creeping about, I've only to throw back my shoulders, let my stride go free . . . Besides, who's observed her walk, in these few days, mostly spent sitting in a char-à-banc, who's studied the set of her shoulders, who'll notice in all the fuss after—after it's discovered—any change in the voice of a fellow-tourist they've known for less than a week? But I—I've known her since we were babies together, I know every look, every mannerism, every overworked slang expression, after all, it's been part of *me*. I helped to build it all up, I know the very thought behind everything she did and said and was: I knew into her mind. And after all these years, am I such a fool that I can't, if I set my mind to it, become what in fact was my other self? Besides . . .

Besides, the rewards were so very great: a new life, freed from the chains that adolescent reserve and diffidence had forged for her, and habit and circumstance ever since imposed—a new life with the beloved of her love-starved heart. And the alternative was death at a hangman's hands.

The eyelashes were the trickiest. Hung by an eyelash! she thought to herself, coolly sardonic; for she dared not appear as Vanda Lane, with Louli's preposterous false eyelashes already in place, and even if she got away with it during her first brief appearance as Louvaine, she could not appear without them when she finally went down to the beach. And surely they would take too long to adjust during her quick change in the bathing hut? Well—she must risk it: the lashes were strung along a line of coarser hair, she had only to lay them along the upper lid and put a dab of adhesive—no time for messing about with the famous white of egg; and if they later came adrift, well, Louli's artificialities were a standing joke with herself and everyone else; and one could produce a hand-mirror and adjust one's make-up every five minutes without exciting comment—Louvaine did, twenty times a day.

One problem remained: how to dispose of the wet black bathing suit, the cap and the shoes. Vanda Lane would obviously have gone back to her room in them: how then, to return them to the room? I must stow them away in the red bag, I suppose, and keep them with me; some time or other, we shall go back up to the hotel in the ordinary nature of things and I must—yes, I must hitch them over the rail outside her room, that shouldn't be difficult. (And pray that none of them would ask themselves why Vanda Lane, having changed, should wrap them all up in a towel instead of spreading them out to dry!)

A clock struck and it was an hour and a half since first the sunshine had been blocked out in the doorway: one hour and a half since Louvaine had come into the room and stood there smiling in the white satin bathing dress. And now it was she, Vanda Lane, who stood in the white satin bathing dress—not smiling. She stood before the looking-glass on the little dressing-table, and looked long and earnestly into the obediently smiling face—a face that so many and many and many a time had looked back into hers: but not from a looking-glass. The same face: the very face: eyes widened and slanted with eye-shadow and pencil to match the slant of the upward pencilled brows, cheeks rouged and shadowed to a new contour, mouth painted to a gash of scarlet—all in a frame of flagrantly dyed red hair. The same face: the same smiling painted face that a thousand times had smiled back into her own: nothing to choose between them but the ghastliness of the smile.

She tore her eyes from the mirror and flung open the window above it to let the bright sunshine stream in on the drying red curls; and somewhere a door slammed, and Inspector Cockrill strolled out on to the balcony. . . .

"You won't want me to explain it to you in detail," said Inspector Cockrill when at last, half-fainting, she had been dragged to her feet and taken away to the waiting car outside. "She showed it all to us—when she decided after her false accusation of Mrs Rodd, to tell the truth and give herself up to the politio. And she did tell the truth—only we none of us recognized it. She walked through the part of Vanda Lane pretending to be Louvaine: and stupid blind fools that we were, we took it that she was acting the part of Louvaine pretending to be Vanda Lane. It was the curl that did it—the curl of red hair blowing across her face from under the black rubber cap: the curl deceived us all, none of us thought for one moment that it really *was* 'dead' Vanda Lane. But she didn't know that: she walked on through the part, she would have executed the two dives, she would have gone through the whole thing: only then something happened. She was doing it because she thought Leo Rodd hated her for what she had done to Mrs Rodd; she was confessing to us all—because she thought he no longer loved her and therefore she had nothing left to lose— that she was Vanda Lane; and then, when she was just about to give herself up to the Gerente, Mrs Rodd stepped in and saved her, and Leo Rodd said, 'I shall be grateful to you for ever, Helen, because of what you've done for Louvaine.' *Because of what you've done for Louvaine.* It was not true, after all, that Leo Rodd no longer loved her, she had something to live for still; and—we all still believed she was Louvaine."

Mr Cecil sat, chin in hand, on the straight-backed chair against the white-painted wall of the little room with its rows of straight-backed chairs against white-painted walls. "That day, afterwards, when she was lying down, I was talking to her about it and she said—yes, that's right, she said, 'You'll never know, no one will ever know, what those words meant to me.' "

"They meant that she was 'Louvaine' again; and no doubt with a growing sense of power because now, really, she must have seemed to herself to be indestructible, the whole imposture must have seemed, after such an escape, as though it were 'meant.' And we were all deceived anew. Puzzled: but still deceived. Puzzled, because we had all in our varying degrees been fond of Louvaine—absurdly fond of her," admitted Inspector Cockrill gruffly, "considering that we had known her a matter of days. But we somehow couldn't be fond of the new Louvaine. All of a sudden her extravagances seemed cheap and silly, she was often unkind where the real Louvaine wouldn't have been unkind, and—she called Mrs Rodd 'ducky.' Louvaine called everyone 'ducky' but not Mrs Rodd—she was injuring Mrs Rodd, deceiving her and injuring her, the real Louvaine had too much true delicacy to force that sort of friendly familiarity on Mrs Rodd. As for Mr Rodd . . ."

Leo Rodd sat beside Helen on the straight-backed chair against the poster-plastered white wall. "I was utterly bewildered. I knew I had loved Louvaine, I knew that Louvaine was—well, a person to be loved; and all of a sudden, I couldn't love Louvaine. I tried, I actually tried to force myself back to being in love with her, but—I couldn't understand it, but it just wouldn't work. It was not a falling out of love, it wasn't the petering out of an ordinary affair." He did not touch his wife, he did not look at her but he knew that for all the pain the understanding cost her, she would understand. "I was in love with Louvaine, I couldn't help myself, it was something that happened to us both and there it was. And suddenly—it wasn't there any more." And he looked down at the spot where she had lain slavering at his feet and said: "Thank God I never loved her, thank God I never held her in my arms. God damn her soul to hell for daring to think that to me she could be— Louvaine."

Mr Cecil burst into the silence, spilling over with gossip and chatter and exclamation like a champagne bottle at long last uncorked. And going for Mrs Rodd like that—and that business of the patchwork skirt, too utterly fascinating, so simple and yet really quite brilliant on the spur of the moment, when you came to think of it . . .

"The skirt?"

"The patchwork skirt—my dears, you do remember? She was wearing it at the funeral, Vanda Lane's funeral—well, her own funeral really when you come to think of it, too macabre and yet rather fascinating, she must have got a sort of dreadful kick out of the whole thing in a way." But actually poor darling Louli's funeral, he added more sombrely; and when one thought of that, one was so glad one had gone to all that expense about the mourning (which anyway, though he did not say so, was going to come in very handy for intime little parties, come the long winter evenings) and had felt quite dreadfully melancholy among all those dreary cypresses. "But the skirt. She wore it to the funeral and then coming home in the vaporetto she had a bit of a tizzy with Mr Rodd, I know it, Mr Rodd, because I was watching you, and then you left her and came over to Mrs Rodd who was sitting with me at my table, and asked her to take a splinter out of your hand. Well, that must have made her mad—Vanda Lane, I mean. She walked away down to the end of the boat, the prow, the van, whatever you call the thing, and my dears, her *face!* She was frightened then; and she was angry. She must have been asking herself how she could be revenged on Mrs Rodd because Mr Rodd always turned back to her like that; and she must have seen then, how at one stroke she could be revenged—and at the same time prevent Mrs Rodd from helping him, drive him to turn to herself when he needed that kind of assistance. As Mr Cockrill says, she was getting a sense of power."

"She has a bad heredity," said Cockie, briefly.

"So she entered like anything into our 'dispersal party' when we got off the boat, and as soon as she was alone, nipped off into the shop and bought a second knife. And afterwards Inspector Cockrill asked if a girl had bought a knife who was wearing a skirt that they simply couldn't have missed—a bright patchwork skirt. And they said that no such person had been into the shop." He eyed them beadily. "A patchwork skirt—lined with scarlet."

"All right, all right," said Cockie crossly. "She turned it inside out: we know that now."

"Yes, we know it *now*," said Cecil. But poor Mr Cockrill had had a horrid time and one mustn't be a tease. "And so then she made an assignation with Mr Rodd for the siesta hour 'as soon as his wife was asleep.' And as soon as he'd left the room, she slipped in—and met him later, under the pines. You see—we all wondered how the attacker could have missed the heart so hopelessly: why the stab should have gone into the right shoulder. It was meant to go into the right shoulder: it was intended to disable—not to kill."

"And yet—why not kill while she was about it?" suggested Fernando. "Mrs Rodd was in her way too."

"I don't think we can know all that really went on in her mind," said Helen. "By that time she was probably—well, half mad."

"A bad heredity," said Cockie, again.

Mr Fernando sat close to Miss Trapp on the small chair, his heavy thigh pressed warmly against her own. She would never get used to it—never; the easy familiarities of the flesh, the unprivacy of it all, the—the earthiness. But there was so much more, so much that transcended these unimportant physical shrinkings and she sat, quietly happy, by his side, grieved for these others with their past pains and their remaining problems, but for herself content. "But, Inspector Cockrill, you didn't know this all along? When did you know?"

A face raised to look up from the terrace, far, far below the topmost tower of the palatio on the hill; an arm stretched forth to take a pair of sun-glasses from a breast-pocket; a hand flung out to catch at a falling attaché case . . .

"She was supposed to be terrified of heights. We knew— we *knew*—that the real Louvaine was terrified of heights. And yet she leaned out over that low parapet a hundred feet above the gardens below, which in turn fell away and away in terraces down the steep hill—and grabbed at the case and caught it and hauled it back. I had been thinking of many other things; but at that moment—I knew. Louvaine couldn't stand heights. This girl didn't mind heights. This girl was not Louvaine."

"But Mr Cecil—the papers—Mr Cecil fainting like that . . ."

Too true, that one did faint most terribly easy, said Mr Cecil, but honestly, honestly, about a silly tarradiddle over one's drawings, well, *no!* No, no, indeed, the thing had been that one had known poor Louli just that shade better than the rest of them and one had, after all, an eye for clothes, that was only natural; and really, there had been something latterly about Louvaine's clothes, all worn quite wrong, wrong tops with wrong skirts, put on all anyhow, and Louli, the real Louli had had a Thing about clothes, she just automatically looked right. So one had been half-prepared, just that step ahead of the rest of them, for that give-away business up on the tower. She had leaned out over the edge—Louvaine, who was supposed to be terrified of heights—and suddenly, as Mr Cockrill said, it had all slipped into place: it wasn't a case of Louvaine losing her sense of dress: it was just that it wasn't Louvaine. And as one had said, one did faint quite terribly easily; and the thing had been so fantastic, so incredible—and yet so utterly obvious when one saw it again from this new angle—that flop! one had gone, out like a light; and bruised oneself like anything on that horrid marble floor, a huge pink mark to this *min*ute on one's tum. . . .

"There was a pink mark on Vanda Lane's shoulder," said Inspector Cockrill, "where she hit the water, deliberately coming down flat in her second dive. To account for it afterwards, when she appeared as Louvaine, she said she had been badly sunburned while she was 'catched' in the bathing-hut. She showed me the supposed sunburn. But later on, when we were all up on the balcony outside Miss Lane's room, her shoulders were perfectly white again. The

269

mark where she had hit the water, had faded. But sunburn wouldn't have faded. And next morning when you were all lying under the sun-shed, I saw her shoulders again. They were perfectly white—no traces of sunburn at all." He said, making it sound like *their* fault, that he ought to have realized then.

"Well, so then I was with the Grand Duke," explained Leo, drawing a red herring across this painful reflection, "and trying to get him to let my wife leave San Juan with us the next day; and Mr Cockrill and Mr Cecil appeared and told us what had happened up on the tower. Mr Cockrill's one idea was to get her—Vanda Lane—back to England; whatever she'd done, there was something, well, almost indecent, in abandoning her to San Juanese justice. And as for me—after the first knowledge of the thing had struck me down, I wanted her got back to England too." His face was terribly grim, his one hand was clenched into a fist upon his knee. " 'Let justice not only be done but be seen to be done.' I want to see justice done; I want to see her stand in the dock in a British court of law, I want to see her condemned to die for what she did to Louvaine; and when the Judge says, 'may God have mercy on your soul,' I want to be there, and not say Amen."

Mr Cecil broke in with his babble again. "So then we hatched up a plot, at least the Grand Duke hatched it mostly. My dears, that Exaltida!—too gorgeous," said Mr Cecil wistfully. "And so masterful! Even Inspector Cockrill had to do just what he said, now didn't you, Inspector?"

"We all had to do what he said," said Inspector Cockrill coldly. "We were all in his power. What the Grand Duke wanted was a hostage—alive or dead, he didn't much care which. What we wanted was to get Vanda Lane back to England. She wouldn't come if Leo Rodd didn't come and he couldn't come if his wife was kept in custody or supposed to be; in fact none of us could go while anyone was supposed to be in the San Juan gaol. We argued it out; and at last the Grand Duke concocted this business about Mr Rodd and—not liking it very much—we had to agree. We worked out a case against him that on the surface would sound convincing—Vanda Lane's no fool: and then Mr Rodd was to swim out to sea and, with the help of his underwater mask, keep out of sight as much as possible, till a boat, with the boatmen under the Grand Duke's instructions, went out to fetch him. It wouldn't be very pleasant for Miss Lane, but that, I think, didn't greatly worry any of us. The men brought him back and he lay as still as he could under the sailcloth, which he says smelt disagreeably of fish, and Mr Cecil and I in turn testified to his being dead." He made a ducking movement of his splendid head in the general direction of Mr Fernando and Miss Trapp. "We must apologize for having had to deceive you; but we had to have someone there who was not just acting. As I say, Vanda Lane's no fool."

An airport official knocked and came in. The bus was waiting which would take them all to Waterloo; if they would please come this way. . . . They got up and went out quietly—Mr Cecil with Little Red Attashy case hugged up under his arm, mincing along with slightly heightened colour, for really the airport officer was madly good-looking in all that dark blue and silver, and did seem rather a *pet;* Miss Trapp in her brown silk dress and the Brussels-Sprouts Hat with Fernando, glistening with affectionate enthusiasm at her meagre side; Helen Rodd, cool and dignified, showing no trace of the doubt and sorrow of the past terrible days, Leo Rodd with ravaged face and haunted eyes, walking close at her shoulder—carrying his own brief-case. Inspector Cockrill let them go out before him, standing aside bowing civilly to the ladies, the white panama hat in his hand. "I won't be a minute," he said to the airport official, when they had all gone through. There was a poster on the wall that had caught his eye and he went and stood before it for a long, long time. It was addressed to visiting foreigners. SPEND YOUR HOLIDAYS IN BRITAIN, it said.

"You have left your straw hat, sir," said the airport official as Detective Inspector Cockrill boarded the bus.

"I know," said Cockie. "I won't be wanting it again."

THE PERENNIAL LIBRARY MYSTERY SERIES

E. C. Bentley

TRENT'S LAST CASE
"One of the three best detective stories ever written."

—Agatha Christie

TRENT'S OWN CASE
"I won't waste time saying that the plot is sound and the detection satisfying. Trent has not altered a scrap and reappears with all his old humor and charm."   —Dorothy L. Sayers

Gavin Black

A DRAGON FOR CHRISTMAS
"Potent excitement!"   —New York Herald Tribune

THE EYES AROUND ME
"I stayed up until all hours last night reading *The Eyes Around Me,* which is something I do not do very often, but I was so intrigued by the ingeniousness of Mr. Black's plotting and the witty way in which he spins his mystery. I can only say that I enjoyed the book enormously."

—F. van Wyck Mason

YOU WANT TO DIE, JOHNNY?
"Gavin Black doesn't just develop a pressure plot in suspense, he adds uninfected wit, character, charm, and sharp knowledge of the Far East to make rereading as keen as the first race-through."   —Book Week

Nicholas Blake

THE BEAST MUST DIE
"It remains one more proof that in the hands of a really first-class writer the detective novel can safely challenge comparison with any other variety of fiction."   —The Manchester Guardian

THE CORPSE IN THE SNOWMAN
"If there is a distinction between the novel and the detective story (which we do not admit), then this book deserves a high place in both categories."   —The New York Times

THE DREADFUL HOLLOW
"Pace unhurried, characters excellent, reasoning solid."

—San Francisco Chronicle

END OF CHAPTER
". . . admirably solid . . . an adroit formal detective puzzle backed up by firm characterization and a knowing picture of London publishing."
—*The New York Times*

HEAD OF A TRAVELER
"Another grade A detective story of the right old jigsaw persuasion."
—*New York Herald Tribune Book Review*

MINUTE FOR MURDER
"An outstanding mystery novel. Mr. Blake's writing is a delight in itself."
—*The New York Times*

THE MORNING AFTER DEATH
"One of Blake's best."
—Rex Warner

A PENKNIFE IN MY HEART
"Style brilliant . . . and suspenseful."
—*San Francisco Chronicle*

THE PRIVATE WOUND
[Blake's] best novel in a dozen years . . . . An intensely penetrating study of sexual passion . . . . A powerful story of murder and its aftermath."
—Anthony Boucher, *The New York Times*

A QUESTION OF PROOF
"The characters in this story are unusually well drawn, and the suspense is well sustained."
—*The New York Times*

THE SAD VARIETY
"It is a stunner. I read it instead of eating, instead of sleeping."
—Dorothy Salisbury Davis

THERE'S TROUBLE BREWING
"Nigel Strangeways is a puzzling mixture of simplicity and penetration, but all the more real for that."
—*The Times Literary Supplement*

THOU SHELL OF DEATH
"It has all the virtues of culture, intelligence and sensibility that the most exacting connoisseur could ask of detective fiction."
—*The Times* [London] *Literary Supplement*

THE WHISPER IN THE GLOOM
"One of the most entertaining suspense-pursuit novels in many seasons."
—*The New York Times*

THE WIDOW'S CRUISE

"A stirring suspense.... The thrilling tale leaves nothing to be desired."
—*Springfield Republican*

THE WORM OF DEATH

"It [The Worm of Death] is one of Blake's very best—and his best is better than almost anyone's." —Louis Untermeyer

John & Emery Bonett

A BANNER FOR PEGASUS

"A gem! Beautifully plotted and set.... Not only is the murder adroit and deserved, and the detection competent, but the love story is charming." —Jacques Barzun and Wendell Hertig Taylor

DEAD LION

"A clever plot, authentic background and interesting characters highly recommended this one." —*New Republic*

Christianna Brand

GREEN FOR DANGER

"You have to reach for the greatest of Great Names (Christie, Carr, Queen . . .) to find Brand's rivals in the devious subtleties of the trade."
—Anthony Boucher

TOUR DE FORCE

"Complete with traps for the over-ingenious, a double-reverse surprise ending and a key clue planted so fairly and obviously that you completely overlook it. If that's your idea of perfect entertainment, then seize at once upon *Tour de Force.*" —Anthony Boucher, *The New York Times*

Marjorie Carleton

VANISHED

"Exceptional . . . a minor triumph."
—Jacques Barzun and Wendell Hertig Taylor, *A Catalogue of Crime*

George Harmon Coxe

MURDER WITH PICTURES

"[Coxe] has hit the bull's-eye with his first shot."
—*The New York Times*

Edmund Crispin

BURIED FOR PLEASURE
"Absolute and unalloyed delight."
—Anthony Boucher, *The New York Times*

D. M. Devine

MY BROTHER'S KILLER
"A most enjoyable crime story which I enjoyed reading down to the last moment." —Agatha Christie

Kenneth Fearing

THE BIG CLOCK
"It will be some time before chill-hungry clients meet again so rare a compound of irony, satire, and icy-fingered narrative. *The Big Clock* is . . . a psychothriller you won't put down." —*Weekly Book Review*

Andrew Garve

THE ASHES OF LODA
"Garve . . . embellishes a fine fast adventure story with a more credible picture of the U.S.S.R. than is offered in most thrillers."
—*The New York Times Book Review*

THE CUCKOO LINE AFFAIR
". . . an agreeable and ingenious piece of work." —*The New Yorker*

A HERO FOR LEANDA
"One can trust Mr. Garve to put a fresh twist to any situation, and the ending is really a lovely surprise." —*The Manchester Guardian*

MURDER THROUGH THE LOOKING GLASS
". . . refreshingly out-of-the-way and enjoyable . . . highly recommended to all comers." —*Saturday Review*

NO TEARS FOR HILDA
"It starts fine and finishes finer. I got behind on breathing watching Max get not only his man but his woman, too." —Rex Stout

THE RIDDLE OF SAMSON
"The story is an excellent one, the people are quite likable, and the writing is superior." —*Springfield Republican*

Michael Gilbert

BLOOD AND JUDGMENT
"Gilbert readers need scarcely be told that the characters all come alive at first sight, and that his surpassing talent for narration enhances any plot. . . . Don't miss."   —*San Francisco Chronicle*

THE BODY OF A GIRL
"Does what a good mystery should do: open up into all kinds of ramifications, with untold menace behind the action. At the end, there is a bang-up climax, and it is a pleasure to see how skilfully Gilbert wraps everything up."   —*The New York Times Book Review*

THE DANGER WITHIN
"Michael Gilbert has nicely combined some elements of the straight detective story with plenty of action, suspense, and adventure, to produce a superior thriller."   —*Saturday Review*

DEATH HAS DEEP ROOTS
"Trial scenes superb; prowl along Loire vivid chase stuff; funny in right places; a fine performance throughout."   —*Saturday Review*

FEAR TO TREAD
"Merits serious consideration as a work of art."
                    —*The New York Times*

C. W. Grafton

BEYOND A REASONABLE DOUBT
"A very ingenious tale of murder . . . a brilliant and gripping narrative."
                    —Jacques Barzun and Wendell Hertig Taylor

Edward Grierson

THE SECOND MAN
"One of the best trial-testimony books to have come along in quite a while."   —*The New Yorker*

Cyril Hare

DEATH IS NO SPORTSMAN
"You will be thrilled because it succeeds in placing an ingenious story in a new and refreshing setting. . . . The identity of the murderer is really a surprise."   —*Daily Mirror*

M. V. Heberden

ENGAGED TO MURDER
"Smooth plotting."
—*The New York Times*

James Hilton

WAS IT MURDER?
"The story is well planned and well written."
—*The New York Times*

P. M. Hubbard

HIGH TIDE
"A smooth elaboration of mounting horror and danger."
—*Library Journal*

Elspeth Huxley

THE AFRICAN POISON MURDERS
"Obscure venom, manical mutilations, deadly bush fire, thrilling climax compose major opus.... Top-flight."
—*Saturday Review of Literature*

Francis Iles

BEFORE THE FACT
"Not many 'serious' novelists have produced character studies to compare with Iles's internally terrifying portrait of the murderer in *Before the Fact,* his masterpiece and a work truly deserving the appellation of unique and beyond price."
—Howard Haycraft

MALICE AFORETHOUGHT
"It is a long time since I have read anything so good as *Malice Aforethought,* with its cynical humour, acute criminology, plausible detail and rapid movement. It makes you hug yourself with pleasure."
—H. C. Harwood, *Saturday Review*

Michael Innes

DEATH BY WATER *(available 4/82)*
"The amount of ironic social criticism and deft characterization of scenes and people would serve another author for six books."
—Jacques Barzun and Wendell Hertig Taylor

THE LONG FAREWELL *(available 4/82)*

"A model of the deft, classic detective story, told in the most wittily diverting prose."
—*The New York Times*

Mary Kelly

THE SPOILT KILL

"Mary Kelly is a new Dorothy Sayers. . . . [An] exciting new novel."
—*Evening News*

Lange Lewis

THE BIRTHDAY MURDER

"Almost perfect in its playlike purity and delightful prose."
—Jacques Barzun and Wendell Hertig Taylor

Arthur Maling

LUCKY DEVIL

"The plot unravels at a fast clip, the writing is breezy and Maling's approach is as fresh as today's stockmarket quotes."
—*Louisville Courier Journal*

RIPOFF

"A swiftly paced story of today's big business is larded with intrigue as a Ralph Nader-type investigates an insurance scandal and is soon on the run from a hired gun and his brother. . . . Engrossing and credible."
—*Booklist*

SCHROEDER'S GAME

"As the title indicates, this Schroeder is up to something, and the unravelling of his game is a diverting and sufficiently blood-soaked entertainment."
—*The New Yorker*

Thomas Sterling

THE EVIL OF THE DAY

"Prose as witty and subtle as it is sharp and clear. . .characters unconventionally conceived and richly bodied forth . . . . In short, a novel to be treasured."
—Anthony Boucher, *The New York Times*

Julian Symons

THE BELTING INHERITANCE
"A superb whodunit in the best tradition of the detective story."
—August Derleth, *Madison Capital Times*

BLAND BEGINNING
"Mr. Symons displays a deft storytelling skill, a quiet and literate wit, a nice feeling for character, and detectival ingenuity of a high order."
—Anthony Boucher, *The New York Times*

BOGUE'S FORTUNE
"There's a touch of the old sardonic humour, and more than a touch of style." —*The Spectator*

THE BROKEN PENNY
"The most exciting, astonishing and believable spy story to appear in years. —Anthony Boucher, *The New York Times Book Review*

THE COLOR OF MURDER
"A singularly unostentatious and memorably brilliant detective story."
—*New York Herald Tribune Book Review*

THE 31ST OF FEBRUARY
"Nobody has painted a more gruesome picture of the advertising business since Dorothy Sayers wrote 'Murder Must Advertise', and very few people have written a more entertaining or dramatic mystery story."
—*The New Yorker*

Dorothy Stockbridge Tillet
(John Stephen Strange)

THE MAN WHO KILLED FORTESCUE
"Better than average." —*Saturday Review of Literature*

Simon Troy

SWIFT TO ITS CLOSE
"A nicely literate British mystery . . . the atmosphere and the plot are exceptionally well wrought, the dialogue excellent." —*Best Sellers*

Henry Wade

A DYING FALL
"One of those expert British suspense jobs . . . it crackles with undercurrents of blackmail, violent passion and murder. Topnotch in its class."
—*Time*

THE HANGING CAPTAIN
"This is a detective story for connoisseurs, for those who value clear thinking and good writing above mere ingenuity and easy thrills."
—*Times Literary Supplement*

Hillary Waugh

LAST SEEN WEARING . . .
"A brilliant tour de force."
—Julian Symons

THE MISSING MAN
"The quiet detailed police work of Chief Fred C. Fellows, Stockford, Conn., is at its best in *The Missing Man* . . . one of the Chief's toughest cases and one of the best handled."
—Anthony Boucher, *The New York Times Book Review*

Henry Kitchell Webster

WHO IS THE NEXT?
"A double murder, private-plane piloting, a neat impersonation, and a delicate courtship are adroitly combined by a writer who knows how to use the language." —Jacques Barzun and Wendell Hertig Taylor

Anna Mary Wells

MURDERER'S CHOICE
"Good writing, ample action, and excellent character work."
—*Saturday Review of Literature*

A TALENT FOR MURDER
"The discovery of the villain is a decided shock."
—*Books*

Edward Young

THE FIFTH PASSENGER
"Clever and adroit . . . excellent thriller . . ."
—*Library Journal*

**If you enjoyed this book you'll want to know about
THE PERENNIAL LIBRARY MYSTERY SERIES**

Nicholas Blake

Gavin Black

☐	P 473	A DRAGON FOR CHRISTMAS	$1.95
☐	P 485	THE EYES AROUND ME	$1.95
☐	P 472	YOU WANT TO DIE, JOHNNY?	$1.95

John & Emery Bonett

☐	P 554	A BANNER FOR PEGASUS	$2.50
☐	P 563	DEAD LION	$2.50

Christianna Brand

☐	P 551	GREEN FOR DANGER	$2.50
☐	P 572	TOUR DE FORCE	$2.50

Marjorie Carleton

☐	P 559	VANISHED	$2.50

George Harmon Coxe

☐	P 527	MURDER WITH PICTURES	$2.25

Edmund Crispin

☐	P 506	BURIED FOR PLEASURE	$1.95

D. M. Devine

☐	P 558	MY BROTHER'S KILLER	$2.50

Buy them at your local bookstore or use this coupon for ordering:

HARPER & ROW, Mail Order Dept. #PMS, 10 East 53rd St., New York, N.Y. 10022.

Please send me the books I have checked above. I am enclosing $ _____ which includes a postage and handling charge of $1.00 for the first book and 25¢ for each additional book. Send check or money order. No cash or C.O.D.'s please.

Name _____

Address _____

City _____ State _____ Zip _____

Please allow 4 weeks for delivery. USA and Canada only. This offer expires 1/1/83. Please add applicable sales tax.

Kenneth Fearing

☐ P 500 THE BIG CLOCK $1.95

Andrew Garve

☐ P 430 THE ASHES OF LODA $1.50
☐ P 451 THE CUCKOO LINE AFFAIR $1.95
☐ P 429 A HERO FOR LEANDA $1.50
☐ P 449 MURDER THROUGH THE LOOKING
    GLASS $1.95
☐ P 441 NO TEARS FOR HILDA $1.95
☐ P 450 THE RIDDLE OF SAMSON $1.95

Michael Gilbert

☐ P 446 BLOOD AND JUDGMENT $1.95
☐ P 459 THE BODY OF A GIRL $1.95
☐ P 448 THE DANGER WITHIN $1.95
☐ P 447 DEATH HAS DEEP ROOTS $1.95
☐ P 458 FEAR TO TREAD $1.95

C. W. Grafton

☐ P 519 BEYOND A REASONABLE DOUBT $1.95

Edward Grierson

☐ P 528 THE SECOND MAN $2.25

Buy them at your local bookstore or use this coupon for ordering:

Cyril Hare

- [ ] P 555 DEATH IS NO SPORTSMAN $2.50
- [ ] P 556 DEATH WALKS THE WOODS $2.50
- [ ] P 455 AN ENGLISH MURDER $1.95
- [ ] P 522 TRAGEDY AT LAW $2.25
- [ ] P 514 UNTIMELY DEATH $2.25
- [ ] P 523 WITH A BARE BODKIN $2.25

Robert Harling

- [ ] P 545 THE ENORMOUS SHADOW $2.25

Matthew Head

- [ ] P 541 THE CABINDA AFFAIR $2.25
- [ ] P 542 MURDER AT THE FLEA CLUB $2.25

M. V. Heberden

- [ ] P 533 ENGAGED TO MURDER $2.25

James Hilton

- [ ] P 501 WAS IT MURDER? $1.95

P. M. Hubbard

- [ ] P 571 HIGH TIDE $2.50

Buy them at your local bookstore or use this coupon for ordering:

Elspeth Huxley

☐ P 540 THE AFRICAN POISON MURDERS $2.25

Francis Iles

☐ P 517 BEFORE THE FACT $1.95
☐ P 532 MALICE AFORETHOUGHT $1.95

Michael Innes

☐ P 574 DEATH BY WATER *(available 4/82)* $2.50
☐ P 575 THE LONG FAREWELL *(available 4/82)* $2.50

Mary Kelly

☐ P 565 THE SPOILT KILL $2.50

Lange Lewis

☐ P 518 THE BIRTHDAY MURDER $1.95

Arthur Maling

☐ P 482 LUCKY DEVIL $1.95
☐ P 483 RIPOFF $1.95
☐ P 484 SCHROEDER'S GAME $1.95

Austin Ripley

☐ P 387 MINUTE MYSTERIES $1.95

Buy them at your local bookstore or use this coupon for ordering:

HARPER & ROW, Mail Order Dept. #PMS, 10 East 53rd St., New York, N.Y. 10022.
Please send me the books I have checked above. I am enclosing $ _____
which includes a postage and handling charge of $1.00 for the first book and
25¢ for each additional book. Send check or money order. No cash or
C.O.D.'s please.

Name _____

Address _____

City _____ State _____ Zip _____
Please allow 4 weeks for delivery. USA and Canada only. This offer expires
1/1/83. Please add applicable sales tax.

Thomas Sterling

☐ P 529 THE EVIL OF THE DAY $2.25

Julian Symons

☐ P 468 THE BELTING INHERITANCE $1.95
☐ P 469 BLAND BEGINNING $1.95
☐ P 481 BOGUE'S FORTUNE $1.95
☐ P 480 THE BROKEN PENNY $1.95
☐ P 461 THE COLOR OF MURDER $1.95
☐ P 460 THE 31ST OF FEBRUARY $1.95

Dorothy Stockbridge Tillet
(John Stephen Strange)

☐ P 536 THE MAN WHO KILLED FORTESCUE $2.25

Simon Troy

☐ P 546 SWIFT TO ITS CLOSE $2.50

Henry Wade

☐ P 543 A DYING FALL $2.25
☐ P 548 THE HANGING CAPTAIN $2.25

Hillary Waugh

☐ P 552 LAST SEEN WEARING ... $2.50
☐ P 553 THE MISSING MAN $2.50

Buy them at your local bookstore or use this coupon for ordering:

**HARPER & ROW, Mail Order Dept. #PMS, 10 East 53rd St.,
New York, N.Y. 10022.**

Please send me the books I have checked above. I am enclosing $ _____
which includes a postage and handling charge of $1.00 for the first book and
25¢ for each additional book. Send check or money order. No cash or
C.O.D.'s please.

Name _____

Address _____

City _____ State _____ Zip _____

Please allow 4 weeks for delivery. USA and Canada only. This offer expires
1/1/83 . Please add applicable sales tax.